# TEN MILLION WAYS TO DIE

## MAGNOLIA BLUFF CRIME CHRONICLES
## BOOK 18

## C W HAWES

CWH BOOKS, KATY, TEXAS

*For Caleb*
*Mentor, Friend, Brother*

# JOIN THE TEAM!

I invite you to become a VIP Reader.

You'll get a free copy of *Vampire House and other early cases of Justinia Wright, P.I.* right off the bat. A collection of novellas and short stories set in the Justinia Wright, PI universe.

Then each month, maybe more often, you'll get curated content and a variety of good things to keep you up to date with my many worlds.

Just click, tap, or scan the QR code to begin the adventure!

*Join the Team!*

# 1

7:04 AM, TUESDAY, 10 OCTOBER

HARRY THURGOOD WIPED HIS HANDS ON A TOWEL. FROM BEHIND THE counter, he surveyed the seating area of the Really Good Wood-Fired Coffee Shop, which he owned, operated, and lived above.

He never tired of looking at the stylish T.A. Tandy tables and chairs, or the classy Henri Vernier flooring and lighting.

And the paintings hanging on the walls. Specially commissioned from two top California artists. They were truly magnificent.

What had been a dump four years ago was now a coffee shop that rivaled anything in New York, Chicago, or San Francisco.

"What the...," he murmured. He slipped on his custom made Tom Jones suit coat and strode around the end of the counter over to one of the Pruett paintings.

Someone had taped a sheet of paper on the wall next to the painting. An advertisement for a barn dance in nearby Llano this Saturday. He tore it down and crumpled it into a ball.

Shaking his head, he returned to the counter, slipped behind it, and tossed the paper into the trash.

"They can post that stuff over at the Spoon," he muttered.

The aroma of high-end brewed coffee filled the air.

Harry heard Miguel, his cook, in the kitchen. He was back

from putting the green Kona beans in the wood-fired roaster, which was accessed from the alley behind the shop, and, from the noise he was making, he was putting away the produce from Elder Smythe's farm that John Paul had delivered earlier.

Estrelita was placing pastries from Bluff Bakery under the three glass domed plates.

Harry snagged one, poured himself a cup of Java arabica coffee, and made his way to his corner table and sat.

*Who would be first this morning?*

He had a pretty good idea who the first two might be. And he wasn't disappointed.

Fergus entered. He was visibly wet from the drizzle. Harry got up and guided him to a corner table. Most mornings, the homeless guy didn't smell the best and this morning was no exception. He'd been out in the drizzle long enough that the water coming off his coat was making little puddles on the floor. His shoes were soaked.

The odor wafting off the wet clothing was very earthy, and not one of good earth.

"Is it safe here?" Fergus asked.

"I think so," Harry replied, and then asked, "Safe from what?"

"The Feds. They were sneaking around in the back alley. I saw them."

A frown descended on Harry's face, which he quickly replaced with a smile. "Probably nothing. Don't worry about it. How about pancakes this morning?"

The worry vanished from Fergus's face and was replaced with a smile. "Yes, sir, Mr. Thurgood. Pancakes are good."

Harry walked to the window behind the counter that looked into the kitchen and told Miguel to make a stack of pancakes and a half-dozen sausages for the fellow.

To Estrelita, Harry pointed at the coffee and nodded towards the homeless vet.

Actually, Fergus was no longer homeless. But the PTSD, a gift from being in Afghanistan, often made four walls seem like a prison.

Harry returned to his table and had just finished his buttermilk doughnut when the door opened and in walked the Reverend Ember Cole. Seeing her brought a smile to his face.

Black jacket. Black pleated skirt. White blouse. Clerical collar. A moderately large gold pectoral cross hung from a gold chain around her neck.

And peeking out from under the black saturno hat was the face of a cherub.

He was grateful for whatever happened last summer that changed her demeanor. There had been a slow thaw. Her resistance to a relationship had softened.

She still insisted that the feelings they had for each other not get out of control, but at least these past few months, she was no longer averse to being seen with him in public.

He got up from his table and slipped behind the counter. Ember closed her umbrella, crossed the floor, and took a seat on one of the stools.

She removed her hat and smiled at him. The smile was warm, with a hint of flirtatious invitation.

Harry loved her smile. He loved that she wore her dark hair in a Dutch Bob. It made her look like those sexy silent film stars from the 1920s. Although she'd doubtless be appalled if she knew he thought that.

"Where were you last night?" she asked. "I was hoping you'd call."

"And good morning to you, too, Reverend Cole. You're a little late. It's after seven."

"I didn't know you kept track."

"I do. I want to know everything about you."

From across the room, Fergus called out, "Mornin' Reverend."

"Good morning, Fergus. How are you this morning?"

Estrelita, having set his breakfast on the table, gave Ember a smile, which she returned.

"I'm good," Fergus said. "Mr. Thurgood fixed me up with pancakes and sausages this morning. Coffee, too. It's really good." He laughed at his joke.

Ember smiled. "I bet it is. Enjoy."

"Yes, ma'am. I am."

Ember turned back to Harry. "I'm glad you give him breakfast every morning."

"Doesn't cost me much."

"So where were you? If you don't mind my asking."

"You can ask. Business. Like the song says, I was taking care of business."

"I see. Okay, Mr. Harry Thurgood, man of mystery."

"And you're the woman of mystery."

"So I am."

"However, if you'll let me, I'd like to take you to dinner and a concert tonight. To make up for my absence last night."

A faint smile tugged at the corners of Ember's lips. "I'll let you, if your business interests don't mind. What concert?"

"Fundraiser for the Burnet College Orchestra."

The door opened and Harry watched a man walk in. He was tall, and had the collar of his car coat pulled up, which partially obscured his face.

"Sit wherever you'd like," Harry said.

The man nodded, chose a table near the window, not far from the door.

In a moment, Estrelita appeared from the back room and walked to the man's table to give him a menu and take his order.

"Don't make it obvious, but do you know the guy Estrelita is waiting on?" Harry asked.

Ember dropped her napkin, got off the stool, picked it up, looked at the man, and got back on to the stool.

"No. I don't think I've seen him in town before."

"Me neither. Might be a tourist. We get a lot of folks here in October."

"We do. Nice weather. Oktoberfest. A whole bunch of music

festivals. You can always check with your friend, Scarlett. She might be able to tell you if he's at the resort."

"I could."

"While we're playing twenty questions, may I have a cup of coffee?"

"Sure. One Ember Cole White Coffee coming right up."

"Very funny."

While preparing her cup, he said, "I am going to put this on the menu one of these days."

"Don't you dare."

"You wait and see."

He set before her a cup that looked like milk with a dash or two of coffee in it. "Here you go. And yes, Scarlett's my friend. And no, the rumors aren't true. We're just friends, with no benefits."

"Says you."

"Says me *and* Scarlett."

"Huh."

"What's on your schedule for today?"

She took a sip of her coffee and set the cup down. "The usual. Work on my sermon. Hospital visitation. Clodine Bauer had her appendix out. At seventy-six. Can you imagine?"

Harry shook his head.

"And the Reynolds boy, Jimmy, had a tonsillectomy. Mavis Finseth—"

Harry held his hand up. "I get the idea."

"And I like to check in on my older parishioners. One or two each day."

"Okay. Same old, same old. Pick you up at six? Concert's at eight."

"Sure. That should work. I can be ready by then."

"And wear a pretty dress. You have one, right?"

"Very funny. Yes, I have a dress. More than one, in fact."

"Good to know. Want your usual?"

"Sure."

"Great. One usual coming right up."

Harry gave the order to Miguel and then turned around. The stranger was still there. It looked like he was scrolling through stuff on his phone.

Who was this guy? Was he connected with what Fergus saw? Or thought he saw?

If so, it might be time to move. Again. Not that he wanted to. He liked Magnolia Bluff and was building a life here. He liked Ember. He liked her a lot. In fact, if he was honest with himself, he was in love with her.

The question was very simple. Did he value his new life enough to make a stand? Or did he fear the Feds more?

# 2

## 9:18 AM, TUESDAY, 10 OCTOBER

MONIKA CROW, RECEPTIONIST, ADVERTISING MANAGER, AND SOCIAL columnist for the *Magnolia Bluff Chronicle*, looked up from her computer screen.

The man looking at her was soaked and was probably leaving a puddle on the floor. A puddle she'd have to mop up. He was tall and on the thin side. His clean-shaven face had probably broken a few hearts along the way.

*Must've been out in the drizzle for a long time*, she thought. *Why doesn't he have an umbrella?*

Instead, she said, "How may I help you?"

"My name's Purnell Tully. I'm with Brother John's Traveling Salvation and Holiness Extravaganza."

Monika kept the emotion out of her face as she studied the stranger. *Not another one of these shysters. Just what we don't need.*

Tully took a folded sheet of paper out of his pocket, unfolded it, and handed it to her.

The paper was slightly damp and was an advertisement for said Extravaganza. Also featured were the Reston Family Singers.

Monika skimmed the text, paused at the couple of pictures, and then re-focused her attention on the man. "Okay. So how may I help you?"

"I'm looking for a place to rent so we can bring to your fair city the Word of the Lord. And what better place than the town newspaper to help me in my hour of need. We were initially referred to a James Thompson—."

Monika cut him off with a nod. "What we call Old Man Thompson's barn. Why not rent the barn?"

"We rented the field, but that nasty Blue Norther last night grabbed our tent and I think most of it is probably in the next county."

Monika nodded her understanding. "Did you ask about the barn?"

"I did, but he said—"

Monika slapped her forehead. "The Fall Fruit and Vegetable Show."

"Yes. No room at the inn, or the barn. So to speak."

Monika nodded. "So to speak."

"Seeing that this is the newspaper office, I'm thinking you may know of an empty building we could rent for a few nights. To bring the Word of the Lord to the hungry hearts and souls—"

"We do have churches here in Magnolia Bluff. Lots of them. Baptist. Presbyterian. Methodist. Catholic. Full Gospel. You name it. And you can find more words from the Lord than you can shake a stick at. Every Sunday morning. Sunday evening. And even Wednesday nights."

"I'm sure. I'm sure."

Monika thought Tully's voice oozed obsequiousness. Quite a contrast with his face. Which she, to her eye, had a somewhat hard edge to it.

He continued, "But have you ever heard the divine voices of the Reston Family Singers?"

Monika shook her head.

"Then your ears, and your heart, and your soul are in for a divine treat. That is, if we can find a place to hold our meetings."

"How long are you planning on being here?"

"That depends on the Lord, ma'am. If the Lord calls forth

many souls, then Brother John will stay as long as it takes to harvest them."

"What sort of place are you looking for?"

"Well, that depends on what's available. The Lord is the One Who provides. Brother John will know if the place is right."

"I see. Do you have money?"

Purnell Tully favored her with a big smile. "It takes money to live in this great country, does it not?"

"It does. Do you have any?"

"The Lord has blessed us abundantly. Does it matter how much He has blessed us?"

"I don't want to see someone stuck with a bill. We look out for each other in Magnolia Bluff. That's something *the Lord* has taught us."

Tully's big smile stayed in place, but Monika swore the temperature went from toasty to frosty.

"I'm sure the Lord is pleased that you take care of each other. Do you think there is a place here in town we could *rent* in order to preach the gospel? A donation would be wonderful, but we do pay our bills. The Lord would not have it any other way."

"I'm sure." Monika thought a minute. "There is a place up on Commerce Street, across from the Piggly Wiggly. Been empty for some time now. Not sure what shape it's in."

She scribbled on a notepad and handed the slip of paper to the man.

"Call Davis Real Estate. They might let you rent it."

"Thank you very much. Miss?"

"I'm Monika."

"Very well, then, Monika, thank you. And keep the flyer. May the Lord bless you."

"Do you need a place to stay?"

"No. We have our bus and campers. They will be fine until we find a building."

"Good luck."

Tully gave her a solemn smile. "The Lord takes care of his children."

"I'm sure he does."

Monika watched the dripping man head back out into the wind and drizzle. When he was gone, she turned back to her computer screen and muttered, "I don't know if it takes all kinds, but there certainly are all kinds."

———

Harry read down the list of green coffee beans available from the wholesaler and groaned. Not for the first time, he told himself, he needed to find a different coffee bean vendor. What coffee seller would not have St. Helena coffee available?

The hum of the conversation and the floral-citrus scent of the brewing Ethiopian Yirgacheffe drifted to and fro like waves gently washing a white sand beach.

He looked up and saw Caroline McCluskey, the town librarian, and her friend, Magnolia Nadine, stand and pick up their umbrellas.

"Leaving already?" he said. "There's still plenty of coffee."

Before either Caroline or Magnolia Nadine could answer, an enormous mountain of a man squeezed through the door and entered the Really Good.

He was wearing a black raincoat that looked big enough to do double duty as a revival tent, and on his head was an oilcloth outback-style hat. The drops of drizzle glistened in the lights of the shop like tiny diamonds.

With his arms spread wide, his deep baritone voice thundered, "May the Lord bless you one and all."

The stranger had everyone's attention.

Reverend Billy Bob Baskin caught the eye of Reverend Ember Cole and raised an eyebrow.

Jack Bonhoffer looked up from the book he was reading at his seat by the cash register.

The man seated by the window stopped scrolling on his phone.

And Graham Huston, owner and editor of the *Magnolia Bluff Chronicle*, the town's only newspaper, pulled out his notebook and pencil and started writing.

Fergus applauded.

Caroline and Magnolia Nadine resumed their seats.

The enormous man continued, "I am Brother John, a wanderer, a pilgrim, a stranger in a strange land. I have been guided to this fair city so that I may raise the lamp of the Lord to look into the hearts of men and women."

Huston's eyes opened wide and he muttered, "Shoot. Bunyan, Heinlein, *and* Diogenes."

"Which of you gentle people is the proprietor of this esteemed establishment?" The man slowly moved his head to take in everyone present.

Harry stood and circled around his table, saying, as he walked up to the man, "I'm Harry Thurgood. I own this esteemed establishment."

"Brother John at your service, good sir." He gave Harry a deep nod of his head. "Perhaps you will be so kind as to grant this servant of our gracious and magnificent Lord a boon?"

From the corner of his eye, Harry noticed Ember was struggling to keep a straight face; which made the task even more difficult for him to do likewise.

"Well, Brother John," he said, "I suppose it depends on the boon."

"A humble request, good sir. I would like to put a placard in your window to inform the good folk of your town that the Lord has seen fit to bring to them and to you, good sir, Brother John's Traveling Salvation and Holiness Extravaganza *and* the divine voices of the Reston Family Singers."

Harry looked over at the table where his friends were staring at the man mountain, then turned his attention back to Brother John.

"Well, sir, that is quite a boon."

"Surely you cannot see it as a huge request. It is but one placard placed in your window."

"It's not a huge request, and it's certainly reasonable. But, you see," Harry pointed to the table where his friends were seated, "there is the Reverend Billy Bob Baskin, pastor of the Presbyterian Church here in Magnolia Bluff, and the woman seated across from him is the Reverend Ember Cole, who is the pastor of the Methodist Church."

Brother John gave each of them a slight nod of his massive head.

Harry continued, "I keep the religious peace, so to speak, by not taking sides. My shop is free from religious favoritism. However, let me make up for declining your boon by offering you a cup of coffee. On the house."

"Very well, good sir. I will take you up on your offer. A hot cup of Java will push away the chill."

"Yes, it will."

"May I have that to go?"

"Certainly."

And before Harry could get behind the counter, Estrelita appeared before the newcomer with a tall cardboard cup and a paper bag. She handed both to Brother John.

The massive man said, "Thank you, young lady," took the items, and peered into the bag. A smile spread across his face.

"May the Lord bless you, young lady. May He make His face shine upon you. And may He give you peace."

Estrelita blushed, and Brother John giving everyone a nod, said, "May the Lord bless you one and all," and squeezed back through the door into the wind and the drizzle.

Harry whispered to Estrelita, "What did you put in the bag?"

"A cheese danish."

"Well, that sure earned you a few brownie points."

She blushed again and walked back behind the counter.

Huston turned from watching the man mountain leave and

said, "I like that, Thurgood. Free from religious favoritism. Of course, we all know that there's a little Methodist to your madness."

Everyone broke out laughing, and Ember turned fifty shades of crimson.

# 3

## 10:33 AM, TUESDAY, 10 OCTOBER

IN A PALATIAL SPREAD ON SANDALWOOD DRIVE, THE ENCLAVE WHERE the monied folk in Magnolia Bluff live to avoid mingling with the Great Unwashed, Mary Lou Fight was looking at photographs in her living room, which was larger than Harry Thurgood's coffee shop by quite a stretch.

Across from her sat a nondescript man. A little taller than average. A little bit broader built than average. Dishwater blond hair, what was left of it. Facial features no one would probably bother to remember.

His suit came off a department store rack quite sometime ago and hadn't been altered. Nor had it ever seen the inside of a dry cleaners.

Mary Lou looked up from the photographs. "Hunter, I'm surprised. These are worthless. They don't tell me anything I don't already know. Everyone knows he sits in his coffee shop and talks to the little strumpet. And this one..." She held up the color glossy print. "Who cares if he ran a red light? This is not like you at all. What else have you found? And don't tell me nothing."

"He's very good, Mrs. Fight. Honest. I can't even find anything to prove his name isn't Harry Thurgood."

"If you're trying to get more money..."

"No, it's not like that, Mrs. Fight. Honest. I don't know who he knows, but whoever it is they are good. Very good."

"And who do you think he knows?"

"Well, if my theory is correct and he paid for a new identity, then we are talking, for an ID this good, someone who works with organized crime."

"You mean like on that nasty TV show?"

"Yeah, something like that."

"I see. So he is a criminal."

"Maybe. Maybe not. But he probably has connections."

"Keep digging. If you need money to loosen tongues, let me know. I want him to pay."

"I will, Mrs. Fight. I'll keep digging. Everyone has a dirty diaper. I'll find his."

"Good. Because I want him gone. I want him in jail so he can never come back. So he can never have his precious little harlot. I want him locked away with a lot of mean and nasty criminals who will humiliate and emasculate him. Do you understand?"

"Yes, Mrs. Fight."

"Good. Now, go."

"Hunter left, and Mary Lou, using her walker, slowly made her way to the floor-to-ceiling picture window. The window that looked out onto her world. And it was her world. Everything she saw, and much of what she didn't see. Her husband, Gunter, owned the bank, and in owning the bank, he controlled the lives of many of the good folk of Magnolia Bluff. And Mary Lou controlled Gunter. Together, they controlled almost everyone in Magnolia Bluff. Everyone except for Harry Thurgood. And that made her angry.

He had thwarted her attempt to get rid of that little minx, Ember Cole, who had the audacity to stand in the pulpit of her church. A church she couldn't even go to anymore because of Harry Thurgood. He had threatened her and thwarted her. Humiliated her in her own town, and that made her blood boil.

She clenched her fists, and in a voice barely above a whisper, but filled with a venom that would make a rattlesnake hide under a rock, she said, "No one humiliates me, Harry Thurgood. No one."

———

Across Burnet Reservoir, in a very large Prairie-style home on the northwest shore, nestled among the trees, Scarlett Hayden stood at her picture window and looked out on her world. The resort that made a rich widow even richer.

She'd been standing there a long time. Long enough for her martini to have lost its icy coldness.

Even though the resort was full, something not uncommon for October, a last hurrah for the tourists, the day was starting out quiet. The Smiths, her very efficient caretakers, had handled everything this morning, leaving her with little to do and a lot of time on her hands.

Scarlett hated the quiet days. Hated them because she always found herself thinking of Harry Thurgood. Daydreaming about what life would be like waking up with him beside her in bed. She wanted him more than anything. But he was only interested in that skinny Ember Cole.

The couple of times he'd visited had convinced her he'd enjoyed her company. And he would've stayed the night. But it was always Ember on his mind.

Her martini was thoroughly warm now. She walked to the kitchen sink and poured the gin and vermouth down the drain. She watched the liquid and her dream flow away.

"Maybe I need to get reacquainted with the football team," she said out loud. "Maybe the high school team as well as the college team."

She barked a harsh laugh and shook her head. "No. If I want the star quarterback, then I'm going to get the star quarterback. I deserve the best and I'm going to get the best. I've had my fill of the milk. I want, no, I deserve the cream."

That decision made, she fixed herself a fresh martini. Drink in hand, she walked to the sofa and stretched out on it.

Scarlett took a sip of the ice cold liquid. "I just have to figure out how to get him away from Ember." The glass returned to her lips and she took another sip of gin, scented with a trace of vermouth. "But how?"

She stared at her genuine Tiffany lamp. The monochromatic yellow-green hues of the glass and the arachnid-like raised veins coming down from the clawed top she found to be soothing.

After some time, she took a swallow of her drink, and said, "There's always Mary Lou and her goddamn groupies. She knows everything. Maybe I need to get back into her good graces. After all, Mary Lou wants Ember gone as badly as I do."

Scarlett took another swallow of the martini. "And then there's Daphne. Women always tell their hairdresser everything. Getting close with her would definitely give me an additional information highway to drive down."

The rest of the martini disappeared in one long gulp."Keep your friends close and your enemies closer. If I were good friends with Ember..." She shrugged. "Why not? If I can poison her opinion of the coffee man and get her to dump him..."

She pursed her lips at the thought, and a big smile spread across her face.

———

Ember Cole stood up and stretched.

Scattered across her desk top were sheets of paper, her Bible, the New Testament in Greek, and several commentaries.

Her eyes came to rest on the statue in the far corner of her office that Harry had given to her at Christmas.

"Why give me a statue of Mary and Jesus?" she'd asked him. "You do remember I'm not Catholic?"

He'd chuckled. "I remember," he'd answered, and added, "It's religious art and you're religious, aren't you?"

"I am."

"So there you have it. And don't throw it out, or give it away."

"What makes…"

He'd held his hand up. "It's valuable. Like very valuable. And incredibly old."

"Really? How old?"

"Let's say that it might have been used by the Druids."

"The Druids? They weren't Christian."

"No, they weren't."

"And?"

"As I said, it is incredibly old."

"I see. You aren't going to tell me. Okay. So why give it to me? And how did you get it in the first place?"

She remembered he'd smiled at her and said, "I want you to have it because I love you. As for how I got it, let's just say it's a family heirloom."

She didn't believe him, but knew she wasn't going to get anymore out of him. So she'd put the thing on a table in the corner of her office, even though she thought it was one of the ugliest works of art she'd ever seen.

"Dull, crusty black metal. Skinny, ugly figures that don't even look like real people."

Harry had laughed at her description.

The statue was wood, and the wood was overlayed with a black metal. It stood a little over two feet in height from the base to the top of Mary's crown.

The Mary figure was tall and skinny and seated on a backless chair. The baby Jesus was seated on her lap, and he was wearing a crown as well, just like his mother.

The statue reminded her of pictures she'd seen of Medieval depictions of Jesus and Mary. Highly stylized. Not at all realistic.

The statue wasn't the only gift Harry'd given her, which made it easier for her to accept the ugly thing.

She walked over to it, squatted before it, and said, not for the first time, "I wonder what makes you so special other than you being old?" She stood. "Sure wish Harry would tell me what's up with you. Maybe Father Lee would know something."

Ember walked back to her desk and sat. Not Father Lee, she thought. Harry. He needs to tell me about his past.

Then she shook her head. "No. If he tells me his dark secret, then I'll have to tell him mine. And I'm not ready to do that. Not yet. Maybe never."

Her eyes darted to the statue. Mystery man. Mystery art. So many secrets. So very many secrets.

# 4

1:11 PM, TUESDAY, 10 OCTOBER

THE LUNCH CROWD WAS THINNING OUT. ONLY THREE REMAINED OF the eleven who'd come through the doors of the Really Good. And one of those three was the man who constantly scrolled through his phone.

Harry was sitting at his corner table observing the stranger. The man didn't look like a Fed. So perhaps he was private. Then again, perhaps he was a tourist.

But if he was a tourist, he doubted the man would have sat at a table drinking coffee for four or five hours.

"Even if the coffee was really good." Harry smiled at his joke.

No, this guy wasn't a tourist, or even someone just passing through. He was working for somebody. The question was, who?

Harry stood and crossed the floor to the man's table.

When he reached it, he said, "Hello. I hope you're enjoying the coffee."

The man looked up from his phone. "It's good." His attention returned to the device in his hand.

Was that a touch of humor in his eyes? Harry asked himself, before saying, "I'm Harry Thurgood. The owner. Today's lunch specials are roast beef au jus and cassoulet made with goose, salt pork, and kielbasa. Or I can serve you up a mean chili or a cheese-burger made with local beef. What do you say?"

The man looked up from his phone, looked out the window at the gray sky and misty drizzle, then turned back to Harry.

"Now that you mention it," he said, "chili would hit the spot."

"Texas-style with no beans? Or Yankee-style with beans?"

"This is Texas, right?"

"Yes, sir, it is."

"I'll take it Texas-style."

"One bowl coming right up. Beans on the side?"

The man thought for a moment and shook his head.

Harry walked around the end of the counter and up to the window, looking into the kitchen. He gave Miguel the order and turned around to observe the man.

The guy was back, looking at his phone.

Near as Harry could tell, his mystery customer wasn't carrying a gun. At least not in a shoulder holster. Nor did it appear, from what Harry observed, the guy was taking pictures.

His accent had a trace of the east coast.

So what was he doing sitting in the Really Good scrolling through his phone hour after hour?

*Who do I know from the east coast who could have traced me to Magnolia Bluff?*

"Order up, Mr. Thurgood," Miguel announced.

Harry took the bowl of chili and plate of cornbread sticks, butter, and honey over to the man. He set it down, walked back to the counter, got himself a doughnut and coffee, and made his way back to the man's table, and sat down.

The man looked at him over a spoon of chili, and said, "I'm not looking for company."

Harry took a bite of his doughnut, chewed, swallowed, and said, "I'm not either. What do you want?"

The man put the spoon of chili in his mouth and slowly chewed. After he swallowed, he nodded and said, "This is good.

And I don't want anything. Just enjoying your coffee and passing the time. No law against that, is there?"

He's a cool one. Matter-of-fact tone to his voice. "No, there isn't. Glad you like the chili. It's an original Texas recipe that one of the women in town gave a friend of mine before she passed away. The woman, that is. Not my friend."

The man nodded, and spooned chili into his mouth.

Harry continued. "Glad you like the coffee. It's from Sumatra. But as for you just passing the time drinking coffee and scrolling the hell out of your phone, I don't think I believe you."

The man shrugged.

Harry went on. "Your accent isn't local, and no one has ever sat in my shop for five hours scrolling through their phone."

"First time for everything." The stranger put butter and honey on cornbread and took a bite. He nodded his satisfaction.

When he swallowed, he said, "Now, if you don't mind, I'd like to eat in peace."

Finally. Now he's getting annoyed. He's not completely unflappable. Harry stood. "Sure thing. And the chili's on the house."

"Thanks," the man said, and turned his attention back to his phone.

Harry took his doughnut and coffee and walked back to his table. He sat and pondered what this guy's presence meant. Wondered if it was the beginning of trouble.

# 5

## 8:04 PM, TUESDAY, 10 OCTOBER

HARRY WATCHED A TALL WOMAN STRIDE ACROSS THE STAGE. HER flaming red hair was gathered in a bun on top of her head. She wore a dark red dress that fell to her ankles. Spaghetti straps crossed her shoulders.

She bowed to the audience, took her seat at the piano, paused a moment or two, and then commenced playing Wagner's piano transcription of his *Tannhäuser Overture*.

Fourteen minutes later, Harry was on his feet clapping and shouting, "Bravo!"

Ember stood and, while clapping, asked, "She was that good?"

"Oh, yes. Amazing."

"Okay. If you say so."

"Not a classical music gal, I take it."

"No, not really."

"Well, she is good." He looked at the program. "Justinia Wright. Wonder why I've never heard of her?"

When the applause died down, a lanky young man in a tuxedo joined the redhead at the piano and the two performed a piano transcription of Beethoven's *Leonore* Overture Number 1 for four hands.

After the performance of Foote's Piano Quintet in A minor,

and Vaughan Williams's Fantasia for Piano and Orchestra, the lights came up for the intermission, and Harry and Ember made their way out to the atrium to stretch their legs and get something to drink.

Ember took a sip of her water. "I liked..." She looked at the program. "I liked the Foote Quintet. It was nice to listen to."

Harry nodded. "Foote doesn't get the recognition he deserves. And she was absolutely amazing. In fact, that was a stunning performance. I hope they recorded it. And the Vaughan Williams piece... It was spectacular. She is gifted."

"I've never heard you go on about musicians before."

"Like anyone else, I have my favorites. I'll have to add Justinia Wright to my list. Wonder if she's made any recordings?"

"According to the bio note, she plays with orchestras in Minnesota, Wisconsin, and North and South Dakota."

Well, let me tell you she is good enough to play with the Cleveland Orchestra, or the New York and Berlin Philharmonics."

"Says here she plays an annual concert with the Minnesota Orchestra."

The lights dimmed twice, signaling the intermission was over.

Harry and Ember made their way back to their seats for the final work on the program: Rachmaninoff's Piano Concerto No. 2 in C minor.

The lights dimmed, the conductor and the tall redhead walked onto the stage to enthusiastic applause. They bowed to the audience. The conductor mounted the podium, and the pianist took her seat at the piano.

The conductor turned to the redhead, who had her head bowed. Then she sat up straight and her fingers touched the piano keys.

When the first movement was over, Harry whispered, "My God, such feeling."

Ember merely nodded.

When the final notes of the concerto sounded, Harry was on his feet shouting, "Bravissimo!" His hands were above his head, clapping vigorously. The rest of the audience stood, as well, to applaud the performance.

The pianist and conductor took their bows, and after four curtain calls, and shouts of, "Encore!", the redhead sat back down at the piano and played a piano transcription of *Heart of Courage* by Two Steps from Hell.

When she finished, the president of Burnet College came on stage, thanked everyone for coming, and asked that they be generous with their donations.

Ember said, "Didn't you have to pay for our tickets?"

"I did. But they didn't cost much. I guess out here they rely on freewill offerings."

"You going to donate?"

"Yes, I am."

"How much?"

Harry showed her the check.

"Oh, my goodness, Mr. Thurgood. You're going to get your name on a plaque for sure."

"Well, if you notice, it's a bank draft and my name's not on it."

"Ah. Once again, the man of mystery."

"Yes, indeed. The man of mystery strikes again. So mum's the word, milady."

Ember put her thumb and index finger together and made like she was zipping her lips.

"Thank you. Fancy a nightcap?"

After a moment, Ember nodded.

"O'Gara's okay? Should be plenty of people there to testify no hanky-panky took place."

"Very funny, Mister. Sure. Let's go."

They joined the crowd leaving the auditorium. Harry dropped his check into the basket held by one of the ushers, and he and Ember made their way to the atrium.

Once there, Harry offered Ember his arm, which she accepted, and the two walked out to Harry's car.

He looked at the woman by his side. *Only Ember could turn that dress into something daring. Just like Louise Brooks. Understated, smoldering, sexiness. How does she do it? She's as far removed from being a sex goddess as is a nun. Doesn't matter. All I can say is that I'm so glad we met. With Ember by my side, all things are bright and beautiful.*

A movement interrupted Harry's musing. He turned his head, and there, several cars over, was the phone scroller who'd spent the day in his shop. Dark clouds blotted out the moonlight.

# 6

11:37 PM, TUESDAY, 10 OCTOBER

EMBER SIGHED. ANOTHER BEAUTIFUL EVENING WAS COMING TO an end.

Harry pulled up to the curb in front of the Methodist parsonage, put the car in park, and shut off the engine.

She released her seat belt and turned to face him. "Thanks for the wonderful evening."

He released his seat belt and turned to face her. "You are welcome. My pleasure, as always."

She laughed at the little bow he gave her. "Sometimes, I wish I was a normal person and didn't have to worry about what other people thought, or have to deal with everyone's expectations."

"You could marry me."

*I could, Harry Thurgood, I could. But you're obviously rich and I'm a poor girl. Would you be satisfied with me? Or would you eventually tire of me? And then there's my past.*

She ran her hand over the soft, textured black leather of the dashboard. "This is new, isn't it? It has that new car smell."

"It is. An Alfa Romeo Giulia Quadrifoglio with everything in it but the kitchen sink and a hot tub."

She giggled.

"No wet bar, either. So you can't drink and drive," he added.

She cast him a sideways glance. "No martini for Scarlett."

"I love *you*, Em. You. Scarlett's a friend. You are the one who has all my love."

"Why? Why do you love me? I'm nothing special." She turned her head and stared into his eyes.

He touched his right index finger to her lips, and she closed her eyes. "You're intelligent. Witty. Dedicated. Honest. Faithful." He leaned over and cupped her face with his hands. "And all of that is wrapped up in the most beautiful package."

She opened her eyes. "But you haven't even seen the package."

"I see your face, and that is enough."

"I bet you tell that to all the girls."

He let go of her face and leaned against the door. "No. I don't. Certainly not since I met you."

"Truly?"

"Truly. You're the one, Em. And I'm going to wait until you're ready."

"Kiss me?"

They both scooched over and their lips touched. The kiss was long and ardent. Then she pulled away.

"I love you, Harry. I do. Can you wait a little longer?"

"Yep. I can and I will."

"Thank you. I don't know what I did to have a person like you to care about me. I thank God every day for you."

"Walk you to your door?"

"Sure."

He got out of the car, walked around the front, and opened her door. He gave her his hand to help her out, and, when her feet touched the sidewalk, she didn't let go. Holding hands, they walked to the parsonage front door.

They faced each other, and he took her other hand in his.

"Both hands, Mister? The neighbors will talk."

"Let them. Nothing untoward going on here. Our relationship

is proof you don't need to engage in sex in order to love someone."

She smiled. "Want to teach High School Sunday school?"

"No, ma'am. I may have been born at night, but it wasn't last night."

She laughed. There was a pause, and then she asked, "What did you do with your old car?"

"The BMW?"

She nodded.

"I'm selling it. Why? Do you want it? I'll give it to you."

"I have a car."

She watched him wrinkle his nose. "Hey, it gets me to where I want to go. And I have a moped."

"The BMW is really nice and newer than that old Korean thing you're driving."

"You're rich, aren't you? You don't just have money. You're really, really rich."

"I have money. Inherited. Why? Don't you like rich guys?"

"No, it's not that."

"Then what is it?"

"You really inherited millions of dollars?"

"I did. I'm independently wealthy. I don't have to work. I can sit on the sofa, eat Big Cherry candy bars all day, and watch reality TV."

"Lucky you."

"More of a curse than a blessing. That's why I opened the coffee shop. Gives me something to do."

"My family's lower middle class. We had no extra money."

"So? I live pretty simply. About the only thing I splurge on are cars."

"And clothes."

He laughed. "Okay, you got me. Clothes. It doesn't matter to me if you grew up not rich. Count yourself lucky. Truly. Now, do you want the car?"

"I'll think about it."

"Sounds good. Let me know soon, though."

"I will." She pulled him to her and slipped her arms around him. "Thanks for dinner and the concert."

"You're welcome. Now, one quick kiss and I'm gone."

They shared a quick smooch. Then she unlocked her door, and stepped inside.

———

Harry trotted down the walk to his car. He crossed in front of it and stopped by the driver's door. Ember waved to him, he waved back, and he watched her close her door. He gave one more wave and got into his car.

He thought about what she'd said. *Maybe I'll just give her the car anyway. It's a better vehicle than the one she has, and I can buy her a new one when we get married.* He chuckled at that. "Stay positive, Harry, me boy."

He started the Alfa and drove off towards home.

Seven minutes later, he pulled into the alley behind the Really Good, parked, got out of the car, and locked it.

The moon was struggling to find a break in the cloud cover. Not unlike him and Ember.

He shook his head, unlocked the back door to the coffee shop, entered, re-locked the door, re-set the alarm, and took the interior stairs to his apartment.

Once inside, he made himself a Corpse Reviver No. 1, crossed to his rocker-recliner, filled his pipe, and told the computer system to play Skempton's *Lento*.

He knew she had something in her past that made her reluctant to get involved in a relationship. Why just this morning she'd called him the man of mystery, and he'd called her the woman of mystery. For months they'd danced around the twin elephants in the room.

And he was willing to dance as long as she was. He didn't

need to know her past. It was past. Dead and gone. It wasn't an issue with him.

But what was an issue was gossip. It could destroy her ministry. It was why she'd been so hesitant at first to be seen with him. She was afraid it would cause tongues to wag. Of course, they'd wag anyway; and the gossips would invent stuff if they had to. And would so even if they didn't.

Then, on top of town gossip, there was Mary Lou Fight and her penchant for destroying those she didn't like. And she didn't like Ember.

And that made for plenty of trouble, right here in Reservoir City.

So he was willing to take it slow, for her sake. Because she had more to lose than he did. And he'd do his best to protect her reputation.

Besides, she was worth the wait.

He got up and walked to the window in his bedroom at the back of the apartment.

The moon was still struggling with the clouds. He opened the window, leaned out, and looked in the direction of the parsonage. He blew her a goodnight kiss and whispered, "Dream a little dream of me."

# 7

11:40 PM, TUESDAY, 10 OCTOBER

PURNELL TULLY TOOK IN THE LARGE EXPANSE OF SPACE. HE'D HAVE to thank that Monika girl tomorrow morning. Her lead had been a good one.

From the newspaper office, he'd gone straight to the real estate agent; having called to make sure they were open.

There was one person sitting at a desk when he got there. Jenny Lynn Davis.

After introductions, Tully asked if she was the owner.

"My father's the owner. But he's semi-retired."

Tully gave her the once over. *Looks awfully young to be a real estate agent. Can't be more than thirty-five and is more likely in her late twenties. Hard to tell with the makeup. Hands still look good, though. And no ring on her finger. So probably younger.*

He said, "Monika at the newspaper—"

"Oh, you're the one who called."

"Yes, ma'am."

"Have a seat. You can hang your coat over there." She pointed to the coat tree by the door. "Let me turn up the heat a bit so you can dry out."

"Thank you, ma'am."

She walked over to where the thermostat was in the back of the office and tapped on it.

Tully liked the way she moved in that pencil skirt. A mighty enticing jiggle there.

She returned to her desk and, once seated, Tully also sat down.

"How can I help you, Mr. Tully?"

He pulled a flyer out of his suit coat pocket and handed it to her.

She skimmed it, set the paper on her desk, and said, "You're looking for a place to hold meetings?"

"Yes, ma'am."

"How long?"

"A week. Maybe two. Depends on if the Lord blesses or not." He'd given her his most charming smile.

"We don't normally do rentals here, Mr. Tully."

"Monika said there's an empty building up on Commerce Street."

Jenny Lynn nodded. "Yes, that's one of ours. The owner is asking—"

"Doesn't matter. We aren't buying. But if we could rent it…"

"I'll have to get in touch with the owner. Why don't we take a look at it, and I'll text him."

She drove Tully to the empty building. The Buick was pretty new.

*Must be doing all right for herself,* he thought. *Might be a hard bargainer. Or it just might be for show. Who wants to use a poor real estate agent?*

They looked around the place. She'd given him the usual patter. Her phone had dinged somewhere in the chatter. When she started talking about square footage, Tully cut her off.

"Okay. Let's cut to the chase, Jenny Lynn. You have an empty building. Been that way for four years. Owner's losing money paying taxes. For the month, I'll give him twelve hundred dollars to rent the entire building. That ought to pay his taxes for the month and then some. I'll give *you* two hundred bucks for a finder's fee and I'll even give you a little getting lucky tip."

He knew he had that forty-something charm that many married women were willing to take advantage of. Single women were more iffy. But nothing ventured, nothing gained. And a little horizontal tango made a slow and rainy day pass the faster.

"To be fair—"

He shook his head. "Take it or leave it. Lots of other empty buildings. Plus, there are churches and school auditoriums. Shoot. We could just buy a tent and rent space in a parking lot. This building would be a whole lot easier, though. For both of us."

They'd looked at each other for the longest time, although Tully suspected it wasn't more than ten seconds. Then she'd stuck her hand out and said, "Okay, Mr. Tully, you have a deal."

Tully smiled at the memory. A handshake, cash, and a roomy SUV in which to pass an hour on a slow and rainy day.

Two of the Reston kids fighting brought Tully out of his reverie.

They were setting up cots along the one wall and apparently two of the brats didn't like sleeping next to each other.

He was glad he slept in the camper unit on the back of the pickup. He had it all to himself. And he liked that. Made life easier that way.

Jearlene, Brother Reston's lovely wife, who usually went by Jerri, caught his eye and smiled. He liked her smile. He liked the rest of her, as well. She was a mighty fine woman. You'd never guess she'd had a dozen kids to look at her.

He didn't see Brother John anywhere. The tub of lard had probably waddled off to his bed in the converted school bus. His bed was big enough to accommodate a harem. Except the enormous man took up all the space himself. Unless, of course, he was having a special prayer session with some sexy young thing.

Joetta caught his eye, smiled, and wiggled her fingers at him. *Just like her mama,* Tully thought. *Only much younger.*

Then there was Oralene, and he couldn't forget Raylene. She'd just turned seventeen.

He smiled at the thought, and said to himself, *No longer jailbait.*

And Raylene was perhaps the most gorgeous of them all. He closed his eyes and licked his lips.

"Mighty fine," he murmured.

He looked at his watch. Everyone was settling in. Good. Tomorrow, the show would begin.

"Goodnight everyone. Get a goodnight's sleep. Tomorrow night will be your time to shine. See y'all in the morning."

He left the building and got into the camper. Getting out of his clothes, he slipped into bed, put his hands behind his head, and looked up at the ceiling.

He thought of the smile Jerri Reston gave him while putting her kids to bed. "If I were a betting man, and I am, I'd give five to one odds she'll be here before morning."

And that put a big smile on his face.

———

*Finally,* Hunter said to himself. *Thurgood's new car sitting out here in a dark alley all by itself. And with no one around.*

He smiled, took a small device out of his pocket, and helped by the flashlight on his phone, stuck the small box on the inside of the left rear wheel well.

When he was certain that the little device was secure, the light went out, and he stood.

"Now I can track where you go, Harry Thurgood," he whispered.

He looked up at the window and thought it was about time he got serious about bugging the coffee shop owner. It might get him what he needed and get Mary Lou off his back.

# 8

7:03 AM, WEDNESDAY, 11 OCTOBER

HARRY SAID GOODBYE TO JOHN PAUL AND ELDER SMYTHE AND
entered the kitchen of his coffee shop. Miguel was busy mincing
onions.

"We got ten pounds of pecans and fifteen pounds of jujubes
from Smythe," he said to Miguel. "We should probably do something special with them."

Miguel looked up from the chopping board and smiled.
"Pecan pie."

Harry chuckled. "Yes. Of course. Good idea."

"And I can use the fresh jujubes like apples."

"Super. We also have twelve chickens. Maybe chicken fried
chicken?"

Miguel nodded. "You'll be competing with the Spoon."

"Good. Your time to shine and do them one better. I also have
a fab white chili recipe. We can use chicken for that. Mix
things up."

"Today?"

"Tomorrow."

Miguel nodded. "I'll make tarts with the jujubes. Individual
tarts. Everyone likes their own tart."

"Sounds good to me."

Harry walked out to the main floor. Jack Bonhoffer was sitting at the cash register on one end of the counter. Estrelita was making sure all the tables had placemats and flatware.

The door opened and in walked Fergus, followed by Ember.

"I'm telling you, Reverend Cole, they were as black as pitch those SUVs."

Ember nodded.

"And they were coming and going on Main Street, both sides, a whole long line of them. Probably twenty or more on each side."

"Uh-huh."

"And then later on I saw them in the alley."

Ember nodded.

"I don't know what the Feds are doing here in Magnolia Bluff, but it can't be good."

"No, it can't."

Harry caught Estrelita's attention and pointed at Fergus. She smiled, nodded, and guided the old vet to a table along the far wall.

Harry turned the man's words over in his mind. *Fergus likes the sauce, and plenty of it, but could there be any truth to what he's saying? Are the Feds in fact here?*

Ember sat on a stool at the counter. She took off her saturno and set it beside her.

"And a good morning to you, Reverend Cole."

"Likewise, Mr. Thurgood."

"Up for another concert?"

"Uh, if it's soft rock, I'm game."

"Are we talking ABBA here?"

"Something like that."

"I guess that explains the white coffee."

"What's that supposed to mean?"

Harry held up his hands and smiled. "Nothing."

"Yeah, right, Mister." A hint of a smile touched the corner of Ember's mouth. "Can I get that white coffee to go? There's some stuff I need to get done at the church ASAP this morning."

"That important?"

"It is. Cally's been on my butt about it."

"What's her position again?"

"Oh, Cally Taylor is the Lay Leader in the church. It's a very important position. She represents the laity. It's also the work-horse position in the church."

"I see. She's kind of like your head boss in the congregation."

Ember laughed. "Yeah. Something like that."

"And she's replaced Mary Lou in the pain in the butt department?"

"That she has. And she wants the reports on her desk this morning."

"Wow. Okay." Harry filled a paper cup with milk and a splash of coffee and gave it to her. "See you later for the Niners meeting."

She touched his hand, smiled, and as she was leaving Harry began humming the old swing song "Heart and Soul".

---

After Jerri Reston had kissed Tully goodbye, he'd pulled out his laptop and checked his accounts.

Even though it was volatile, cryptocurrency was still the best way to go, in his opinion.

"No banks, and still unusual enough that people won't think to look to see if you have any or not," he said out loud to himself.

And had some he did. In fact, Purnell Tully had quite a bit of cryptocurrency. He wasn't a Bitcoin billionaire, but a very big smile appeared on his face when he looked at the balances in his accounts.

*Two hundred and fifty-one thousand dollars. Right here. Right now. And after we're done with our con in Magnolia Bluff, I can get the heck out. Go some place nice and leave the Restons behind.*

He'd miss Jerri and her daughters. But women like them were a dime a dozen. Every town had its beauty queens. Yes, indeed. A dime a dozen. And he had plenty of dimes.

# 9

## 8:33 AM, WEDNESDAY, 11 OCTOBER

HARRY WAS STANDING BEHIND THE COUNTER, WONDERING WHY Gunter Fight had come in for a cup of coffee. Nothing fancy. Just wanted a large Yemen Mocha Mattari to go, with cream and sugar separate.

Fight had looked around the place, told him good morning, and then said, "Nothing Texas about this place."

Harry had replied, "I'm not from Texas. It's modeled after Buckles in New York, and Jeremy's in Chicago."

"Look out that window, Mister. Does that look like New York or Chicago to you? This here is Texas. And if you're plannin' on stayin', you best get some Texas in this place. I suppose you got all your money in some New York or Chicago bank." He shook his head, and said not a single word more. When Harry gave the banker his coffee, Fight turned around and left.

Harry watched him go out the door and muttered, "He didn't even say thank you."

Five minutes after Fight left, Ember walked through the door and sat on a stool at the counter.

"Another coffee?" Harry asked.

"Yes, please."

In a flash, Harry placed a cup before her. The liquid looked like beige milk.

The bell over the door tinkled. Ember turned, and Harry's eyes shifted to see who had just walked in. His mouth almost fell open.

Standing just inside the door was an impossibly tall redhead. The pianist from the previous night's concert.

Her hair was gathered into a bun on the top of her head. She wore a wide-pleated teal skirt suit, the hem of which fell just below her knees. She wore a white blouse, white stockings, and teal shoes with three-inch stiletto heels.

A large onyx and gold pendant was the only jewelry she wore. A teal handbag dangled from her shoulder on a gold chain.

Harry thought she must be over six feet tall.

"Do you have tea?" she asked.

Ember whispered, "There's your dreamboat."

Harry whispered back, "You're my dreamboat." To the potential customer, he said, "Yes. I can offer you tea."

"Is it quality?"

"I source my tea from Mark T. Wendell, Simpson and Vail, Upton, and TeaSource."

"Good." The statuesque redhead took a seat.

"Excuse me a moment, Em."

"Make sure she autographs your shirt cuff."

"Very funny."

Harry walked over to the table occupied by the pianist.

She was looking at her iPad. Without moving her head, she said, "I'd like toast, white bread, and Mark T. Wendell Irish Breakfast, if you have it."

Harry smiled at her, but she didn't see it. "MTW Irish Breakfast and toast coming right up."

He walked back to the counter, gave the order to Miguel, and returned to the woman's table.

Her eyes rolled up and fixed on his face. "Yes?"

"I just wanted to say I loved the concert last night. Your playing was magnificent."

She set the iPad down. "Thank you. I'm glad you enjoyed it."

"Do you have any recordings? My name's Harry Thurgood, by the way. I'm the owner."

"I'm Justinia Wright. Pleased to meet you, Mr. Thurgood."

"Likewise, Ms. Wright."

Harry was surprised by the pained expression on her face, which was all scrunched up as if she'd bitten into a lemon. "Are you all right? Did I say something?"

"*Miss* Wright. I'm not married. Ms. is the abbreviation for a manuscript and I am not a sheet of paper."

"I'm very sorry, Miss Wright. Honorifics have been warped by the PC crowd. It's quite unusual for a woman these days to insist on proper etiquette."

"Yes, indeed. To answer your question, my brother manages a website and sells recordings of my concerts and recitals. All the proceeds go to support a student at the Minnesota School of Music."

She reached into her purse, took out a card and a CD, and gave them to him. "The college burned that for me. It's a recording of last night's concert and the card has the website address."

"Thank you very much."

"You're welcome. Oh…" She reached into her purse, took out a pen, and held out her hand. "I'll autograph the label on the CD."

Harry gave her the CD, she signed it, and handed it back to him.

Estrelita brought the toast and tea.

"I'll leave you to your breakfast."

The redhead's nose was buried in her iPad.

When she didn't respond, Harry walked back to the counter and sat on a stool next to Ember.

She said, "I told Estrelita to get a mop to clean up all the drool."

"Very funny, Em. She's really an outstanding performer. Truly world class. Could be right up there with Yuja Wang and Khatia Buniatishvili."

"If you say so. Whoever they are."

Harry rolled his eyes. "Just two of the best younger pianists performing in the world today."

Ember's mouth formed an O.

Harry shook his head. "Did you finish what you needed to do to get Cally off your behind?"

"I hope so."

Graham Huston and Reverend Billy Bob Baskin entered the shop and walked over to a table.

Harry looked at his watch. "They're early."

Huston called out, "The usual, Estrelita."

The two men sat, and Harry and Ember joined them.

Huston whispered, "Who's the redheaded bombshell over there?"

"I'd have thought you'd have the scoop on her," Harry answered. "She was the pianist at last night's fundraiser for the college orchestra."

"Carter covered that. Gave the story about five lines yesterday. Three of which were too many."

"But that was before the concert."

"Next edition is Saturday, and that story is now ancient history."

Police chief Tommy Jager came in with Caroline McCluskey, the town librarian, and her friends Magnolia Nadine and Daphne Leigh.

"You get yourself a new sports car, Thurgood?" Jager bellowed. "What the hell is it? Never seen anything like it."

"It's Italian."

Everyone looked at the towering redhead who had said the words. She fished a bill out of her purse, put it on the table, and walked over to the group.

"It's a Lamborghini Sesto Elemento, and it's mine."

The police chief stroked his chin. "Italian, huh."

"Am I double parked?" she asked. Her eyes giving Jager the once over.

"No, ma'am. But is it street legal?"

She smiled. "No, it's not. Arrest me?"

"I can't let you drive it."

"Well, Chief Jager, if you can catch me, then I guess you can arrest me."

Harry laughed. "Good luck with that, Jager. She'll be in Dallas before you're outside the city limits."

Jager looked from the tall redhead to Thurgood, then back to the redhead. "How do you know my name?"

"I'm a private detective. It's my job to know things. So I do." She turned to Harry. "Thank you for the tea and toast. Enjoy the CD. And watch your back. I used to be in art. It can be an exceedingly dangerous field."

Harry's eyes grew large, and his eyebrows met his hairline.

She turned and walked out the door.

In a moment, the rumble of 562 horses could be heard. The group moved to the window and watched the sleek embodiment of some future's midnight pull away from the curb and disappear down Main Street.

The group returned to the table and sat.

"They built only ten of those cars," Harry said. "That's about two and a half million dollars's worth of art."

"I didn't know you had a thing for cars," Caroline said.

"You haven't seen that new one he's driving?" Magnolia Nadine said.

"I'm more interested in her comment about art," Jager said. "Any idea what she meant, Thurgood?"

"Don't have a clue."

# 10

Purnell Tully stood before the building he'd rented for not much more than a song. And in its present condition, was hardly worth even that.

He didn't see any sign of Jearlene or the Reston kids. The bus and van in the parking lot were empty.

*They're probably still out distributing flyers,* he told himself.

On either side of the door was a large window. On display in the left window was a huge sign announcing the arrival to Magnolia Bluff of Brother John's Traveling Salvation and Holiness Extravaganza.

In the other window were signs that read "Full Gospel," "Charismatic," "Faith Healing," and "Snake Handling." There was also a large picture of the Reston Family Singers.

He smiled. Snake night always brought out a huge crowd. And a huge crowd usually meant the offering baskets overflowed with cash. And Purnell Tully very much liked cash. Even more than Brother John did.

Carefully juggling the two bags he was carrying, Tully unlocked and opened the door. Once inside, he secured the door, and looked at what would be the worship area. The cots were gone, and the area was now filled with folding chairs.

He'd had a busy morning. Trying to find a place that would rent him folding chairs had proven to be a bear. He'd ended up driving to Marble Falls to get the chairs for the Extravaganza.

Now they just needed warm bodies with lots of cash to fill those chairs. That was the best part of the Lord's work. Tonight might not be so good. But word spreads fast in small towns. Tomorrow night would certainly be better.

Tully smiled at that and made for the door with the faded "Employees Only" sign on it. Now for the unpleasant part of his work.

He pushed through the door and crossed the floor to an office from which bright light spilled out of the window and open door.

The back area of the building was huge, and the light made a sharp contrast with the inky blackness of the unlit area.

Standing in the doorway of the office, Tully looked at the massive man parked in a chair that was much too small for him. He was leaning back, shoulders resting against the wall. His eyes were closed, and his folded hands rested on the expanse of his gut.

"Got lunch, Reston," Tully said. "Good deli at the Piggly-Wiggly."

The big man opened his eyes and let the chair come forward. He grabbed the bag Tully held out to him and looked inside.

A smile appeared on his face. "Never get tired of fried chicken. And this stuff smells pretty damn good."

Tully pulled up a chair and sat on the other side of the desk from Brother John. From out of his bag, he took a container of tuna noodle salad and one of beef and broccoli soup.

"What the hell is that you're eating, Tully? No wonder you're so damn skinny."

Tully shrugged. "Can't accuse me of gluttony."

Brother John lowered the chicken leg. His eyes narrowed. "You sayin' I'm a glutton?"

"I don't know what part of my statement referred to you. Care to enlighten me?"

"You're a wiseass, Tully, and disrespectful of the Lord's Servant. If you weren't so damn good at bringing in the suckers, I'd drop you in that reservoir over there with some heavy scrap metal tied to your ass."

Tully spooned soup and, after he'd swallowed, said, "No need to get nasty, Reston. We're business partners, remember? You need a setup man, and I need a voice that sounds like God's thunder on Mount Horeb. I have what you need. And you have what I need. Eat your chicken."

Reston snorted a laugh. "I can always find a setup man. But finding a voice like mine? And the ability to move a crowd? Good luck with finding that, my friend."

Tully spooned more soup. *We aren't friends, Reston,* he said to himself. *And as soon as I get my take from this hick town, I'm gone.*

Reston shoved chicken into his mouth. "Are we all set for tonight?" he mumbled.

"I believe so. Jearlene and the kids handing out flyers?"

Reston nodded.

"Then it all depends on you wowing the ones who come tonight. The gossip will do the rest."

"Do we have someone who needs healing? That's always a good start."

"I have someone lined up. Never ceases to amaze me that so many buy into that stunt."

"Why Purnell Tully, I do declare you are beginning to talk like an infidel. Everyone is sick with something. A little persuasion to help them get healed is doing the Lord's work."

"Gotcha. Sorry I doubted. Although I fail to see how what we do is any different from selling indulgences."

"What are you saying, Tully? I have no idea what you're talking about."

"Never mind. All's fair as long as we can name it and claim it."

"Now you're talkin'. When they get back, make sure Joetta and Oralene have their duet ready."

"Sure thing. I'll also make sure they're ready to interpret if someone speaks in tongues. And when Jerri sings her solo, they'll be swooning in the aisles."

"Oh, that'll be good. Slain in the Spirit by the angelic voice of Jearlene Reston. Hope that newspaper man is here to see that."

"You were at the newspaper?"

"I was. And I can tell you I wouldn't mind bending that young woman over her desk."

"Monika?"

"That's her name. Gorgeous little thing."

"Good luck with that. I don't think you're her type."

"And how would you know that?"

"I think an angel whispered it."

"Ha. Very funny, Tully. Don't go into comedy."

Tully shook his head and spooned soup.

The chicken all gone, Reston started in on the mashed potatoes and gravy.

*Sure hope he doesn't get a heart attack before we hit our big payday,* Tully said to himself, and moved soup from bowl to mouth. Out loud he said, "You going to do the snakes or wait until tomorrow?"

"I'll wait. Suspense. Feed the gossip channels. Probably pack the house tomorrow."

"Sounds like a plan."

Potatoes and gravy gone, Reston stuffed the cornbread into his mouth. When it was on its way south, he said, "Now skedaddle. I gotta work on my sermon."

Tully finished his soup, put the tuna noodle salad back in his bag, and left Reston's office. He walked out to what would soon be the worship area and sat in a folding chair.

He took the container of tuna noodle salad out of the bag and dug in. As he ate, he wondered where Jerri was. If she was too busy with those flyers, maybe he'd track down Raylene. The two of them could go out to the Reservoir and take in all the beauty nature had to offer.

He was so glad she had turned seventeen.

"Probably the prettiest of Reston's girls, and that's saying something," he murmured. "And she's no longer jailbait."

# 11

12:05 PM, WEDNESDAY, 11 OCTOBER

WHILE TULLY AND RESTON WERE EATING LUNCH AND DREAMING dreams, the Reverend Ember Cole left her office and walked the eight blocks to Harry Thurgood's Really Good Wood-Fired Coffee Shop. She opened the door, stepped inside, and froze.

Harry was at his table in the corner, drinking coffee and eating a slice of pie. Jack Bonhoffer was at the cash register, taking money from a customer. Estrelita was waiting on a table. And on the opposite side of the floor from Harry sat Mary Lou Fight and five members of the New Order of the Crimson Hat Society. After last year's debacle, Mary Lou created a new group, with new members, to serve up the same old tittle-tattle and muckraking dirt as before.

Ember, regaining her composure, stepped further into the shop.

Mary Lou gave her former minister a pernicious smile before raising the teacup to her lips.

Ember, in turn, gave her former parishioner an angelic smile and then marched right over to Harry's table.

"What the hell is that woman and her minions doing here?" she demanded to know in a loud whisper.

"Whoa, Reverend. Have a seat. I don't serve bourbon, but a good strong coffee might do just as well."

Ember sat. "Why is that woman and, and those people here?" she hissed.

"They're having lunch. But more likely they're here to spy on me. Maybe you, too."

"Exactly. So why are you serving them?"

"They're wearing shirts and shoes. How could I say no?"

"This isn't funny, Harry."

"Who's laughing? I was just as surprised as you. Is Mary Lou still going to Billy Bob's church?"

"Yes. As far as I know."

"At least you're in the clear there."

"No one on this planet will be in the clear until she is dead."

"Not sure you should say that out loud."

"You know, if I wasn't trying my best to be a good servant of Christ, I'd show her what it really means to be a bitch."

"Whoa! Where is the sweet Emmy I've come to know and love?"

Ember took in a lungful of air and slowly exhaled.

"You do realize that there are bigger issues in the world than Mary Lou Fight. At best, she's a big fish in a very tiny pond."

"You're right. I'm sorry."

"No need to apologize to me. My sentiments are the same as yours. I just don't say them where or when anyone might possibly hear me. Besides, I don't know if you want Mary Lou dead. Can you imagine her and Satan tag teaming?"

"This isn't funny."

"Who's laughing?"

"You're making light of this. Her being here is serious."

"Next time she shows up, I'll text you."

"Thanks."

"Now, how about a real strong cup of coffee and a bowl of chili?"

Ember closed her eyes, folded her hands together, said a brief prayer, opened her eyes, and nodded.

Harry stood and walked behind the counter to give the order to Miguel and to get the coffee.

While he was filling her cup, a young woman glided from the table of Crimson Hats to stand next to Ember.

"Mrs. Fight would appreciate it if you would join *us* at *our* table for luncheon."

Ember's eyes took in the condescending Rubenesque woman. A red hat with a very wide-brim sat on her head and a long bright yellow feather boa was draped around her neck; the ends trailed down her front and back.

Her tight purple and white dress emphasized all of her many curves. In addition, the neckline was cut very low, revealing a mile of milky white cleavage. Ember wondered how the woman avoided a wardrobe malfunction.

Realizing she was probably staring, she said, "You're Pearline Applewhite, aren't you?"

"That's right. My husband teaches music at the college."

"Yes, I remember now."

"So, will you be joining us?"

"Unfortunately..." Ember looked at her watch. "I'm going to have to eat and run. I have an appointment."

"I see. How unfortunate."

"Please give Mrs. Fight my regrets. Perhaps next time."

"There might not be a next time," Pearline hissed through the smile on her lips."

Harry brought Ember's coffee and chili to the table."

"I'll let you eat, Reverend Cole, and I will give Mrs. Fight your regrets."

"Thank you, Mrs. Applewhite."

As Pearline Applewhite glided back to her table, Harry asked, "What was that all about?"

"Mary Lou sent her minion over to invite me to lunch with them."

"Seriously?"

Ember sipped her coffee. "Not kidding."

"That's a new tactic."

"It is, and it can't be good."

"I dare say not."

Ember brought a spoonful of chili up to her mouth and blew on it.

At the same time, the bell over the door rang, and in walked Scarlett Hayden.

The tall and shapely blonde was wearing a dark brown mid-calf heavy cardigan sweater. Underneath the open sweater, she was wearing a winter white dress that clung to her hips and breasts and revealed an ample eyeful of cleavage. Three-inch winter white stilettos covered her feet, and a winter-white beret sat on top of the long cascade of soft blonde curls. Hanging from a gold chain that was over her left shoulder was a small, winter-white purse.

Ember groaned. "And this day started out so well."

Scarlett smiled at Harry and made a kiss with her lips. She smiled at Ember, and walked over to the Crimson Hat table, where she exchanged greetings with the women. She then took a seat at her own table.

Estrelita hurried over to take her order.

Ember's eyes moved from Scarlett to her coffee and then to Harry's face. "Would you box all of this for me? I have to go."

"Sure, Em."

Harry left the table, and got a to-go cup for the coffee, along with a heavy paper bowl and plastic lid for the chili, and a paper bag. He returned to the table, transferred food and drink, and put them in the bag.

"Here you go, Reverend. Hope the rest of your day is better."

"Me, too. Bye, Harry."

Ember walked swiftly to the door. As she reached out to open it, the door swung open, and in walked the strange man who'd spent the previous day sitting by the window scrolling through his phone.

# 12

## 12:42 PM, WEDNESDAY, 11 OCTOBER

HARRY WATCHED THE PHONE SCROLLER LOOK AT THE RETREATING Ember Cole. *What is this guy looking for?* he asked himself. *He's obviously keeping an eye on me, but Em, too?*

Once Ember had disappeared down the sidewalk, the man entered the Really Good, walked up to the counter, and took a seat.

Estrelita was busy at a table; so Jack Bonhoffer grabbed a menu and slid off his stool, but Harry's upraised hand stopped him.

Harry got up and walked over to the man. "You're back, I see."

Phone scroller nodded. "I am. Coffee. Black. And a bowl of that chili."

"Coming right up," Harry said, and he slipped behind the counter to give the chili order to Miguel.

To the man, he said, "Colombian light medium roast okay?"

"Yeah, sure, that'll work."

Harry poured the coffee and placed the mug before him.

The man took a sip and nodded his acceptance.

"Order up, Mr. Thurgood," Miguel said.

Harry retrieved the chili and cornbread and set the bowl and plate on the counter.

"Thanks," phone scroller said, took his food to the table by the window, and once he was seated, began to eat.

Harry watched the six pairs of eyes at the Crimson Hat table study the new arrival.

*I bet they'll all be losing sleep trying to figure out who the stranger is.*

He smiled at that thought, walked over to Scarlett's table, and occupied the chair across from her.

"That smile for me?" she asked.

"Do you want it to be?"

"I can tell I'm high on your list." She nodded her head towards the phone scroller's table. "Who's the hunk?"

"No idea."

"Hope he stays around."

"You'll have to ask him."

"I just might, since I can't even get a smile from the guy I care about."

"So, to what do I owe the pleasure?"

"My desire for a good cup of coffee."

"I see." He got Estrelita's attention, made a drinking gesture, and pointed to Scarlett.

In a moment, the sultry blonde had a piping hot cup of coffee on the table before her.

"And coffee's the only reason you're here?"

Scarlett took a sip. "No."

"Ah. Pray tell what else are you here for?"

"Nothing's free, you know." She drank coffee.

"Very true. There's always a cost to someone somewhere. How about an IOU?"

Scarlett smiled. "You know, if I didn't like you I just might tell you to go copulate with yourself."

He laughed. "Well, I guess I should be glad you like me."

"Yes, you should."

"Would you believe me if I told you I am?"

Scarlett's gaze shifted to one of the paintings hanging on the wall, and she closed her eyes for a moment. When she opened them, her gaze turned back to Harry's face. "Yes. I believe you."

"Good. An IOU then?"

She sighed. "Very well. You're being followed." She turned her head toward the Hats and lifted her chin.

"Let me guess. The Queen Bee over there has something to do with that."

"As sure as honey comes from the comb."

"I see. I suppose I'd better watch my steps."

Scarlett nodded and touched the coffee cup to her lips.

————

Ember was practically running back to the safety of her church. She clutched the bag to her chest. Her focus on the sidewalk in front of her.

First, Mary Lou and her hatted minions. Then Scarlett Hayden. Scarlett. The one woman who could take Harry away from her.

"Why, oh, why can't I forget my past?" she muttered. "I know Jesus has forgiven me. Why can't I completely forgive myself? Harry loves me. I know he does. If he truly loves me, won't he forgive what I've done?"

Tears welled up in her eyes, and she swiped at them with the back of her hand.

"Please God. Please. Don't let what I've done scare off the man I love. Please."

As Ember cried out to her God, a man wearing blue jeans and a black hoodie followed her.

## 13

### 1:17 PM, WEDNESDAY, 11 OCTOBER

JOETTA AND ORALENE RESTON HAD FINISHED HANDING OUT FLYERS on both sides of Madison Street and were taking a brief break.

"Who you daydreamin' about this time?" Oralene asked her older sister.

"Nobody."

"Oh, don't be givin' me that, Jo. I know that look. Is it Purnell again? What's he promisin' you this time?"

"You're just jealous."

"Me? How do you know he ain't jumpin' my bones?"

"What?"

"Just sayin'. I don't think our Mr. Tully is overly particular about where he dips his wick, just so long as it's wet."

"I can't believe you're sayin' that about Purnell, Oralene. That's just downright nasty, that is."

"Oh, come on, Joetta. You know he's doin' Mama, right? And Raylene's been talkin' an awful lot to him. Hell, he's all over us like white on rice."

"No need for swearin'."

"Since when did you get all high and mighty?"

"I'm not."

"You know John-John and Purnell got into a big fight when we was in Zwolle, don't you?"

"Yeah, Raylene told me. John-John caught him and Mama at it. Did he tell Pa?"

"I don't think Pa cares none. He's been sniffin' around Wendolyn."

"What? She's only twelve."

"Yeah, so? When has that ever stopped him? You oughta know that."

Joetta said nothing. With head bowed, she stared at the flyers in her hand.

"Come on, Jo, let's do this next block."

Joetta nodded. "I'll take this side."

"Okay. I'll race you to the end."

Joetta laughed. But her heart wasn't in it. *Oralene's smart. Maybe the smartest one in the family.*

And she knew her younger sister was right.

————

John Reston, Junior, called John-John by his family, and his brother Lofton were over a block from Joetta and Oralene handing out flyers.

The brothers worked opposite sides of the street. As they neared the end of the block, John-John saw his mother hurrying down a cross street.

"I bet she's meeting Tully again," he muttered. "And leaving Ray to finish handing out the flyers by herself." He shook his head. "Ain't right."

He remembered that time he caught them in adultery. He'd hit the older man really good. Knocked him down. Told him he'd kill him if he didn't leave his ma alone. And he'd meant it.

"Looks like I'm going to have to do something about this. Again. Pa won't. Can't understand that. No man's screwin' *my* wife."

When no one answered his knocking, he opened the screen door and slipped in a flyer.

He stared at the cross street in the distance. "Looks like me and Tully are gonna have to have another talk. And not the kind with words."

# 14

3:42 PM, WEDNESDAY, 11 OCTOBER

In Room 12 of the Cozy Corners Motel, Purnell Tully was pulling up his slacks. Still lying on the bed was Jearlene Reston. She hadn't bothered to cover herself with the sheet.

"You know, Purnell, it might be nice if once in a while you took me someplace real pretty."

Tully slipped his arm into a shirt sleeve. "You know I would, Babe, if I could. Our situation is difficult right now. But it won't be that way forever."

"I've seen how you've been lookin' at Raylene." Jerri sat up.

Tully found it difficult not to stare at her breasts. She had beautiful breasts.

He said, "She's a pretty young girl. And that's it."

"Keep it that way. You can't be screwin' a mama and her daughter. It's not right."

"I love you, Jerri." He sat on the bed next to her. His hands found their way to her breasts, but she pulled away from him.

"C'mon now. Don't be jealous. I'm with you. And when we get enough money socked away, we're gonna leave that tub of lard behind. I still don't see what you saw in him."

"I was sixteen and he was forty-one and I was pregnant with

Joetta. And my daddy had a shotgun. That's what I saw in Johnny. I told you all this before."

"So you did, Sugar. Sorry."

"We have to take Mary Jean and Jacob with us. They're too young."

"Sure, Sweetheart. Whatever you want."

"I'll feel bad, awful bad, leavin' the other kids, but Joetta and Oralene can look after them. At least until we can send for them."

"Absolutely, Honey."

"You're not just sayin' that, are you?"

"Heck, no. I mean it."

"Promise?"

"I promise."

"Then kiss me before you go."

"Sure we don't have time for more than a kiss?"

"If you hurry, we do."

Purnell Tully stood, undid his belt, and let his trousers fall to the floor.

# 15

4:57 PM, WEDNESDAY, 11 OCTOBER

LANDON COLE PACE COULDN'T BELIEVE HIS EARS. "WHAT DID YOU say?" He had his hands on his hips.

Graham Huston leaned forward in his chair. "I want you to go to the revival show tonight. It ought to be good and I want it in the paper."

"But what about—"

Huston cut him off. "I'm the editor and you're the intern. Now get out of here and go do some reporting. It's the only way you're going to learn this job."

"Is that how *you* learned the job?"

Huston leaned back in his chair and put his hands behind his head. "Sit down, Mr. Pace."

Landon dropped his hands to his sides, hesitated a moment, and then sat in the chair and faced Huston from across the desk.

"I'll admit I came to this profession late in life. But that also means I had a lot of life before I got to sit in this chair. I don't know a lot about journalism, but I do know something of life and death. Especially death. And I learned a little bit about newspapers from the former editor and publisher, Neal Holland. I also found his body on that printing press in the back room. He was murdered and I caught his murderer. Probably murderess would be more accurate.

"I was in Afghanistan and saw a lot of men die. My best buddy died and it should have been me. But it wasn't and I have to live with that for the rest of my life.

"Now the one thing I know about this business is that to sell papers I need stories people want to read. But the money they pay to read them doesn't pay for the electricity to keep the lights on or your salary. Advertising pays your salary and keeps the lights on. And advertisers will only pay me money if they know people are reading the paper.

"Now I know you had some interview all lined up with a winery snob and his hot little wife. But that interview won't sell a quarter of the papers that a story about Brother John and his extravaganza will sell.

"So get out there and get me one helluva story. A story that will keep the lights on and let me buy enough paper and ink for the next edition. And give you a paycheck. Do I make myself clear?"

"Yes, sir, Mr. Huston."

"Good. And if you need your hand held, take Monika with you. Now get out of here. There's no news here."

Pace got up from the chair and just about ran out of the *Chronicle* office.

Standing on West Main, he looked up and down the street. The traffic was normal for a late afternoon.

He took his phone out of his pocket.

*Damn. I was sure looking forward to the interview tonight because Clemmie Zollerndorfer is easy on the eyes.*

He sent a text to Theodore Zollerndorfer, owner of Zollern Cellars, which was a short drive west of town, to tell him he needed to reschedule the interview.

That done, he checked the time and slipped the phone back into his pocket.

*Two hours to showtime. Perhaps I can interview Brother John or someone on the team.*

He smiled. *Yeah. That would be a good start.*

———

The signs in the windows announced that this was the place where the good people of Magnolia Bluff could hear the preaching of the Word and the divine voices of the Reston Family Singers.

Landon tried the door and found it was unlocked. He pushed it open and stepped inside.

The building looked like it had once been a grocery store, or possibly a department store. Now it was just an empty shell. There was a slight musty smell to the air.

Fourteen people were standing on the small stage singing some song about Jesus.

He studied the group. It was very clear he didn't need the picture in the window to tell him these were the Reston Family Singers, as they all bore a certain family resemblance.

The enormous bear of a man was Brother John. That much was obvious. Landon guessed he was in his sixties. He spotted Jearlene, Reston's wife.

*Maybe early forties,* he thought. *And she still has a good figure, in spite of all those kids.* She was a MILF if he ever saw one.

The largest boy, who looked like he was the oldest, was a near carbon copy of his dad.

*Probably around my age.*

Landon's eyes swept over the girls. The oldest looked to be about his age. And were they ever gorgeous.

*I just might have to talk to them to see if my soul can be saved.* Then he laughed to himself, because salvation was the last thing on his mind.

Standing over to the side of the large room was a man looking

at a tablet. Landon guessed he was maybe in his forties, like Jearlene Reston.

*I think I'll start with him. Might give me some background.*

Landon walked over to him.

"Excuse me, I'm Landon Pace and I'm with the *Magnolia Bluff
Chronicle.*"

The man looked up from the tablet. "I'm Purnell Tully. I'm
Brother John's personal assistant."

Tully held out his hand and Landon took it.

"You here to witness the power of the Lord?" Tully asked.

"I'm here to see, observe, and write a story for the paper."

"That's good. It's good to spread the word of the Lord by any
means."

"You doing any snake handling tonight?"

"Not tonight. Tomorrow. Are you a man of faith, Mr.Pace?"

"Call me Landon. Sure. I have faith in money and in the fact
that people will screw you over the first chance they get. So it's
best to screw them over first."

"That's a mighty cynical position for a man your age."

"All you have to do is take an honest look at the world, Mr.
Tully. It's dog eat dog. And even those who try to do good end up
doing bad. It's a sad state of affairs. But, hey, we can eat, drink,
and be merry, can't we?"

"I suppose you can if you don't believe in God, or in any form
of human goodness, then that's about all that's left to you. And if
that's what you believe, and you want nothing to do with Jesus,
then you might as well cut to the chase and just die soon. You
avoid all the nonsense that way."

"Huh. A little bit of Nietzsche there. Interesting."

"I believe it pays to be smart. Dogma's for dolts. And you,
young man, are spouting off a lot of poorly thought through nega-
tive dogma."

"So what does the smart man do?"

"He plays the long game and keeps his eyes open. Now, if
you'll excuse me, I have work to do for tonight."

Landon watched Tully cross the floor and head for a door on the far wall.

*I wonder what he meant by the long game and keeping your eyes open?*

# 16

7:43 PM, WEDNESDAY, 11 OCTOBER

BROTHER JOHN WAS RAINING HELLFIRE AND BRIMSTONE DOWN ON THE four dozen people sitting in the folding chairs.

Landon wished he hadn't had that fourth beer at O'Gara's. Either that or had gotten a second order of french fries. The forcefulness of the preaching wasn't doing his head any good.

Then suddenly, with an instinct born out of natural ability and honed talent, Brother John shifted gears and his tone modulated. Becoming almost pleading. Landon was thankful. The softer tone didn't hurt his head as much.

"We are unworthy sinners. That's a truth as concrete as this floor. Yet, yet there is One Who has washed away your sins, my friends. He has freed you from Hell. All you have to do is believe in His gift. Let Him enter your heart and sweep out the filth. Sweep out the unbelief.

"And Who is this person Who will save your wretched soul? He is the Lord Jesus Christ. Yes, my friends. Jesus will save you and give you eternal life. All you have to do is confess your sin and let him enter your heart."

On one side of the stage, Joetta and Oralene began softly singing "Just as I am", and then, on the fourth line, Jerri Reston added her angelic voice: "O Lamb of God, I come, I come."

"That's right, my friends," boomed Brother John, "just come to Jesus. Right now. Get out of that chair and come right down here. Unburden that wicked heart. Let Jesus take over. Become a new creation in Christ Jesus."

Several people got out of their seats and went forward.

While they were responding to the altar call, a woman jumped up and began babbling words belonging to no known language of planet earth. At least that Landon was aware of.

*What the hell is that?* he asked himself. And right then, he made a promise to ask Huston why he gave him this assignment.

He checked to make sure that the recorder was on. It was. He'd listen to the gibberish again later.

Brother John, though, kept right on with the service and raised his hands. "We have a word from the Lord. Is there anyone here who can interpret God's Word for us?"

On cue, Joetta stepped forward. "Thus saith the Lord," she began, "I am the Healer. The One Who casts out the demons that cause disease. There is one here who is ailing, who is beleaguered by the Devil. She has a tumor. Step forward and be healed, says the Lord!"

Landon rolled his eyes. "Who the hell can be this gullible?" he said under his breath.

He watched as a tall woman, young, perhaps a senior in high school, stepped forward. She was conservatively dressed, but it would have taken a burlap sack to hide the curves on her body.

She stopped in front of Brother John and spoke to him.

The mountain of a man invited her to step up onto the stage.

Landon noticed Reston placed his hands probably where he shouldn't have as he helped her up onto the platform.

Brother John said, "This young woman has a tumor recently discovered by her doctor. And it is growing rapidly. But tonight she will experience the power of the Lord Jesus Christ. She will be healed!"

The preacher touched under the young woman's breast. "Oh,

yes, I feel a large tumor here. Jearlene, come and feel this manifestation of the demon."

Jearlene Reston crossed the stage and put her hand on the girl. "Oh, yes. Yes, I can feel it. I can feel the power of Satan."

Jerri Reston stepped back and Brother John stepped forward. He placed one hand on the tumor and another on top of the young woman's head.

Landon was taking video of the healing on his phone.

"Do you believe in the Lord?" the preacher asked.

"Yes, I believe," the young woman answered.

"Then believe that you shall be healed," Reston thundered.

He closed his eyes and bowed his head. A moment later, his head shot up, his face pointed towards the ceiling, and he began uttering a string of gibberish.

Landon shook his head and wondered how long this circus sideshow would go on.

After a good half-minute had passed, the girl threw her head back, screamed, and collapsed.

Jearlene caught her and laid her down on the platform.

Brother John turned to the congregation. "The demon has left her." He kneeled beside the girl and Landon thought an awful lot of the big man's hand was on her breast.

"I do not feel the tumor. But we will get confirmation when she comes out of her swoon."

"Seriously? *Swoon?*" Landon muttered.

Brother John was speaking again. "The Lord Jesus wants you. Come forward. Be saved. Confess your sins and turn your life around. Be healed. Let Jesus make you whole, my friends."

Joetta and Oralene were softly singing "Just as I am", and Landon wondered if either one had a boyfriend.

After about five minutes, he muttered, "A sane person can only take so much." He stood and left.

Standing on the sidewalk outside the building, he wondered if all new reporters had to go through this.

"I'll have to ask Carter. Maybe he can tell me if all new reporters have to endure crap assignments."

Landon looked at his phone. *Still early enough for another beer at O'Gara's. But after this circus show, I think whiskey. Neat."*

# 17

9:28 PM, WEDNESDAY, 11 OCTOBER

CLOUDS SCUDDED ACROSS THE BLACK, MOONLESS SKY.

*At least the drizzle has stopped,* Hunter told himself.

He was transferring the contents of the Really Good's dumpster to black plastic trash bags and putting the bags into the back of his pickup.

This was the fifth time he'd collected Thurgood's trash, and thus far he'd hauled away nothing but useless refuse. Perhaps he'd get lucky tonight. Maybe Thurgood would finally get sloppy.

What he actually needed to do was to break into Thurgood's apartment. He'd been resisting doing so because it was dangerous. But the Fight woman was putting an awful lot of pressure on him.

He'd tried drones and external microphones to no avail. The guy was good.

No, it was time to do a bit of breaking and entering.

He looked up at Thurgood's window. A light was on.

Hunter sighed and went back to collecting trash, doing his best to avoid the garbage.

He hoped the GPS tracker would give him something good. And if he got something from the trash, that would be even better.

If not, though, a search of the man's apartment should reveal something. It had to. Just as long as he didn't get caught.

———

A man dressed all in black sat on a bench in the green across from Thurgood's store. He watched the light in the apartment above the store go out. A few minutes later, he saw Harry Thurgood come out the street door, lock it, and walk briskly down the street.

The man took out his phone, texted a message, and then began scrolling through the contents while he waited for a reply.

———

Hunter tossed the last bag into the pickup. He looked up once again at Thurgood's window and noticed the light was out.

"He won't be gone long," he muttered, "but it might be long enough for me to plant a bug. Then I can come back later and do a thorough search."

Hunter opened the back door of his truck, rummaged around in a box, found what he was looking for, locked the vehicle, and trotted down the alley to the street corner. He rounded the corner and continued on to Main Street.

He noticed the lack of traffic.

*A normal small town,* he thought. *The sidewalks roll up when the sun goes down. Which is just perfect. Perfect for me.*

# 18

9:53 PM, WEDNESDAY, 11 OCTOBER

HARRY ENTERED OLIVIA'S PIZZERIA, LOOKED AROUND AND CAUGHT Ember's wave. He raised his hand to acknowledge that he'd seen her wave.

There were about a dozen college students in the place. Harry didn't notice any locals. *Probably too late at night*, he speculated.

Crossing the floor, he took a seat at the table Em had claimed for them. He was no sooner in his chair, when Olivia was at the table with an extra large pepperoni, mushroom, and black olive pizza; a bottle of Texas Zinfandel; and two glasses.

In a stage whisper to Harry, Olivia said, "I skipped the anchovies. Just in case. You know?"

Ember turned bright red.

Harry laughed, and said, "I'm sure the Reverend here appreciates your gesture."

Olivia poured wine into the glasses. "Just call me Miss Cupid." And with a hearty laugh, she was off to get another order.

"God, I'm so embarrassed," Ember said.

"Why?"

"Because of what people think we're doing."

"What we're doing? I don't know about you, but I think we're going to eat pizza and drink wine."

"You know what I mean."

"Just be thankful. Now, I won't have fish breath."

Ember laughed. "Well, there is that."

"Did you order this?"

"Nope. Just Olivia doing her thing."

"Kind of spooky how she knows what you want before you even get here."

"Kinda is. It does save time, though."

"That it does." Harry raised his glass. "To time. Our friend and our enemy."

Ember touched her glass to Harry's and drank a swallow of the rich and spicy red wine. "That was a strange toast."

"In what way?"

"It was quite philosophical."

Harry shrugged. "I'm a philosophical kind of guy."

"I guess that's one of the things I love about you. You know everything. Genuinely know everything." She leaned forward. "And I love an intelligent, confident, and thoughtful man. One who can take charge, with no hesitation."

Harry reached across the table, took her hand in his, and gave it a squeeze.

There was a yell from a couple tables over, and a pitcher of pop shattered on the floor, breaking the spell.

"Well, let's get going on this pizza, Mister, before it gets cold."

"Let's."

They ate pizza and chit-chatted until they were the only ones left and Olivia finally shooed them out.

Harry left a hundred dollar bill on the table, and arm in arm, they left the restaurant and walked to Main Street.

When they rounded the corner, they saw flashing lights.

"Those lights look like they're in front of the Really Good," Ember said.

"So they do. Wonder what's up?"

The two picked up their pace, and when they were twenty feet away from the storefront, it became very obvious why the police were there. A body was sprawled on the sidewalk. From the way the one arm was stretched, it looked to Harry as if the person had been reaching for something.

*Whatever it was he was trying to grasp,* Harry thought, *he isn't going to be finding it in this world.*

# 19

## 12:13 AM, THURSDAY, 12 OCTOBER

"AH, THURGOOD." REECE SOVERN, THE INVESTIGATOR FOR THE Magnolia Bluff Police Department, ambled over to the couple.

When he reached them, he took the unlit and soggy cigar out of his mouth. He nodded his head slightly to Ember. "Reverend." Stuck the green corona back in his mouth, sank his teeth into it to make sure it didn't get away, and focused on Harry.

"Any idea why there's a murder victim on your doorstep?" he asked.

"No."

Sovern pushed his glasses up his nose. "Come here and take a look. Maybe you recognize him."

Harry and Ember followed the detective. They stopped next to a man dressed entirely in black. He was sprawled across the sidewalk.

"Recognize that face?" Sovern asked.

"No," Harry answered.

Ember shook her head.

Sovern grunted in reply, then asked, "Name Hunter Sulzer mean anything to either of you?"

Ember shook her head.

Harry asked, "How did he die?"

"Three gunshots to the back. From the scorch marks, I'd say very up close and personal. Still waiting on Wylie to make the official announcement that he's dead."

"Someone who knew him?"

"It's a thought," Sovern answered, and then continued, "Have to wait for the ME to find out the caliber. But we haven't found any brass. So either the perp was super good at finding three casings in the dark, or he used a revolver."

Harry nodded. "Probably a revolver."

"My guess, too," Sovern said, then asked, "Recognize the name, Thurgood?"

"No. Should I?"

Sovern shrugged. "You tell me."

"Never heard of him."

Ember asked, "Did anybody see or hear anything?"

Sovern shook his head. "Not even a call saying gunshots were heard. And apparently no one around at the time."

"Fergus might know," Ember said.

"Yeah, he might," Sovern admitted. "Testimony's not worth a damn since he's usually drunk."

"How did you know the body was here?" Ember asked.

"Officer Winkler drove by and noticed it."

Ember nodded.

"I need to ask," Sovern began, "where have you two been?"

Harry answered. "We were at Olivia's since about nine, nine-thirty. I was walking Em home when we saw the lights."

"You agree with that, Reverend?"

"Yes."

"Before nine?"

Harry answered first. "I was here. Upstairs. Left by this door around nine. There wasn't a body here when I left."

Sovern studied Harry's face. "And you've no idea who this person is and why he'd be here?"

"None."

"Reverend, where were you before getting your pizza?"

"I was at the hospital visiting with patients until five-thirty. Went home and fed Wilbur, my cat. Then went to a committee meeting at the church. After the meeting ended, I walked to Olivia's. Took Monroe Street over."

"Why didn't you meet Thurgood?"

"The Really Good is out of the way. Straighter route if I take Monroe."

Sovern pursed his lips, thought a moment, but let it drop. "You walking the Reverend home?"

"I am. I believe I already said I was."

"So you did. Go on then. Get her home safe and sound. And don't take any long trips, you two, unless you tell me. Okay?"

"Deal," Harry said.

Ember nodded.

"We should have the body out of here as soon as Wylie shows up. Don't know what's keeping the man."

"It is late," Harry said. "Might be sleeping."

"Might. Lucky devil if he is," Sovern said. "Goodnight."

Harry took Ember's hand and they headed off toward the parsonage.

"Every month," Ember said.

"Yes?"

"Every month for the past year someone has been murdered."

To himself, Harry said, *And I wonder who's next?*

# 20

6:51 AM, THURSDAY, 12 OCTOBER

REECE SOVERN PITCHED HIS SOGGY CIGAR TOWARDS THE WASTEBASKET that occupied a corner of his office. It missed going in and joined four others on the floor. He took a fresh corona out of the desk drawer, removed the cellophane, and stuck it in his mouth. He never lit one.

The detective picked up the dead man's wallet and looked once more at the driver's license. Hunter Sulzer. Dallas address. A business card identified the man as a private detective.

Reece set the wallet down and picked up the set of lock picks that had been found next to the body.

"Was probably picking the lock on the street door to Thurgood's apartment when he was shot," Reece muttered. "So who hired him, and why?"

He picked up the S&W Model 638 snub-nosed revolver and turned it over in his hands.

*Nice concealed carry gun.*

The revolver had been found in a holster tucked into the small of the dead man's back.

*Someone obviously snuck up on Mr. Sulzer before he had a chance to defend himself.*

"Now for the million dollar question," he muttered, "who the hell shot him and why?"

The revolver, however, had no answer for the police detective, so he set it down, put his hands behind his head, and leaned back in his chair.

His eyes were pointed towards the ceiling, but they weren't focused there. They were staring past the dingy white paint into a place that hopefully held answers. But none were revealing themselves.

*What it looks like is that someone hires this Sulzer guy to get something on Thurgood. Then someone sees him at Thurgood's door and shoots him dead. Now, who would want to do that? If Thurgood didn't do it himself, who's his guardian angel?*

Reece closed his eyes. He'd called the number on the victim's business card, but the call went to voicemail.

Suddenly, he sat up. "Phone," he said. "There was no phone on this guy. Who doesn't have a phone these days?"

Reece leaned back again in his chair. His hands behind his head. Eyes closed.

*So the perp takes the guy's phone, but not his wallet. Which means this wasn't a robbery. Whoever shot Sulzer wanted him dead. And wanted whatever was on our Mr. Sulzer's phone. But why not take the hundred and sixty-eight bucks in the wallet? I mean, Sulzer's not gonna need it.*

The cigar moved over to the other side of Reece's mouth, and he continued his analysis.

*Maybe the person who killed him didn't need the money, so he, or maybe even she, didn't even bother to look. Now who around here doesn't need a buck or two?* He snorted. *Too many. Although, I'm not one of them.*

Reece sat up and looked at his coffee mug. He picked it up. It was a third full and the mug was no longer warm. He walked out of his office and headed for the lunchroom.

There was half a carafe sitting on the warmer. He poured the cold coffee out into the sink, refilled his mug, and returned to his office.

Once again seated at his gray metal army surplus desk, he pitched the soggy stogie at the gray wastebasket, missed, and drank coffee.

Somehow Thurgood was mixed up in this. The detective knew it in his bones. The guy was friendly and certainly nice enough, but there was something off about the coffee shop owner. Something not quite on the up and up with the man. But Reece couldn't put his finger on it.

And then there was that comment from the stranger in the coffee shop, the red-headed bombshell that Jager had told him about. What was it? He'd made sure to write it down so he could add it to the collection of tidbits he was gathering on Thurgood. He paged through his notebook until he found it.

"I was in art," the woman said, "and it can be a dangerous business."

*Now what the hell did she mean by that?* Reece asked himself. *According to Jager, the woman gave every indication Harry knew what she meant.*

Reece set the notebook down. "If that's the case," he muttered, "then that means Thurgood is or was in the art business and this woman was warning him about the unsavory side."

*That would be things like forgeries and theft. Is that what Thurgood is into?*

Reece sipped his coffee and leaned back in his chair, holding the mug against his chest.

Thurgood obviously has some means of support he's kept mum about, because the coffee shop's now in its fourth year.

Reece chuckled. "And it doesn't make enough in one day to keep me in cheap cigars. Let alone Thurgood's fancy suits and cars."

*So where is the money coming from? The word on the street is that the account at Fight's bank doesn't contain enough for a pot to pee in.*

*The other million dollar question, though, is how does the Thurgood mystery connect with the dead private dick? Who is it that suspects something about our coffee shop dandy and decided to hire a private to check him out?*

Reece drank coffee. "It makes sense," he said. "In fact, it makes a whole lot of sense. So who'd hired Sulzer to get the goods on Thurgood?"

The more Reece turned that question over in his mind, the more he wanted to find the answer to it. And the deeper it fell into a dense fog.

# 21

8:57 AM, THURSDAY, 12 OCTOBER

TWO TABLES WERE PUSHED TOGETHER AND AROUND THEM SAT
Reverend Billy Bob Baskin, pastor of the Presbyterian church;
Reverend Ember Cole, pastor of the Methodist church; Graham
Huston, owner and editor of the *Magnolia Bluff Chronicle;* Police
Chief Tommy Jager; LouEllen Mueller, owner of LouEllen's
Lounge, and still in the running for the Dolly Parton lookalike
contest; Caroline McCluskey, head librarian of the Magnolia Bluff
library; Magnolia Nadine Roane, conservator of the Women's
Building; and Harry Thurgood.

The group made up the nine a.m. regulars at Harry's coffee
shop.

Estrellita set two pots of coffee, a tray of Bluff Bakery doughnuts, and a Czech poppyseed roll of Harry's making on the table.
After making sure nothing was lacking at the tables, she returned
to her post behind the counter.

Jager poured himself coffee and took a doughnut. "So, Thurgood, who do you think is digging into your life?"

"What do you mean?" LouEllen asked. "Everyone knows
Harry has more secrets than Carter has pills, as my momma used
to say."

Huston stopped the slice of poppyseed roll from entering his mouth. "Some private detective was shot to death last night. Right out there." He pointed out the window and then guided the poppyseed slice to his mouth.

"I just don't know what our town is coming to," Magnolia Nadine said. "For nine years we had those awful May murders, and now people are dying left and right, and we have sex traffickers camping out on our doorstep. I'd hate to think what my—"

Jager cut her off. "Yeah, Nadine, we all know what your great-grandmother would think. You, though, didn't answer the question, Thurgood."

"I was already questioned by Sovern."

"Yeah, that's why *I'm* asking you."

Harry took a sip of his coffee. "I'll tell you what I told Reece: I have no idea."

"You must have one helluva interesting secret life," Huston said, "if someone's willing to hire a private detective to bring it to light. Sure you don't want to give me exclusive rights to your story?"

"No, Graham, I do not," Harry answered. "Besides, there's nothing exciting in my life. I just value my privacy, and apparently there are some people in this town who can't stand that."

"That's what the guilty always say," Jager chimed in.

"Well, one thing's for sure," LouEllen said, "someone isn't going to get their money's worth."

———

Across Burnet Reservoir, in a cabin tucked away in a remote part of Hayden Resort, a man dressed in black sat at a table absent-mindedly scrolling through his phone. He looked at the time. She was late.

*But then she was always late,* he reminded himself.

There was a knock, and the door opened. In walked the tall, buxom blonde. She was wearing a light blue blouse with too many buttons unbuttoned, and a dark blue, ankle-length, full skirt. Around her waist was a belt and on the belt, a small pouch. In her left hand, she was carrying a backpack.

She lifted the backpack and said, "It's in here. You want to count it?"

The man stood. "Nah. If it's not all there, I know where you live." He favored her with a smile.

The woman held out the backpack, and he took it with his left hand.

Hefting it, he said, "Feels about right."

"Good. Pleasure doing business with you."

"I give a discount for repeat customers." His eyes took in the expanse of flesh the unbuttoned blouse revealed.

"I'll keep that in mind."

"Well, then, until next time." He gave her a lazy salute and headed for the open door. When he passed her, he recognized the perfume. It was one he liked.

*Such a tease*, he thought.

When he'd reached the door, he heard her voice behind him say, "Thanks for the memories."

Then there was a deafening roar, and a burning finger of pain touched his back and shoved him forward.

He dropped the backpack, grabbed hold of the doorjamb, and turned around. There was a revolver in her hand.

Another deafening blast, a flash, and a red hot poker pierced his chest, followed by another.

"Damn, never expected this," he uttered, before he sank to his knees and pitched forward into the beckoning black hole that suddenly appeared before him.

## 22

10:01 AM, THURSDAY, 12 OCTOBER

PURNELL TULLY WONDERED YET AGAIN HOW THAT LITTLE DESK CHAIR supported the bulk of Brother John.

"You listenin' to me, Tully?" Reston took a big bite out of his cheese Danish.

"Everything's ready for tonight."

Reston swallowed. "The snakes been fixed?"

"The poison sacs were removed. At least that's what the fellow said."

"Good. Wouldn't want there to be a mishap that would cast doubt on the power of the Lord Jesus."

"Couldn't have that, could we?"

Reston looked at Tully with squinted eyes, shook his head, muttered, "heathen", and took another huge bite out of the Danish.

"Don't get your shorts in a knot. There won't be any problems."

"Good. That's what I want to hear. Anyone in the audience willin' to trust the Lord tonight?"

"A couple coming from Driscoll who want to be blessed by the divinely anointed servant of the Lord."

"You payin' them extra to say that?"

"Nope. They're giving us that one for free."

"Mighty generous of them."

"You'd be surprised what a hundred bucks can still buy."

"A hun… You're gonna send us to the poorhouse, Tully."

"Keep your shirt on. We did quite well last night. And I think that reporter will be back."

"That's good. A mention in the paper never hurts."

"No, it doesn't. You do your part, Reston, and it'll all be fine. Don't you worry."

———

Landon Pace couldn't believe it. His boss was sending him back to that circus show.

"And get pictures of the snake handling," Huston had told him.

Landon, after his protest had fallen on deaf ears, had walked out of the *Chronicle* office and on down to Bluff Bakery.

He got himself a large coffee, a dozen doughnuts, and gone down to the library, with his laptop, to do a little research on Brother John's Traveling Salvation and Holiness Extravaganza.

*The guy's a con artist. Maybe I can get something a whole lot more interesting on him than just pictures of some snakes.*

———

Ember Cole had never seen a snake handling service and was surprised when Harry said he'd go with her.

When she'd asked why, he merely shrugged, and said, "I want to see who's in the running for this year's Darwin Award."

She laughed. "So, what's your real reason?"

"Everyone will be talking about it tomorrow. Might as well see the show with my own eyes."

"And that's it?"

"Well, you never know. You might need protecting should one of those snakes escape."

"Protecting?"

"Yep. I mean, doesn't it say somewhere in the Good Book about snakes and women causing the world a whole lot of grief?"

"Very funny, Mister. Besides, my name's not Eve."

Harry laughed. "No, it isn't. And with the look on your face right now, we'd have fried rattlesnake for supper. Too bad that story wasn't about Harry and Ember, instead of Adam and Eve."

"What do you mean?"

"We'd still be in paradise. But you know what?"

"What?"

"With you around, this is paradise."

Ember felt her face flush. She merely said, "See you later," and left the coffee shop. Once outside, though, a huge smile spread across her face.

# 23

IT DIDN'T TAKE LANDON PACE ALL THAT LONG TO GET THE SCOOP ON Brother John and his extravaganza. The web and a few phone calls convinced him that Reston was, in fact, a fraud. A con artist. A snake oil salesman. And the man behind the curtain, the man who made the magic happen, the magic that filled the offering baskets with cold, hard cash, was Purnell Tully.

Therefore, it made sense to Landon that he have a little talk with Tully. A talk that just might net him some green. After all, he wasn't rich. At least not until his parents died. And his pocket would feel very good with a little extra green in it. Besides, Tully probably had to grease a lot of wheels. He, Landon Pace, would just be one more wheel that needed a bit of grease to not squeak.

In his opinion, there was no better place than this quiet little stretch of beach on the west side of the reservoir for his talk with Tully to take place.

Out on the water was a boat some fifty yards offshore with a couple of old guys in it fishing. They had probably arrived in the beater Chevy truck and trailer that were parked along the side of the road.

Landon looked at his phone. Tully was late. But he was confident the confidence man would show. Confident Tully would want his silence.

———

Purnell Tully was annoyed. Annoyed that the young reporter had become a potential problem. He slipped a little snub-nosed revolver into his pocket. Just in case he needed it for persuasion.

This wasn't the first time some newspaperman thought he could get the jump on Purnell Tully. And it wouldn't be the last. So far, not one had succeeded. And he doubted this wet-behind-the-ears greenhorn cub reporter would be the first.

He looked at his phone. He was late. Good. Make the kid sweat. Let him get cocky. Cocky was better. Worried was good, too.

Tully typed a text message:

*Got held up. Leaving now.*

He got in his truck and drove out to the west side of Burnet Reservoir. The kid had said to look for an old, dinged-up white Toyota.

*Probably wants money,* Tully thought. *Thinks he has some hot item to blackmail us with.*

He spotted the car, took several pictures as he drove past, and took a few more as he pulled up behind the car.

He chuckled. *Pictures and Photoshop can make anything a reality.*

Tully got out of the truck, walked up to the passenger side of the Toyota, and got in.

He looked the lanky young man up and down. The boy really needed to ditch the mustache and beard.

"What do you want to talk about?" Tully asked.

"Some information I ran across."

"I see. Get out of the car."

"What?"

Tully opened his door. "Get out," he said, as he exited Pace's car, leaving the door open.

When the kid continued to sit behind the wheel, Tully leaned down and said, "Get out, or we ain't talkin'."

He watched the youngster exit the car. When he was standing on the road, Tully closed the passenger door and said, "Come here."

"Why?"

"Because I'm going to give you a pat down. No listening devices. No recording devices."

"What?"

"You heard me."

He watched the kid roll his eyes. *Kids these days,* he said to himself.

"Look, son, this may be your show, but it ain't my first rodeo. I'm calling the shots. Now, get your ass over here so I can frisk you."

Tully watched the kid's face. At first, he thought Pace might tell him to get lost, but after a moment or two the young reporter stepped around the car and let Tully frisk him.

"Satisfied?" Pace asked. "Or do you want to feel me up some more?"

Tully's right fist shot out and connected with Pace's stomach. The reporter doubled up and dropped to his knees. Tully grabbed the kid's long hair and yanked his head back. There was anger in his eyes.

*Good,* Tully thought. *This one has some fight. Can't stand it when they're fawning wimps.*

"No, I'm not satisfied," Tully said. "Give me your phone." And he yanked the kid to his feet.

Pace took a deep breath and winced. He exhaled and said, "What?"

"Are you deaf? Your phone. Get it out and shut it off in front of me and then put it in this handkerchief."

"Are you serious?"

"Yep. As I said, this ain't my first rodeo. I've had your kind try to pull all manner of tricks. Only got caught once. And that was when I was your age. Wised up awful fast because of that. Now quit jawin' and get out your goddamn phone."

Pace took his phone out of his pocket, shut it off, and placed it in the handkerchief.

Tully stuffed the handkerchief and phone into his coat pocket. "Now, get in the truck."

Pace walked over to the pickup and got in. Tully climbed in behind the wheel.

He looked at the kid for close to a minute before saying, "Tell me what you *think* you have."

"Brother John is a fraud and I can prove it."

"So?"

Tully watched surprise and then puzzlement wash over the youngster's face.

"I can write up a story for the paper and you'll be finished here."

"Look, Mr. Pace. Do you honestly think you're the first person who's called Brother John a fraud? He's been doin' this for forty-three years. Probably twice as long as you've been out of diapers. I've been with him for nineteen years. Probably almost as long as you've been alive.

"Do you want to know how many reporters, both TV and newspaper, that Brother John has had for lunch? Probably more than you can count, since they don't teach math anymore."

"Yeah, but—"

"Yeah, but nothing. I suggest you write us up a really good story, and if Brother John is pleased with it, and it brings in the people, he might — and I say, might — reward you. But if you try to blackmail him?"

Tully pulled the revolver out of his pocket. "I bet there are some mighty deep places over there in that reservoir. My guess is you probably don't want firsthand knowledge of them. Dead or alive. You savvy?"

Pace's eyes were as big as saucers, and Tully was pleased. It was obvious that in spite of his spunk the kid was pretty green when it came to the ways of the world. That would make him in the end much more pliable. Easy to manipulate.

"I asked you a question, Mr. Pace. Do you savvy?"

"I do."

"Good. Now, remember: do a good job of reporting and Brother John just might give you a nice reward."

"You mean he might pay me?"

"Might. But he has a couple of very pretty daughters, and maybe you'd like to meet them. Spend some time with them."

"Uh, if it's all the same—"

"You, my friend, don't have a say in the form of payment. Just do as you're told. Consider yourself a temporary employee of Brother John's Traveling Salvation Show and Spiritual Extravaganza. Now get out. I have work to do and you've taken up enough of my time."

Pace got out of the truck. "What about my phone?"

Tully took the handkerchief-wrapped phone out of his pocket and dropped the device into the kid's outstretched hand. He watched the boy walk to his car, get in, and drive away.

*Now I go to work and make some blackmail pictures. Just in case the kid decides to get a pair.* Tully shook his head. *Kids these days.*

He started the truck, put it in gear, and drove back to town.

# 24

6:51 PM, THURSDAY, 12 OCTOBER

HARRY THURGOOD HELD THE DOOR WHILE EMBER ENTERED AND THEN walked in behind her.

He was surprised to see so many people. A quick head count told him at least five dozen had showed up for the snake handling service.

Ember said, "There's Chris Hayes and Billy Bob Baskin over there."

"Are the Baptists and Presbyterians joining forces to fight the evils of religious populism?"

"What are you talking about, Mister?"

"Never mind. Over there are Caroline McCluskey and Magnolia Nadine. Curious to see them here."

"Why do you say that? They're probably interested for the same reason we are."

"You're probably right on that. Curiosity killed the cat, and satisfaction brought it back."

Ember laughed. "I don't see Graham, but I see he sent his intern and Monika."

"Smart man that Graham Huston."

"You didn't have to come, you know."

"No, I didn't. But, as I told you earlier, someone has to be here to protect you from any deadly snakes that get loose. And it's my job to protect my woman."

"*Your* woman? Aren't you making a huge assumption, Mister?"

"Okay. If you don't want to be my woman—"

"I didn't say that."

"Okay. How about this: I want to protect any fair damsel in distress — especially the fair damsel I care most about."

Ember pursed her lips for a moment, before saying, "You've made your point. How about we grab a seat?"

"Lead on."

Ember walked over to where Chris and Billy Bob were sitting with their wives.

"Mind if we join you?" she asked.

"Not at all," Rhoda Hayes answered.

Ember and Harry took the last two chairs in the row. Harry was on the outside and Ember was next to Emillene Baskin.

While Ember and Emillene chatted, Harry let his eyes room the old building.

An enormous room that had been stripped down to bare cinderblock walls, and was now filled with folding chairs and staging platforms.

There was nothing on the walls. The center aisle divided the rows of chairs six to a side. Harry counted nine rows.

At the front, the raised platform was about two feet off the ground. A couple of steps led up to it from the center aisle. There was a backdrop with a large cross painted on it.

The stage was empty, except for four microphone stands. There were large speakers on stands situated on either side of the stage.

Off to the side of the building, across the floor from where he sat, Harry noticed a tall, thin man. He was looking at what was probably a tablet.

And then to the sound of cymbals and tambourines and a

chorus of voices, Brother John and the Reston Family singers emerged from behind the backdrop to the front of the stage.

They were singing some praise song Harry had not heard before. Two of the girls were shaking and tapping the tambourines, and another two were tapping finger cymbals in time with the melody.

Brother John bellowed over the song, "Welcome to Brother John's Traveling Salvation and Holiness Extravaganza, with the divinely blessed voices of the Reston Family Singers!"

Harry watched a beautiful woman step forward and begin singing some song about Jesus he'd never heard before. But he could tell Ember knew it, because she was mouthing the words.

On the chorus, the other singers joined in, and quite a few of the audience. Including Ember.

After half-a-dozen songs, Brother John launched into a fire-breather of a sermon on faith.

Harry focused on the psychology of the delivery.

*Brother John is good, no doubt about it. All the power and control of the best demagogues. Kurelek should come out and hear him. I bet he'd have a lot to say about Brother John's methodology. Maybe even use the evangelist as an example in one of his psychology classes.*

After about thirty minutes or so, the big man swung into the altar call. There were a couple of women who spoke in tongues, and one of Reston's daughters, at least Harry assumed she was a daughter, interpreted "the Word from the Lord".

*Convenient,* Harry thought. *Control the narrative.*

Then it was the moment everyone had come for. The snake handling.

Brother John threw his arms wide and proclaimed in the lowest register of his baritone voice, "Faith! It is what makes us new creations in Christ."

His arms moved as if he was a shepherd gathering in his flock. His voice was soothing. "Come to me all ye who labor and I will give you rest. Let me heal you from your sin and your diseases. Thus saith our Lord Jesus Christ."

The mountain of a man descended the two steps to the floor and moved a few feet down the aisle.

"Tonight, you can test the depth of your faith. Our Lord Jesus said to his disciples: 'Go ye into all the world, and preach the gospel to every creature. He that believeth and is baptized shall be saved; but he that believeth not shall be damned. And these signs shall follow them that believe; in my name shall they cast out devils; they shall speak with new tongues; they shall take up serpents; and if they drink any deadly thing, it shall not hurt them; they shall lay hands on the sick, and they shall recover.' That, my friends, is the world of the Lord."

Ember whispered to Harry, "Those verses aren't legitimate. They were a later addition."

"Oh, really?"

Ember nodded. "The original ending of Mark's gospel is lost."

Harry mulled that over in his mind, and decided that the preacher was a very good conman, basing all of this show on a spurious text. Unless he actually believed it to be the genuine ending of Mark.

The tall, thin man's movement interrupted Harry's musing. The man and a good-sized kid, who was in the choir, and was a smaller version of Brother John, disappeared behind the backdrop and came out again carrying a large box.

When they set the box down, the tall man opened it and the two of them took out four smaller boxes and set them down at the front of the stage.

"Now, my friends, who'd like to test the word of the Lord?" Brother John's massive head swung from left to right, taking in the audience.

"I know you may have doubts. There may yet be hidden sin in your heart and you are afraid. But now is the time for you to purge that sin. Confess it now to the Lord Jesus and be free. Free to experience the power of the Lord! Free to cast out demons. Free to heal the sick. Free to drink poison and not be injured. Free to handle serpents, the symbol of the devil, and not die."

Brother John walked over to a box, opened the lid, reached in, and pulled out a snake.

"Oh, my God," Ember blurted.

"Must be eight feet long," Harry said.

"Witness the power of the Lord!" Brother John exclaimed.

He let the snake move along his arms and up across his shoulders. The preacher let that go on for thirty long seconds, then said, "Who's next? Who here is a faithful servant of Jesus?"

Harry watched one of Brother John's daughters step forward and pick up a snake. She wore it like a feather boa, and for some strange reason he thought of Quetzalcoatl, the Aztec deity, whose name translates to Precious Serpent, or Feathered Serpent.

*I wonder if the Aztecs were into serpent handling,* he mused.

Brother John was speaking, "Prove your faith. Let the power of Christ protect you."

A woman stepped forward from the audience. She exchanged a few words with Brother John, who then reached into a box, took out a six-foot long rattlesnake, and draped it over the woman's shoulders.

"Our sister, Rosie May Turnbull, who worships at Star of Bethlehem Foursquare Gospel Tabernacle, right here in your fair city, is demonstrating her faith in the Lord. Come—"

The scream from Rosie May silenced Brother John. The tall, thin man was suddenly at her side. He removed the snake from the woman and put it in a box.

Jearlene Reston helped her back to her seat and, from what Harry could see, looked to be bandaging her arm.

Brother John, his arms outstretched, said, "Sister Rosie May is all right, my friends. Her faith is strong."

He turned to the bitten woman. "You believe in Jesus?"

She nodded.

"You believe He heals?"

She nodded again.

"Go forth from here this night and tell everyone of the power of Jesus."

Two paramedics rushed into the building. One of them said, "We got a report that a rattlesnake bit someone here."

"Do not fear," Brother John said. "We have no need of you. We are filled with the power of the Holy Ghost! And He is stronger than any man-made medicine."

A sprinkling of "Amens" could be heard from folks in the audience.

"Was someone bit?" the paramedic asked. His voice registering concern, and possibly anger, Harry thought.

A person in the front row stood and said, "This woman here."

Rosie May Turnbull stood. "I'm fine. Don't need no help."

"Were you bitten by a rattlesnake?" the other paramedic asked.

"Yes, but I am fine. As Brother John said, I have no need of any help from mankind. Serpents cannot harm the servants of Jesus."

"Are you refusing to go to the hospital?"

"That's right. I'm not sick."

"Will you at least let us check you?"

Before Rosie May could speak, Brother John said, "Please do. You will find her unharmed and fit as a fiddle."

Ember said, "Do you think the snake actually bit her?"

"Probably," Harry answered.

"Then how…"

"If I were a betting man, and I often am, I'd say we're looking at a con game by a very good con artist."

"You think so?"

"I do. People, though, tend to be gullible. And whoever called the paramedics did Brother John a great big favor."

# 25

REECE SOVERN RANG THE DOORBELL.

*For all their money,* he thought, *the Fights sure have one ugly house. It's just a massive architectural monstrosity.*

He rolled the cigar to the other side of his mouth and pushed his glasses up his nose.

*I don't know much about architecture, but I do know a butt ugly house when I see one. And this one is butt ugly.*

He took the cigar out of his mouth and pressed the doorbell again.

The door opened, revealing a middle-aged woman wearing a maid's uniform. Black A-line dress with a white apron.

"May I help you?" she asked. Her accent placed the land of her birth somewhere south of the border.

Sovern put the cigar back in his mouth, fished out his ID, held it up so she could see it, and said, "Reece Sovern. Magnolia Bluff police. Mrs. Fight called."

"Just one moment."

The door closed, and Sovern counted to two hundred and ninety-seven before it reopened.

"Mrs. Fight will see you."

"I should hope so. She's the one who called." He entered the huge entryway.

The maid closed the door. "Follow me, please."

Sovern followed her through one room, then a second, before he was let into a small sitting room.

When he entered, Mary Lou Fight turned off the TV. "Please have a seat, Mr. Sovern."

She was lying on the sofa. Reece sat in a chair across from her.

"How may I help you, Mrs. Fight?"

"It is I who shall help you."

Sovern raised his eyebrows, got out his notebook, while his cigar migrated to the other side of his mouth.

"Never refuse help. So how are you going to help me?"

"I know who killed that man you found."

"And what man would that be?"

"Come, now, Mr. Sovern, don't be coy. The man you found dead in front of Harry Thurgood's coffee shop."

"I see. Did you know the deceased?"

"Yes. I had employed Hunter to conduct some business for me regarding Mr. Thurgood."

"And what business might that be?"

Mary Lou laughed. "Oh, you don't need to trouble yourself about that. There is, though, only one person who could have killed Hunter."

"And who's that?"

"Why Harry Thurgood, of course."

Sovern lowered the notebook to his thigh. "And what makes you think Thurgood killed the man?"

"Isn't it obvious? Hunter was attempting to break into Mr. Thurgood's residence."

"And how do you know that? Did you instruct him to break into Thurgood's apartment?"

"Heaven's no. I employed Hunter to get results. I assumed he knew how to do so."

"So how did you know the deceased was trying to break into Thurgood's apartment?"

She smiled. "I have my ways."

"Thurgood has a solid alibi. He was somewhere else at the time."

"Oh, I don't mean he'd shoot Hunter himself. I can't imagine him getting his hands dirty. No, men like Harry Thurgood pay others to get their hands dirty."

"So you're saying Thurgood hired a hitman to stand guard and shoot anyone who just might happen to try to break into his building? Seems a bit farfetched to me."

"No. I'm saying he found out I'd hired Hunter to follow him, and that's why Mr. Thurgood had him killed."

"So why did you hire the deceased to follow Thurgood?"

"That's my business. But he was compiling information on Mr. Thurgood's activities."

"So your theory is that Thurgood found out, hired a hit man, who then killed Hunter Sulzer."

"It's not a theory. That is what happened."

"Any proof?"

"Oh, my, detective, I can't do *all* of your work for you. You do have to do something to earn the salary I'm paying you."

Sovern stood. "All right, Mrs. Fight. I'll check it out. Thanks for the information."

Mary Lou rang a bell, and in a moment the maid appeared.

"Marie, please show Mr. Sovern out."

"Yes, ma'am."

"Oh, one more thing, Mrs. Fight. When did you find out your private detective had been killed?"

"About half-past ten this morning."

"Thank you, Mrs. Fight."

Sovern followed the maid back out to the front door, and when he was once again standing in the fresh October night air, he found himself shaking his head.

"Ten hours," he muttered. "Took her ten hours to find out. God. If only we could work that quickly. Wouldn't be a criminal left on the street."

He shook his head again, pitched his soggy cigar somewhere out onto the Fights's lawn, and walked to his car.

# 26

HARRY THURGOOD SAW A FAMILIAR CAR PARKED IN FRONT OF HIS store. He altered his destination, so he ended up by the driver's door. He watched the window roll down.

"Evening, Thurgood."

"Good evening, Reece."

"Passenger door's open. Why don't you get in?"

"You could come up to the apartment."

"Here's fine. Get in."

Harry sighed, walked around the car, and got in.

"Well, Detective, what's on your mind?"

"Mary Lou Fight. Had a chat with her earlier this evening."

"I bet that was interesting."

"It was. She said you had the private detective, Hunter Sulzer, killed because you knew she had hired him to follow you. That true?"

"Which part of your question are you asking me is true?"

"I'm a simple man, Thurgood. Just answer the question."

"Actually, you asked two, Detective. You want to know if I hired a hit man to kill Hunter Sulzer and you want to know if I knew that Mary Lou had hired Mr. Sulzer to follow me. The answer to both questions is no."

"So you were completely unaware that Mrs. Fight was looking to get something on you?"

"Now, you see, Reece, that's a different question altogether."

"For God's sake, did Lauderbach coach you or something?"

"And why would my attorney need to coach me? It's simple English, Reece. You're now asking me if I'm aware that Mary Lou is digging into my past. That is, trying to get something on me. Let me put it this way: I suspect that Mary Lou has been trying to find something on me for the past year and a half. But proof? No, I don't have any proof she actually is trying to get something on me. After all, this is Mary Lou Fight we're talking about."

Sovern nodded. "That it is. And she's rarely wrong about anything."

"Very true. But in this case, she is. I suspect she's probably trying to find something with which to blackmail me, because that's her usual *modus operandi*. Did I know for sure? No. Therefore, I couldn't have hired someone to kill her PI, because I wasn't aware she'd hired one — let alone know his identity."

"I'll have to pass this on to Jager. So don't go anywhere."

"Don't worry. I have nowhere I got to be, except here."

"Good. Now get out of here so I can go home."

"With pleasure, Detective. Goodnight."

Harry got out of the car and watched the police investigator drive off into the night. He thought of the information Scarlett had told him yesterday and wondered how she'd come upon it.

"Guess it doesn't matter," he murmured. "It looks as though someone eliminated my follower."

He walked over to the street door to his upstairs apartment. While unlocking the door, he thought, *Why would someone kill the guy? But more importantly, who would do so?*

# 27

HARRY PUSHED THE DOORBELL A SECOND TIME, AND THIS TIME THE door opened.

"Well, well, well. Harry Thurgood ringing my doorbell at quarter to midnight. Are you lonely?"

"Hello, Scarlett. No, I'm not lonely; but I would like to talk."

"I was just going to bed. Join me?"

"Not tonight."

"Now *that's* an interesting response. Very well, come on in."

The tall blonde walked away from the door. The red babydoll she was wearing ended a little below her butt cheeks and barely covered her breasts. Not for the first time, Harry wondered if the woman had any inhibitions at all.

He followed her into the living room after closing the door.

She sprawled out on the sofa, and said, "I'd like a martini. Especially one made by you. And make yourself whatever you like."

He favored her with a smile and crossed the room to where a small portable bar was positioned against the wall.

"The ice is fresh, by the way. So what do you want to talk about in the dark of the night?"

"I had a visit from Reece Sovern." He removed the gin bottle and a glass from the mini-freezer.

"And what did he have to say?"

Harry told her while he put a couple drops of vermouth in the glass, and rotated it so the herbed wine coated the inside of the glass. He emptied the excess vermouth and added the gin plus two olives.

"Very interesting," Scarlett said, when Harry finished the story.

"Here you go."

She took the glass and tasted her drink. "Mm. That is pure seduction."

"If you say so." He sipped brandy.

"So what does Reece talking to you have to do with me?"

"The juxtaposition of Reece's conversation and your earlier warning to me." He shrugged and sipped brandy.

Scarlett swallowed a mouthful of her drink. "And?"

"I'm curious how you got your information."

She licked gin off of an olive and put it in her mouth. She chewed it slowly, and swallowed. Olive gone, she drank more of the martini.

Harry kept his eyes focused on her face, and when hers met his, he said, "I'm a cat. Kill me."

"Never. I love you."

"Satisfaction will bring me back."

"Really? How interesting. I would love to satisfy you. You would be sated with love till death do us part."

He smiled. "You are persistent."

"You rang my doorbell just before the witching hour."

"So I did. I'm a cat. Curiosity. I couldn't wait."

"You're not a cat, Harry Thurgood. You're a lion. You are the king. You are my king."

"So you're not going to tell me."

"No. I'm not. At least not now. Spend the night with me and

you might find me much more talkative tomorrow morning in the shower, while you wash my back."

Harry finished his brandy and stood.

"Leaving so soon?"

"I am."

Scarlett got off the couch and moved next to him so that they were face to face and so close a breath of wind would have found it difficult to pass between them.

"I love you, Harry Thurgood, and I will do anything to protect you."

"I need protecting?"

"You underestimate Mary Lou Fight. I know her."

"I do know her kind."

"But I know *Mary Lou.*"

Scarlett put her arms around his neck, pulled him to her, and kissed him.

Her hunger was very apparent, and Harry enjoyed her passion, but he did not return it.

She pulled away. "You're thinking of her. Aren't you?"

"Ember's always on my mind."

"Is she aptly named?"

"I'm a gentleman. I'll never tell."

"Hm." She touched her finger to his lips, then walked back to the sofa and sat.

Harry couldn't help but find the view enticing.

"You are. A gentleman, that is. And that's why I love you."

"I'm sorry, Scarlett."

"I believe you are. Watch yourself with the Queen. But also remember what I said."

"I will. Goodnight."

"Until we see each other again." She ate the other olive and closed her eyes.

Harry turned and left.

Driving home, he thought about what Scarlett had said. There was no doubt in his mind that she believed she was in love with him.

Could she have acted on the information she'd discovered about Mary Lou hiring a PI? Could Scarlett have killed Hunter Sulzer?

# 28

BROTHER JOHN WATCHED THE YOUNG WOMAN GET OUT OF BED AND start putting on her clothes. She'd told him her name was Melissa, and he had no reason to doubt her. She was too young for guile.

"I have an early class," she said, "otherwise I'd stay for morning devotions."

"Perfectly understandable."

"But I may come again tonight. You know, if I need more prayer and counseling?"

"You may, indeed."

She cupped her ample breasts, wiggled her butt, and winked at him.

Brother John intoned, "The lost lamb must be found and, when found, comforted."

"Oh, yes. Comforted. I need a lot of comfort."

"I am here, my child. Together, tonight, we can beseech the Lord on your behalf."

"Yes. I love the beseeching. And especially with the rod of correction." She winked at him, slipped on her shoes, and departed.

Brother John sighed a sigh of satisfaction. Just as David had his two comforters, so the good Lord provided him, Brother John, servant of the Lord, with a little comfort.

He liked the young ones. They were so eager and willing to please.

Jearlene had once been eager and willing to please, but now she was a Jezebel, a harlot, a common street strumpet.

They didn't think he knew. But he did. He'd known for quite a while now and had been calmly deciding what to do about both of them. The Lord no longer struck down the unfaithful, as He had done in the desert to purge the Children of Israel. Pity that.

But it didn't mean He cast a blind eye towards sin. Those who rebelled against Moses, even his own brother, paid for their sin.

He, Brother John, servant of the Lord, had turned the other cheek. Now, it was time to cast the sinners out of the temple of God.

"Just as Jesus did," Brother John whispered. "And I'm the servant of Jesus." He curled his massive hands into fists.

————

Tully gave Jerri Reston one last kiss before he watched her leave.

He had a situation on his hands. Jerri was a fine woman, but she constantly thought about those kids. And if he was honest with himself, he didn't want to deal with the brats. But Jerri wanted them with her.

On the other hand, Joetta and Oralene were young and had no baggage. And if he could, he'd take Raylene over her sisters in a heartbeat.

But that was unlikely because Joetta was just too damn clingy. He'd have to do something about that. Just what, though, he wasn't sure. Although, he could just take off with Joetta in tow and break the clinginess once he got her away by herself. Besides, she was a fine woman. So eager to please, and he did like that.

Oralene, though, had the brains. And brains were always useful.

Tully got out of bed and put on his clothes. He didn't have to decide today. But he had to decide soon.

———

John Reston, Junior, or John-John as his siblings called him, was standing in the shadow cast by the building in the soft dawn light. He was watching the small parking lot where the bus was parked and where his father was sleeping. When the door opened and a woman came out, his suspicions were confirmed.

And to make matters worse, his mother was with Tully. Again. He'd seen her go into his camper, which was parked up the street. He'd have to have another session with the man. Re-emphasize that he needed to leave his mother alone.

And something had to be done about his father. The constant parade of women, and even his own sisters.

John-John knew he was now a man. And with manhood came duties and responsibilities. If his father had fallen into the ways of sin, it was now up to him, his namesake, to purge the sin from the Reston family. The mantle of the Lord had fallen to him, as it had to Elisha. And now he would use it to strike dead the sinners.

# 29

## 6:51 AM, FRIDAY, 13 OCTOBER

JOETTA TAPPED ON THE CAMPER DOOR. IT OPENED; SHE ENTERED AND pulled the door closed behind her.

Tully took her hand and tried to pull her to the bed, but she didn't move.

"What's the matter, Jo?"

"I don't like you doin' Mama."

"Who says that I am?"

"I seen her leave this mornin', and I doubt she was doin' your laundry."

He let go of her hand. "I see. Let me explain."

Joetta held up her hand. "I also heard you're doin' Oralene. Is that true?"

"Now, where did you hear that?"

"Oralene. She said you was jumpin' her bones."

"That wasn't my fault—"

"You mean your zipper just magically undid itself? I thought you loved me. You said you did. But you're doin' Mama *and* Oralene... You doin' Raylene, too?"

"Look, Jo, let me explain."

"What's to explain, Purnell? We were goin' away. You said you was takin' me away from all this. You said you loved me. But you don't love me. I don't think you ever did. It's just like Oralene said. You just like gettin' your wick wet."

"Aw, c'mon, Babe."

"Don't *Babe* me. I ain't your babe. You're just a two-bit cheater." She opened the camper door. "And I hope you go to hell, Purnell Tully. I hope you go to hell and burn forever. And when I tell Mama, I bet you'll run there yourself just to get away from her holy wrath."

---

Tully cringed at the sound of the slamming door. He felt the camper shake with the force Joetta used.

He was in deep trouble now.

"I have two choices. I drive off with the money I've skimmed off so far. Or I try to make amends to Joetta or Jerri or, if need be, both."

He opened the drawer underneath the bed, moved aside the clothes, and took out the pistol and silencer.

*Just in case my only option is none of the above.*

# 30

## 7:11 AM, FRIDAY, 13 OCTOBER

EMBER ENTERED THE REALLY GOOD. SHE NOTICED FERGUS WAS sitting in a corner off to her right.

"Good morning, Fergus," she said.

"Mornin', Reverend. You best be prayin' the Feds go away. Saw the big, black SUV again last night."

"Why would the Feds be here?"

"Secrets. Too many secrets. Too much gossip. Too many dead people walkin' the streets. The Feds don't like dead people. Especially walkin' dead people."

"I see. What are you having for breakfast?"

"Mr. Thurgood fixed me up with some corned beef hash and eggs. It's really good." He laughed and his attention returned to his food.

Ember walked up to the counter and sat on a stool. Estrelita set a cup of coffee before her.

"Where's Harry?"

"He said he had a call he had to make. I think he's upstairs or out back. Do you want your usual?"

"Yes, please. To go."

Ember drank her coffee and, when the cup was empty , Estrelita set a bag in front of her.

"Here you are, Reverend Cole."

Ember gave her a ten and a five and told her to keep the change.

"You'll tell Harry I was here?"

"I will."

Ember gave her a smile and left.

She walked briskly down East Main, continued on past the library, where west and East Main come together, and on down to Magnolia Street.

The morning was chilly by Texas standards. Sweater weather, though, where she grew up. She found it amusing to see the natives bundled up in coats and boots, while she simply slipped on a sweater under her black ministerial suit coat.

She walked past the Flower Bed and Breakfast. Five blocks later, she turned down Church Street, and then trotted up the steps to the double doors of her church. Father Lee Gorman was waiting for her.

"Good morning, Lee."

"And a good morning to you, Ember."

She unlocked the doors, pushed one open, and they entered the narthex.

"Follow me. My office is in back."

"That's where they usually put us," Father Lee quipped.

"Except when we're needed."

"Isn't that the truth. So what do you want to talk about?"

"It's more what I want to show you."

"Okay."

Ember walked down a side aisle of the nave to a door on the right of the chancel. She opened the door and entered a short hall that lead to the back of the church where the offices and meeting rooms were located.

She led Lee to her office, turned on the lights, and pointed to the statue in the corner. "Tell me about that."

Ember watched Lee's eyes open wide.

"Oh, my," he said, crossing himself before walking over to the statue.

"What is it?" Ember asked.

"It's a Black Madonna and Child. Where did you get it?"

"Is it valuable?"

"I'd say this one is. The metal is silver, blackened due to age."

"Did you say silver?"

"Yes. Some Black Madonnas were intentionally painted that way. Others, like this one, became black over time when the silver oxidized."

"Is it very valuable?"

Father Lee squatted and studied the piece. When finished, he stood, made the sign of the cross, and turned to Ember.

"I'm not an expert on art. As a religious relic, I'd guess it's priceless. As a work of art, probably more than a million."

"What? A million dollars?"

"Probably more. There aren't a lot of Black Madonnas around. Let me take a few pictures, and I'll ask one of my seminary profs what he thinks."

"Sure. I'd like to know more about her."

Father Lee took several pictures and then Ember let him out the back door.

When she was seated at her desk and eating her breakfast sandwich, she turned Harry's story over in her mind.

She chewed and swallowed a bite of her sandwich. "Family heirloom, my foot," she said out loud. "There is something really odd about this. Really odd. What is Harry involved in? And do I want to go there?"

# 31

REECE SOVERN SAT AT HIS DESK WITH A HOT CUP OF COFFEE, A FRESH corona in his mouth, and an open notebook.

Now he knew the general lay of the land. Mary Lou Fight hired Hunter Sulzer to dig up dirt on Harry Thurgood. Which meant Mary Lou was convinced there was dirt to dig up. Then someone comes along and kills Sulzer.

Logically, the first person he'd look at was Thurgood. But the coffee shop guy's alibi was ironclad. Not only the Reverend but also Olivia put him at the pizza place at the time someone was dishing up lead to the private dick.

Unless Thurgood shot him before going to Olivia's. However, the ATF had no record of Thurgood having purchased a .380 caliber handgun. And, according to the ME, three .380 caliber bullets terminated Sulzer's life.

Of course, that didn't mean Thurgood didn't have one. There were many ways to get a gun without the ATF knowing about it. And Sovern wouldn't put it past Thurgood to know all about them.

There was something about the guy he just didn't trust. Call it his cop instinct. But Sovern was willing to wager his retirement pension that Harry Thurgood was not at all the coffee shop dandy he pictured himself to be.

But just exactly what he was in reality, Sovern couldn't even begin to guess. A cursory search had turned up nothing. Well, nothing illegal. What it had turned up was that Harry Thurgood didn't exist prior to eight years ago.

That, in and of itself, wasn't illegal. Maybe the guy changed his name. Lots of people change their name for lots of reasons.

Then he shows up in Magnolia Bluff four years ago. Pays cash for a building. Then pays more cash to renovate it. And has for the past four years kept the business running with minimal clientele.

And that too was a mystery, because the coffee and food were both good. Although the prices he charged weren't Hill Country prices, that's for sure.

Perhaps that is why most of his customers were tourists. At least from what Sovern had observed.

His coffee was cold. His cigar, soggy. Sovern stood and pitched the stogie towards the wastebasket. It went in.

"Huh. Maybe my luck's changing."

# 32

8:47 AM, FRIDAY, 13 OCTOBER

CAROLINE McCLUSKEY AND MAGNOLIA NADINE ROANE WALKED into the Really Good. Harry waved as he came over to help them move a couple tables together for the morning coffee klatch group.

At the same time, Stanton Mirabeau Lauderbach and Gloria McBride entered. They were deeply engrossed in a discussion over the fine point of some abstruse subparagraph of the legal code.

Harry motioned for Estrelita to take care of the coffee klatch group, while he saw to the desires of the lawyers.

"Good morning, Stanton, Gloria," he said. "How are you two on this fine Friday the thirteenth?"

"Just peachy," Gloria answered.

"Just another day on the treadmill, Harry," Stanton said, then added, "Although, I'm glad my treadmill is here instead of Dallas or Houston."

"Ain't that the truth," Gloria said.

Harry chuckled. "That's why I'm here and not in the big city. What can I get for you two?"

"You have any of that Tanzanian Peaberry in the light roast?" Stanton asked.

"What the hell is that?" Gloria said.

"Simple magnificence," Stanton answered.

Harry shook his head. "Not today. But I have some Brazilian Obata. Subtle floral notes, with some honey in the taste."

Stanton nodded. "I'll try that. Cream on the side."

Gloria said, "I'll have a Colombian Latte Macchiato."

"Coming right up."

Harry made his way back behind the counter to make the coffees when in walked Police Chief Tommy Jager, Reverend Billy Bob Baskin, Graham Huston, and Reece Sovern.

Jager, Baskin, and Huston took seats at the coffee klatch table. Sovern continued on to the counter and sat on a stool opposite Harry.

"Morning, Reece. What can I get you?"

"I'd have to win the lottery to afford your coffee."

Harry poured him a cup of Kenya AA city roast. "Here. My treat. Happy Friday the thirteenth. I assume you want to talk."

Sovern nodded and sipped coffee.

"Let me drop these off and I'll be back."

Harry, with a large tray in hand, walked over to the lawyers. He gave them their coffee and left a plate of pastries for them.

Back behind the counter, he faced Sovern. "So, what do you want to talk about?"

"I'd like to go over the timetable for Wednesday night with you."

"I've already given my statement. I've nothing to add and can't be more precise."

"Well, that's the thing, Thurgood, the ME says death occurred sometime between nine and eleven Wednesday night."

"And?"

Sovern took his notebook out of his pocket and flipped a few pages. When he found what he was looking for, he said, "You told me you were at Olivia's from nine or nine-thirty on."

"Yes. I did."

"Well, Olivia said it was closer to ten when you showed up, and the Reverend confirms that."

"Okay. I guess I got my timing wrong."

"That's just the thing. If Olivia's right, you had plenty of time to shoot Hunter Sulzer."

"I suppose so. The problem is, I didn't shoot him. I didn't even know him. Nor did I know that Mary Lou hired him."

"So that's your story?"

"It is. And I'm sticking to it." Harry pointed at Lauderbach. "If there is anything else, Detective, talk to Stanton."

"You don't have to get all huffy, Thurgood. I'm—"

Harry held up his hand. "I know. You're simply doing your job. Fine. We all have jobs to do. You can do yours with Stanton. Now, if you'll excuse me, *I* have a job to do."

"Suit yourself. And thanks for the coffee."

Sovern stood up and left the coffee shop.

Harry stood staring at the half-drunk mug of coffee for a moment or two, then picked it up and hurled it through the open window into the kitchen.

# 33

PURNELL TULLY DROPPED THE BAG ON THE OLD BEAT-UP DESK IN THE tiny office, and carefully set down the cups of coffee.

Brother John let the chair fall forward and opened the bag. "Looks good, Tully. That Bluff Bakery has some mighty fine pastries. If the Israelites had those every morning, they'd have never rebelled against the Lord."

Tully watched Brother John take out of the bag a very large cream cheese Danish.

Looking in the bag, he took a raised glazed doughnut for himself.

"So you're telling me, Reston, that a hick town bakery makes better food than the Almighty Himself?"

"There you go again, Tully. I said no such thing. Of course, the Lord's food's better. I was only payin' a compliment to the baker. Why are you so cantankerous? Are you gettin' enough? Seems to me you should be. I see that camper bouncing all hours of the night."

"I'm not going there. Our take last night was a little over a thousand dollars. Fifteen forty-seven for the two nights. How long do you want to stay here?"

"Might try for two weeks. Whoever called the paramedics was a godsend."

"Then we're going to have to have more snake handling, more healings, and you might want to consider raising someone from the dead."

"That one's always tricky. But I hear you. If we really want to cash in, we'll have to have a raisin'."

"I'll see what I can do."

"Do so. Just make sure you leave enough so the kids can eat."

"What's that supposed to mean?"

"Every servant of the Lord is bedeviled with a Judas, Tully. Someone who loves filthy lucre more than Jesus."

"You sure you want to go down this road, Reston? Wouldn't be good for us if that college freshman told the newspaper about your special prayer meetings and the laying on of hands."

"You are a Pharisee, Tully. Get out and drum us up some business for tonight."

"I'll do that. Enjoy your pastries. Make sure you have your heart attack *after* the service."

Tully stormed out of the office and out of the building. Standing on the sidewalk, he looked down the street at his pickup.

"The smart move would be to get in that truck and just drive right outta here," he murmured. "But am I that smart?"

# 34

10:38 AM, FRIDAY, 13 OCTOBER

THE BELL OVER THE DOOR JINGLED. EBEN MOSER LOOKED UP AND SAW a brute of a kid enter his shop.

"Hello. Can I help you?" Moser asked.

"I-I'd like to buy a pistol."

Moser looked the young man up and down, and one thing was for sure: the lad looked mighty nervous.

"How old are you, son?"

"I'm twenty."

"Can't help you, I'm afraid. Have to be twenty-one to buy a pistol. I can sell you a rifle or a shotgun."

The kid shook his head. "That won't work."

"The only way you can get a handgun is from a private party."

"Oh. Okay. Um, thanks."

The kid went back out the door, and Moser followed. He watched the youngster get into a Ford Excursion that was no longer black from too much southern sun.

Using his phone, Moser took several pictures of the vehicle, including one of the license plate.

When the car was gone, Moser returned to his store and called the sheriff's office.

"Hello, Moby? Yeah, this is Eben over at Southern Star

Firearms. Had a young fella come in tryin' to buy a handgun. Looked a mite nervous. Might be some trouble there. Got pictures of the car. Can I text them to you? Sheriff Blanton might want to check up on this."

———

Mary Lou Fight picked up her phone and told it to call Goody Preminger.

"Good morning, Mary Lou," Goody said. "How are you?"

"I'm as well as can be expected. Yourself?"

"The sun is out. James is at the golf course. Just got in from my swim. Life is good."

Mary Lou digested all that for a moment and wondered if it was true that Goody swam in the nude in that heated pool of theirs.

*Probably something a drone would be useful for,* she thought. Out loud, she said, "I have a favor to ask of you. Actually, it's Crimson Hat business."

"Sure. What would you like me to do?"

"I'd like you to get to know Harry Thurgood."

"Is he the coffee shop owner? The handsome guy with the gorgeous blond hair?"

"Yes, that's the one."

"Okay. I can do that."

"What I'm asking is that you get to know him very well."

"I don't think Jim would like that."

"You do like being a member of the Crimson Hats, don't you?"

"Of course."

"Good. After all, you're a Braxton. Your family was a pillar of the Republic. And a Braxton should be a Crimson Hat."

"Yes, of course."

"I also know that you might not want Jim to be made aware of a certain indiscretion—"

"I see. Well, let me meet this Harry Thurgood and see what happens."

"That's all I was asking, Goody. I'm glad we understand each other. I knew right away you'd make a wonderful Crimson Hat member. I'm glad I wasn't wrong."

"I'll introduce myself as soon as I can."

"Wonderful. Good day, then, Goody."

Mary Lou disconnected and smiled. "Yes, Goody Preminger. Still trim, and with a body men always admired. Tall. Beautiful alabaster skin. Luscious dark hair. If she is anything like she was in high school, she'll have Harry Thurgood eating out of her hand in no time."

# 35

## 1:08 PM, FRIDAY, 13 OCTOBER

FATHER LEE GORMAN LOOKED AT THE TEXT ON HIS PHONE FROM Doctor Gerald Betzenstein, his former professor, who was a specialist in obscure relics.

It read:

*Am flying to Dallas. If your Black Madonna is what I suspect it to be, it will be the greatest religious find of the century. Should arrive in Magnolia Bluff tomorrow night.*

He texted back, asking Dr. Betzenstein to keep him posted so he'd know what time to expect him, and received a thumbs up from the doctor.

Lee slipped his phone back into his pocket and decided he should probably let Ember know.

He took the phone back out of his pocket and called the church office. When the secretary answered, he asked for Reverend Cole.

"I'm sorry, but she's not in her office right now. Would you like to leave a message?"

"This is Lee Gorman."

"Oh, hello, Father Lee. Reverend Cole is visiting at the hospital."

"Okay. I'll catch her there."

"Very good."

"Say…"

"I'm Anna Stocker."

"Oh, yes, of course, say, Anna, is there a lock on Reverend Cole's office door?"

"There is, but I don't think she ever locks the door. I'm not even sure she has a key. Come to think of it, I don't know if we even have a key for it."

"Hm. It's just that…"

"Is something the matter?"

"Uh, no, nothing. I'll catch up with Ember. Thanks, Anna."

He ended the call, put the phone back in his pocket, and got into his suit coat.

Heading for the door, he stopped, got out his phone, and dialed the Methodist Church's number.

"Hi, Anna. Lee Gorman again. Do you have Reverend Cole's personal phone number? It's important that I get hold of her."

"Sure. Ready?"

Lee said he was and the secretary gave him Ember's number. He thanked her, hung up, and called the number. After five rings, he got her voicemail.

"Ember, Lee Gorman. Doctor Gerald Betzenstein should be here in Magnolia Bluff tomorrow night. He seems to think your statue is a very important religious relic. Call me as soon as you can so we can make sure the statue is in a safe location. Bye."

Call ended, Lee put his phone back into his pocket. He thought for a moment and decided to head over to the hospital. That statue had to be put somewhere safe. Maybe in the bank's vault. Because if it was lost again…

# 36

## 1:10 PM, FRIDAY, 13 OCTOBER

H ARRY'S EYES TOOK IN STANTON MIRABEAU LAUDERBACH. *HE'S A lot like me. At least in the clothes department. Lauderbach's always impeccably dressed.*

The lawyer was behind his desk, sitting in what had to be a custom-made chair. His hands were folded on his desk blotter. His suit was custom-made as well. It was the deepest charcoal gray Harry had ever seen, without being black. The lawyer's tie was blood red, with tiny gray dots covering it.

His dark hair was combed straight back from his high forehead, but was not slicked down, giving it a very full appearance. He had an aquiline nose and thin lips. But what Harry always found most impressive were the lawyer's piercing, almost feral eyes. And his smile: genuine, but rather too genuine.

"I didn't catch all that Sovern was saying, Harry. Care to elaborate?"

Harry told Lauderbach about Hunter Sulzer, Mary Lou, and Sovern's newest suspicion that Harry may have had time after all to kill the private detective.

When he was finished, Lauderbach leaned back in his chair and put his hands behind his head.

"I have to say, Harry, Sovern enjoys having you in his sights."

"Seems that way. But I'm not the real target."

"So you say."

"Gee, thanks. I thought you were my lawyer."

"I am. And I will defend you. But guilt or innocence is for judge and jury to decide. My job is to be persuasive enough so that the decision of said judge and jury is in your favor."

"You have trouble sleeping at night?"

"Never. I sleep sounder than a baby without colic."

"Glad you qualified that."

Lauderbach smiled and sat up. "Sovern is fishing. He's casting here and there and seeing if he gets any bites. Your job? Don't bite."

"Okay. I won't bite."

Lauderbach stood, and Harry did likewise.

"Leave everything to me," the lawyer said. "I'll have our detective casting his line in a different stream."

"Good. And thanks."

They shook hands, and Harry left.

On his walk back to the Really Good, not for the first time did the thought come to him that a cabin in the woods some place might be a whole lot better than living amongst his fellows.

*I wonder if I could convince Ember to join me?*

———

Joetta found Tully in the Silver Spoon. He was sitting in a booth in the back of the restaurant.

She walked back and slipped into the seat across from him.

He looked up from his plate of chicken fried chicken, mashed potatoes and gravy, and collard greens.

"Didn't think I'd see you," Tully said.

A waitress came to the table, and Joetta shook her head when the older woman asked if she wanted to order.

When the waitress left, Joetta said, "You and Pa are fightin'. When you planning' on leavin'?"

He set his fork down. "We are. Don't know for sure about leaving. Would like to have more money, but I told you that earlier."

"Don't leave me here, Purnell. You said you loved me. I don't know if you do, but I love you. I'd be a real good wife for you. I would. We can start over. I'll forget all about Mama and Oralene. Just please take me with you."

"Why the change of heart?"

"No change of heart. I was just angry this mornin'. I know a man sometimes wants another woman and I guess I was just jealous is all. I want to be the only one. I know I can be woman enough for you, Purnell. Just gimme a chance."

"We need money, Jo. You know that."

"You been sayin' that for over a year now. How long is it gonna take?"

"I have to be careful. Your father's already suspicious."

"Well, maybe you need to make sure there are plenty of young women who want his special blessin' so he don't have time to be suspicious."

Tully chuckled. "Aren't you the devious one."

"I know what Pa is like. And I know what he likes."

"I suppose you do. The other problem is your brother."

"He hit you again?"

"No. But he was in my face. Maybe you can settle him down."

"John-John's mighty protective. Thinks he's the man of the family. He's gettin' mighty religious, too."

"Yeah, I know. Not good."

"So, how soon can we leave?"

"I don't know. I have a few things to settle, and it depends on our take here."

"Well, I hope it's soon. Real soon."

"Why? What's the rush all of a sudden?"

"I think I might be pregnant."

# 37

## 2:07 PM, FRIDAY, 13 OCTOBER

LANDON PACE WAS NOT A HAPPY CAMPER. FRIDAY NIGHT WAS coming and his hot date was another dance with the faith-healing, snake-handling circus sideshow.

At least Huston liked the story he'd written about last night's show. But what was more important was if that Purnell Tully liked it. And if he'd see anything from the con artist for his efforts.

Pace sat on a park bench and waited for Tully. While he waited, he watched a couple of catboats running to the south end of the large expanse of water. They appeared to be racing each other.

Purnell Tully slid onto the opposite end of the bench.

"You have a habit of showing up late?" Pace asked.

"Only when it's important."

"Did you like the article?"

"It was good."

"It'll be in tomorrow's paper. When do I get my pay?"

"You aren't in the driver's seat and I didn't say your pay would be money."

"I'd rather have cash."

"Wouldn't we all. But Joetta Reston is a mighty fine woman. Might even make you a good wife."

"How do you know I'm not married? Maybe I am."

"You're not."

"How do you know?"

"Because you look hungry, you don't look pussy-whipped, and you definitely don't look like you've been nagged into submission."

"If all that is true, why the heck would I want to get married?"

"You're young and hungry. Marriage is the best way to guarantee satisfying that itch. And Joetta would make a wonderful wife. She wants to please her man."

"When does the other stuff kick in?"

"Six months to a year. Depends on how fast you stop meeting her needs. And that's something almost all men end up doing. Take note. That was some free advice. Cost you a hundred bucks if you got that from a shrink. More if you're talking to a lawyer."

"Thanks. I think I'll stick with money. So now what? I wrote you a nice article."

"Keep on writing really nice articles."

"Payment. You said—"

Tully held up his hand. "I don't have to pay you a dime. Savvy? Because I have pictures of you with one of the Reston girls in your car. And when she starts hollerin' rape — why, you best have a full tank of gas in that jalopy of yours."

"Rape? I've been nowhere near those girls."

"That's not what the pictures say."

"What pictures?"

"The ones Mister Photo Shop took."

Pace jumped up and stood before the huckster. His hands balled into fists.

"Better not hit me, young man. Because an assault charge won't look any better."

"I can't believe this. You're blackmailing me." Pace turned around and faced the reservoir.

After a moment, Tully stood next to him. One hand clapped his shoulder, the other held an envelope.

Looking at the water, Tully said, "Take the envelope. A down payment. But don't forget what I said about Joetta. She's a mighty fine woman and wants a man she can please."

Pace looked at the con artist's profile, then took the envelope.

"Good man," Tully said, and walked away.

Pace shook his head and turned his back to the water. *O'Gara's,* he thought. *I could use a good stiff drink.*

"God, what a mess," he murmured.

Even though he wanted a drink, he decided to play it safe. Because once he started, he might just keep on drinking. And that wouldn't solve any problems.

No, he'd get a burger and fries, and an iced tea at Storm's Drive-In.

*Let's hope I can sort this mess out before it blows up in my face.*

# 38

2:15 PM, FRIDAY, 13 OCTOBER

HARRY WAS SITTING AT HIS TABLE IN THE CORNER OF THE REALLY Good checking his accounts. The bell tinkled over the door and he looked up. At first he thought it might be the phone scroller, but what he saw was someone entirely different.

She appeared to be in her late forties and was fairly tall for a woman. After removing her sunglasses, her eyes took in the shop.

Her outfit was conservative, but appeared to be of high quality. Burgundy slacks, white blouse, a light gray cardigan, and burgundy high heels. Simple, yet it radiated class.

A burgundy fedora-style hat with an extra wide brim sat at an angle on her head. The hair that spilled out from under her hat was a luscious dark brown, fell past her shoulders, and had a bit of a curl to it. A burgundy purse completed the outfit.

Her skin was very fair. What some called paper white. Although Harry preferred the term alabaster. Her makeup was lightly applied, although her eyes were rather dark and her lips were bright red.

The woman had an attractive figure, and Harry thought she probably exercised and watched her diet.

He looked at the half-eaten glazed buttermilk cake doughnut

on the plate next to his coffee cup. "Doesn't eat many of those," he whispered.

She was definitely a looker and Harry wondered why he hadn't seen her about town before now. Although the back of his mind was telling him there was something familiar about the woman.

When her eyes finally settled on him, she smiled; and Harry couldn't help but feel there was a bit of come hither to it.

She selected a table and sat; her face pointed toward the board listing the specials of the day.

Estrelita walked to the table, took the woman's order, and Harry's attention went back to his laptop and his accounts.

But when a shadow darkened his table, he looked up to see the woman standing there looking down at him.

"Excuse me. Are you Harry Thurgood?"

He stood. "I am."

"My name is Goody Preminger. My husband and I are fairly new in town. He retired early and we decided to relocate to where I grew up."

"Please, have a seat." *Where have I seen her before?* he asked himself.

She set her coffee cup down and sat in the chair across from him. Harry returned to his seat.

"If I remember, this was a shoe store back when I was a little girl. Trager's Shoes, I believe, was the name."

"All I know is the building wasn't in the best state of repair when I bought it. What it had, though, was location."

She smiled. "Very important. Location, that is."

"It's everything in real estate."

"So they say."

"Are you checking out the downtown?"

"Yes. A lot has changed. But a small town is still a small town."

"So I'm learning."

"You're new here?"

"My accent doesn't give me away?"

She laughed. "I can tell you weren't born in Texas."

"I wasn't. I'm not brand new in Magnolia Bluff. Been here four years now. I'm told my great-great-grandchildren might not be considered newcomers."

She laughed. Harry thought she had a very infectious laugh. He also wondered what it was she wanted.

"Very true. I'm suspect myself because I married a Yankee."

"Feelings run deep."

"They do here in the South. But even that's changing."

"I suppose so. The only constant is change."

"Isn't that the truth."

Suddenly it came to him where he'd seen her before, albeit only briefly. But he decided to keep that to himself. At least for the time being.

"So, how long have you been back home?"

"Six months. My husband was a senior partner in an architectural firm in Chicago."

"What do you do?"

"Now that the children are out of the house, I mostly just play. I swim most every day. Take our sailboat out on the reservoir as often as I can. Keep up my fencing skills by playing bouts with members of the college fencing club. And I grow old roses."

"Busy schedule, if you ask me."

"It is. What do you do? Aside from running this shop, that is?"

"Art and music are my passions."

"No exercise? You look so trim."

Harry chuckled. "Metabolism. No, I'm not much for exercise. Although, since moving here, I do a lot more walking."

She finished her coffee. "I've taken up enough of your time. Best get on with my self-guided tour of the new downtown."

Harry stopped her when she opened her handbag. "No need to pay. On the house."

"Thank you. How very nice of you." She stood and Harry did as well. "It was nice meeting you. Perhaps I'll see you out walking."

"Perhaps. Otherwise, I'm usually right here."

"Thanks for the coffee."

"Have a good afternoon."

He watched her leave and wondered what the Queen of the Crimson Hats was up to this time.

# 39

2:34 PM, FRIDAY, 13 OCTOBER

EMBER COLE SAW GOODY PREMINGER LEAVE THE REALLY GOOD while she was crossing the street.

"That's odd," she whispered. "What would she be doing at the coffee shop this time of day?"

She opened the door, entered, and realized she'd just become the afternoon crowd.

"Hey, Em," Harry called out.

"Hi, Harry. Has Goody ever been in here before?"

"No. You know her?"

"She and her husband joined the church when they moved to town, but don't attend much. I think she's a spy for Mary Lou."

"I thought she looked familiar. Had a vague recollection of her in the swarm following the Queen Bee maybe a month or two ago."

"I heard she was a Hat. Don't know how active she is. She's old money, and her husband is apparently very loaded. Might have more bread than what's in Gunter's bank."

"Don't say."

"I do." Ember sat across from Harry.

"So, what are you up to? I don't usually get the pleasure of your smiling face this time of day."

"I heard the evangelist is going to have another snake handling service tonight. And rumor has it, Brother John might raise someone from the dead."

"Kind of doubt he'll pull that one off."

"Be interesting to go, though."

"If that's your cup of tea."

"I'm going tonight."

"You are?"

She nodded.

"What on earth for?"

"I find it fascinating."

"I can think of other things that are far more fascinating than that charade."

"Well, I'm going. I'd like you to go with me."

"It's Friday night."

"So?"

Harry groaned.

"Fine. If you don't want to be with me…"

Harry held up his hand. "You know I do."

"Good. I'll be right out there on the sidewalk at six-thirty."

"And I'll be waiting for you."

"I love you, Harry Thurgood."

"I love you, Ember Cole."

"Are you sure you want to be a minister's husband?"

"Yes. Why do you ask?"

"Just checking. Because you'll be opening the door to a whole lot of religion. Think you can handle it?"

"I can handle religion. Not sure I'll be able to handle you."

"And what's that supposed to mean, Mister?"

"That you're one feisty, determined woman."

"Too much for you to handle?"

"Not if I learn to say 'how high'."

"If you think I'm domineering now, wait until I give you a taste of my riding crop."

"Whoa, Nelly. You said what?"

Ember giggled. "Tit for tat. Still want to marry me?"

"You bet I do. And I'm fine being a minister's husband. As long as you're okay being a coffee shop owner's wife."

"I'm thinking about it. There's something to be said for free coffee."

Harry laughed. "I guess there is."

Ember stood. "Gotta go. See you later."

"Ciao."

Ember left and was standing on the sidewalk when she heard her phone ding. She looked at it and saw a text message from Lee Gorman.

She read, *Did you get my voicemail?*

She checked her messages, found Lee's, and played it.

A very important relic? So important someone is coming all the way to Magnolia Bluff from Minnesota to look at it?

She considered turning around and asking Harry about the statue. She wanted to tell him she wanted the entire story. But he'd been so guarded.

No, she was going to listen to what this expert had to say, and then go from there. Because when she was ready to discuss the history of the statue with Harry, she wanted all the aces in her hand.

# 40

4:07 PM, FRIDAY, 13 OCTOBER

WITH NO CUSTOMERS, HARRY DECIDED TO CLOSE THE SHOP EARLY. Estrelita and Jack had already gone home. Miguel was finishing cleaning up and doing a bit of prep for tomorrow.

"Make sure you take any leftovers home for your family," Harry told him.

"Thank you, Mr. Thurgood. There's a family at church that can use the food. I'll take it to them."

"That's wonderful. Glad to hear it. I don't want to throw it away."

"No worries there, Mr. Thurgood."

"I'm off to the bank. If you're not here when I get back, have a good evening."

"Same to you, Mr. Thurgood."

Harry left, locked the door, and crossed East Main. He spotted Fergus sitting on one of the benches on the Green and detoured to say hi. But Fergus spoke first.

"The Feds."

The hair on Harry's neck stood up. "What about them?"

"It's the statue. They're here because of the statue."

"Statue? What statue?"

"Cars black as midnight. Statue black as midnight. Driving

around town in the black of midnight. Not good. Not good at all."

"What statue?"

"Only the devil's spawn is out at midnight."

"What are you talking about? Devil's spawn?"

"That's what Brother John said. Devil's spawn at midnight. Black SUVs at midnight. Devil's spawn."

Harry wondered what the heck Fergus had been drinking. "It's chilly today. Want me to walk you home?"

"Nah. Magnolia Nadine will see to that. This is her town, you know."

"So she says. Have to run to the bank. Catch you later."

"Not midnight. No devil's spawn parading black statues. You're safe, Mr. Thurgood."

"Thanks. Glad to know it."

Harry took off for the bank. He wondered who'd mentioned a black statue to Fergus. And if Fergus was talking about a black statue, Harry was willing to wager his Alfa Romeo that everyone was gossiping about a black statue. And that wasn't good.

———

Reece Sovern was at loggerheads. Somebody had killed Hunter Sulzer. Mary Lou Fight pointed her finger at Harry Thurgood. But then everyone knew she had a thing with Thurgood. And it wasn't a good thing.

However, other than Mary Lou's word and Thurgood's revised timetable of events, there was nothing concrete to pin on the coffee shop man.

Jager agreed Thurgood seemed the most likely suspect, but in the end it was Thurgood's word against Mrs. Fight's. And now that Lauderbach was involved, it was going to take more than the pronouncement of Mary Lou Fight to pin this on Thurgood.

On a lark, he ran the case by Sheriff Blanton. Buck had simply looked him in the eye, his grin taking on a stern cast, and said,

"Why do you want to mess with the best cup of coffee in town? And for a private dick outta Dallas?"

"But what about Mrs. Fight?"

Buck leaned back in his chair, hands behind his head, grin shining like a floodlight, and said, "If Mrs. Fight wants to take someone down, she doesn't need us to do it. She's just toying with Thurgood. Which means you, me, and Thurgood can be happy for that."

Sovern had digested that bit of insight, and decided there were more productive cases he could investigate. He still thought Thurgood was somehow involved. But it was going to take a bigger shovel than what he had available to move enough earth to get to the bottom of this one.

He picked up Sulzer's file, looked at it for the longest time, and then slipped it into his desk drawer.

The stogie moved to the other side of his mouth.

Then, again, maybe a haircut down at Daphne Leigh's just might be the thing to give his mind a new line of thought.

# 41

7:04 PM, FRIDAY, 13 OCTOBER

HARRY AND EMBER WERE SITTING THREE ROWS FROM THE STAGE. Ember had insisted. She wanted to watch the snake handling up close. Harry'd acquiesced. The things one does for love, he'd told himself.

He was surprised to see the place packed. Who would've thought a snake handling, faith healing, speaking in tongues, and a hellfire and brimstone service still had that kind of appeal in the enlightened twenty-first century?

Then again, he was from the godless north. What did he, Harry Thurgood, know about faith?

The Reston Family Singers were belting out some lively praise song. About half the audience were clapping and singing with them. He looked at Em. Her eyes were closed, her face turned upward, and she was clapping and singing, too.

Harry noticed Mike Kurelek was four rows back. Maybe he was here to observe applied psychology in action. Good anecdotes for his classes at the college, Harry thought.

Graham Huston was absent. But Monika Crow and that intern were sitting two rows ahead on the other side of the audience, representing the interests of the paper. All Harry could say was that Huston was one smart guy.

The praise song morphed into "Gimme that old-time religion" and almost everyone was on their feet, clapping and singing.

Harry studied the singers on stage. In the center was Mrs. Jearlene Reston. She was singing and moving to the music.

Mezzo-soprano, Harry thought. There's a bit of weight to her voice.

The three older girls formed a trio on the right, and the three older boys formed a trio on the left. In the center, behind Jearlene Reston, were the remaining six children, along with Brother John.

After two more songs, the family moved to the back of the stage, and the enormous mountain of a man that was Brother John took center stage.

In his booming baritone, he said, "'Comfort ye, comfort ye my people, saith your God. I am here tonight to bring you comfort, my friends. I am here tonight to prepare for you the way of the Lord! To make straight in this desert a highway to God for each and every sinner, each and every tarnished soul."

Brother John thundered on for another thirty minutes and then segued into the altar call.

"Who may abide the day of His coming?" Brother John asked. "Who shall stand when He appeareth? For he is like a refiner's fire!"

Mrs. Reston and the three older Reston daughters began singing softly in the background. "Just as I am," and Brother John pleaded for the sinners and backsliders to come forward.

Harry watched a half-dozen people answer the preacher's call.

When the sinners and backsliders had been attended to, the spectacle moved on to the main event of the evening. Main event for most of the audience, Harry guessed. The snake handling.

As before, the tall lanky man and the oldest Reston boy brought out the boxes and set them on portable stands so that the boxes were waist high.

Brother John lifted the lid on one of the boxes, reached in, and took out a long, fat snake, and draped it across his shoulders. He reached back in and took out two more snakes, holding one in each hand, and held them up.

"Who wants to experience the power of the Lord Jesus? Who wants to challenge the authority of that old serpent, Satan?"

He stepped down off the stage and held out a snake to a woman in the front row.

Harry watched her shake her head.

Brother John moved down the row. A woman directly in front of Ember, but in the front row, screamed, jumped up, and took off running.

Harry saw first one, then a second snake bite the enormous man.

Brother John's eyes grew wide. He staggered back until his legs collided with the staging, and then he toppled over backwards.

One of the stands came crashing down with him, and now there were snakes crawling everywhere.

The older Reston children, along with Reston's wife, rushed forward, and in the melee sent two more boxes of snakes crashing to the floor.

People were screaming and running for the front doors.

Harry noticed a few of the younger members of the audience were taking video of the scene with their cameras.

"Probably be on TikTok in the next ten minutes," he muttered.

Harry took Em's hand and stood. "Come on. Let's get out of here."

"But I'm a Christian," she said.

A gunshot rang out. Then another.

Harry pulled Ember to her feet, stooped, pulled her across his shoulders, and stood.

"Put me down!" she said, her voice just shy of yelling.

Harry took a quick look at the crowded front doors and ran for the door marked "Employees Only".

When they were through the door, Harry set Ember down.

Her hands were on her hips. "What did you do that for?"

He shook his head. "You're the one who told me that snake handling text was bogus. Then some nutter starts shooting."

The sound of sirens came to their ears.

"So this minister's husband made sure the minister could preach on Sunday."

"We're not married."

"Getting in practice."

They heard Chief Jager bellowing something.

Harry breathed a sigh of relief. "Now that Tommy's here, we ought to see things settle down."

Ember took Harry's hand. "Come on. Let's see if everyone's okay. Hope Brother John isn't badly hurt."

They walked back out into the auditorium, and could see the younger Reston children crying.

Chief Jager was issuing orders. "Everyone stay put. I and my men will take your statements."

"Oh, no," Ember said. "This sounds serious."

Harry spotted Officer Hans Winkler and walked over to him. Ember followed.

"What's going on?" Harry asked.

Winkler turned to face him. "Where were you two?"

Harry hooked his thumb towards the door they'd come through.

Winkler nodded. "Snakes bit several people. Paramedics are taking care of them. That big guy, though, is dead."

Ember's eyes grew wide. "Dead?"

Winkler nodded.

Harry's eyes swept over the Reston family and the first thing he noticed was that none of the older children, nor Mrs. Reston, were crying.

# 42

## 11:37PM, FRIDAY, 13 OCTOBER

REECE SOVERN SIGHED AND SHOOK HIS HEAD. "YOU TWO. I should've known."

"What's that supposed to mean?" Ember asked.

From the tone of her voice, the police investigator knew a long night was just about to get longer. He decided his best course of action would to be simply plow on.

"Why is it you two seem to show up every time we have a murder?"

"Aren't you exaggerating a wee little bit, Reece?" Thurgood said.

Reverend Cole added, "We weren't anywhere near those bodies they found on Blue Bonet's place. And we were nowhere around when they fished that college student out of the lake. And that crazy stuff with the dogs? We had—"

Reece held his hand up. "Okay, Reverend, I get your point. So tell me what happened. You first, Reverend."

Reece listened to the minister's and then Thurgood's versions of the night. When the coffee shop owner finished, Reece asked, "That's it? Nothing else?"

"Did the snake bites kill Brother John?" Thurgood asked.

"So far, that's what it's looking like," Reece said, "but Wylie Garrison, he's the Justice of the Peace—"

Both the Reverend and Thurgood nodded their heads. And Thurgood added, "I know Wylie."

Reece continued, "Wylie noticed an odd puncture wound, not consistent with a snakebite. So we're shipping the body off to Austin for the Medical Examiner to do an autopsy."

Thurgood pressed, "So his death is actually suspicious."

"Yes. And you two leave it alone. Now, anything else you noticed?"

"You might want to focus on the older Reston children and Mrs. Reston. They didn't appear to be grieving. In fact, they almost looked relieved."

"And you could tell all that from a brief look at their faces, Thurgood? Maybe you should become a partner with that voodoo shop owner."

"Trinity isn't into voodoo, she's—"

Reece raised his hand to silence the Reverend's verbal lava flow. "No offense intended. If you think of anything else, no matter how insignificant it seems to you, please let me know. Now get outta here."

Reece watched the couple go. He pursed his lips and wondered if their being present had any significance. Or was it just one of those coincidences?

*The thing is,* Reece said to himself, *I don't believe in coincidences.*

# 43

HARRY SAT IN HIS ROCKER RECLINER. A HANDEL CONCERTO PLAYED softly on the sound system. He puffed on his pipe, savoring the smoky, leathery taste of the latakia blend. A Corpse Reviver Number One was on the table next to the chair.

On the way to the parsonage, Ember had talked about "that poor family" and "those poor kids".

He smiled. That was Em. She was genuine. A selfless soul. Perhaps too selfless at times.

But his mind had only half-focused on what she was saying. The other half was thinking about what he'd seen after he and Em had re-entered the auditorium.

Or perhaps more accurately, what he hadn't seen.

Namely, that tall lanky fellow. The guy who was probably the manager.

He helped bring out the boxes of snakes. But when the fiasco started, that's when he seemed to disappear.

"I wonder if Reece knows about him?" he said out loud.

He reached for his phone, thought better of it, and left it on the table.

"I'll tell him in the morning." He chuckled. "Later in the morning."

Harry puffed on his pipe and took a sip of his drink.

The conversation with Fergus weighed heavily on his mind. If what the old vet said was true, there was probably going to be trouble. Right here in River City.

"And the one thing I don't need right now is more trouble."

He took another sip of his drink and puffed on his pipe.

After a few minutes, he decided he probably needed to derail that trouble before it gained a beachhead.

———

Joetta Reston was mad. She kicked the tire on the trailer and hit the side with her fist. The can she found in the street she kicked a good twenty feet.

"That no good two-timin' scoundrel took off and left me. He left all of us. Wonder if he has some hussy stashed away in one of those podunk towns we've been through?"

She paced back and forth in the space where Purnell Tully's truck had been parked, then stooped, picked up a rock, and hurled it at the trailer.

"All of us. He left Mama and Oralene and Raylene and me."

She started crying.

"And me in the family way."

The back of her hands wiped away the tears.

"God. Damn. You. Purnell Tully!"

She shook her fist at the dark, empty street.

"God damn you to *Hell*, you two-timin' worthless skunk."

Then she sat in the street. Her sobs hung heavy on the chill night air.

———

Jerri Reston had finally gotten the younger children to bed. Their cots lined the one wall of the old building.

The older ones had gone off some place. She wasn't sure where. Didn't matter. They'd be back.

She sat on the edge of the stage. Her feet on the floor.

Finally, after all these years, she was free. Freedom was scary. But it meant a new life. And she'd wanted a new life for a very long time. Now she held it in her hand.

She was glad. So very glad the fat, old sinning scoundrel was dead. He was probably in Hell right now.

"And that's where he shoulda been a long time ago. I just never had the guts to send him there," she murmured.

Now, it was just a matter of how to get out of town. Because the police chief and that detective were watching them. And she needed to get while the getting was good.

# 44

9 AM, SATURDAY, 14 OCTOBER

ESTRELITA WAS SERVING COFFEE TO THE MORNING REGULARS, WHO were all clustered around two tables listening to Chief Tommy Jager talk about the fiasco that ended last night's revival meeting. And Brother John's life.

Harry noticed the phone scroller wasn't around. *That makes for two days now. Wonder where he's off to?*

He mentally shrugged it off and brought to the morning coffee klatch an assortment of doughnuts, turnovers, kolaches, and a cranberry and orange marmalade tart.

"I made the tart using my own homemade orange marmalade," Harry said with a bit of pride in his voice.

"You were there, Harry," Jager said.

"Yes. Em and I were both there."

"You think he was murdered?" the police chief asked.

Harry shrugged. "Possible. Do you know if those snakes were fixed?"

"What do you mean?" LouEllen Muller, looking every bit like she was on her way to a Dolly Parton lookalike contest, asked. "You worried about them reproducing?" She laughed loudly.

Graham Huston shook his head. "You asking if their poison sacs were removed?"

Harry nodded. "Yes. My opinion is that Brother John was a con artist."

Huston nodded his head.

Jager said, "So you think he was scamming folks."

"I do," Harry answered.

Huston said, "Then maybe someone who was scammed paid back the scammer."

"Yes. That's why I asked if the snakes had their poison sacs removed."

"Good point, Harry," Jager said. "I'll have Sovern check into that."

Harry continued, "Because if someone slipped non-fixed snakes in with the fixed ones, then I'd say someone murdered Brother John."

"What a way to die," Caroline McCluskey said.

"They really got to take that chapter out of Mark," Reverend Billy Bob said.

"Horrible way to die," Magnolia Nadine said, and drank coffee.

"What about the other people who were bitten?" Ember asked.

Huston said, "Three adults and a ten-year-old were taken to Austin because we didn't have enough anti-venom. One person fell in the rush to get out. Someone stepped on her and broke her arm."

Magnolia Nadine shook her head. "I hope those folks will be all right. We don't need any more deaths around here."

"Someone once told me," Harry began, and sat before continuing, "that there are ten million ways to die. And every one of us will avoid all but one."

"Geez, Harry, that's too heavy for my Saturday morning." Jager stood. "I'm outta here. Catch y'all later." He downed his coffee, grabbed a cream cheese kolache and an apple turnover, and walked out the door.

Graham Huston said, "Whoever told you that, Harry, was on

the money. It's a reality very few of us are willing to face. But it's there staring us in the face every single day."

Harry nodded. "The Fates hold all of our life strings in one hand and a knife in the other."

There was a moment of silence, and then Huston said, "For whom does the bell toll?"

And Ember added, "It tolls for thee."

# 45

---

## 10 AM, SATURDAY, 14 OCTOBER

EMBER USED HER KEY TO UNLOCK THE BACK DOOR OF THE CHURCH.
For some reason, Graham's quoting of Donne's famous line bothered her.

Life was so fragile. Graham had been in Afghanistan. He understood how fragile it was. And she had a sneaky feeling that Harry's secret life gave him a perspective on the world similar to Graham's.

She pushed open the door and entered the church, closing the door behind her, and locking it.

The building was quiet. There was a light on in one of the offices. Cally Taylor's office. She was the Lay Leader and had become the thorn in Ember's flesh upon Mary Lou's departure.

Cally led the faction that wasn't happy with her leadership. And her position gave her a lot of clout. If it wasn't for the staunch support of Benton John Widdon, the chairperson of the church council, Ember realized she'd probably be anywhere but Magnolia Bluff.

She poked her head into Cally's office, gave her a cheery "good morning", and was answered with a perfunctory "morning" in reply.

Ember turned around and walked down to her office, shaking

her head, and asking herself why were people so bent on being mean.

Mean-Spirited Christians. They made no sense.

"We're all new creations in Christ. Most of us, though, act like last year's model."

She opened her office door, flipped on the lights, entered, closed the door, and crossed to her desk. When seated, she picked up her sermon notes.

"One more practice run and I should be ready for tomorrow."

She glanced over to the corner where the ugly statue sat and gasped. It was gone.

———

Lee Gorman stood in Ember's office. He shook his head. "And you're sure all the doors were locked?"

"Yes, Lee. You've asked me this twice before. I'm from the city. I always lock my doors. All the church doors were locked when I arrived. There's no key for my office door, but the church doors were locked."

"Sorry, Ember. It's..."

"I know. You think it's valuable, and now it's gone."

"Yes. Doctor Betzenstein will be crushed. Did you report the theft to the police?"

"Yes. And you've asked me that twice before, too."

"Sorry. It's just that this statue is quite possibly the *La Madone noire de la crypte* from the Chartres Cathedral. What's of interest is that this particular statue may have even begun life as a Druid votive piece and was then reworked into a Christian statue. Everyone thinks she was destroyed during the French Revolution. But your statue perfectly matches the description we have of the piece from eyewitnesses before she disappeared."

A buzzer sounded.

"That must be the police," Ember said. "Excuse me."

Lee nodded, and Ember left. His eyes roamed Ember's office. Spartan was the word that came to his mind.

"She would have made a good nun," he whispered.

Ember returned with Reece Sovern, who nodded to Lee and said, "Father."

"Good morning, Reece," Lee said in return.

"So what's going on?" Sovern asked.

"I had a statue, given to me by Harry Thurgood—"

Sovern shook his head. "I shoulda known he'd be involved."

Ember put her hands on her hips. "Just what is that supposed to mean, Mister Sovern? My taxes do pay your salary, you know."

"Nothing. So Thurgood gives you a statue and now someone has stolen it."

"Yes."

"When did you notice it missing?"

"About half an hour ago. Cally was here since six, but she said no one was in the church when she arrived and all the doors were locked."

"Locked doors. Any sign of them being forced?"

"No."

The police detective looked at Lee. "And you're here, why?"

"Ember asked me about the statue the other day. Asked if I knew anything about it. I told her I thought it was valuable, and I'd ask an expert I was friends with to look at it. But now it's gone."

"Why isn't Thurgood here?"

"Because I haven't told him it's missing."

"Why?"

"That's my business, Detective."

"Do you have a picture of it?"

"Yes. Let me send it to you."

Sovern gave her his email address, and asked, "So what is so special about this statue?"

Lee told the detective about the missing Black Madonna from

Chartres and his suspicion that Ember's statue was the missing statue.

When he finished telling his story, he watched the detective look at the floor, shift the cigar to the other side of his mouth, and then lift his head so they were eye to eye.

After a moment, Sovern said, "But this is all speculation on your part. You don't know for sure that the Reverend's statue is your missing Black Madonna."

"That is correct. That is why I spoke with a former professor and friend of mine, Doctor Betzenstein, to ask if he'd give us his opinion. He thought my guess was a good possibility. That's why he's coming here. Only now there's no statue."

"Anything else missing?"

Ember shook her head. "No. Not that I can tell. Nothing obvious, at any rate."

"So, what you are saying is that someone broke in without damaging any doors or windows and steals a rare and valuable piece of religious art that's been missing for a couple hundred years. Is that what I'm hearing?"

Lee turned to Ember, she looked him in the eyes, then they both turned to the detective, and said, "Yes."

"And you got this statue from Thurgood in the first place."

Ember nodded.

"Where did he get it from?"

"Just said it was in his family and that they'd pass it around at Christmas as a white elephant gift."

"Uh-huh." The cigar moved to the other side of Sovern's mouth and he pushed his glasses up his nose.

"All I can say is good luck getting it back. Wherever it ends up, it ain't going to be around here. I'll do my best. But two murders have higher priority. I'd check with Thurgood, if I were you. Good day."

Lee and Ember watched Sovern leave.

"Well, I guess that's that," Ember said.

"Perhaps Reece is right," Lee said.

"Talk to Harry?"

Lee nodded.

"Good luck with that."

"I'm very sorry about this, Ember."

"Me, too." She sighed. "I never did like it. I wish I would've just given it to you."

"What's done is done. I regret I won't have a chance to confirm my suspicions."

"Maybe *you* should talk to Harry."

Lee thought a moment, smiled, and said, "Maybe I will."

# 46

HARRY THURGOOD, DRIVING AN SUV BORROWED FROM REVEREND Billy Bob Baskin, pulled up in front of the building Brother John had used for his revival meetings and in which he'd met his end.

Police tape crisscrossed the windows. A police officer, unknown to him, stood by the door.

He got out of the SUV and approach the officer.

"I brought food for the Reston family. May I go in?"

"And why are you interested in the family, Mr. Thurgood?"

*Huh. Knows who I am.* Harry read the shiny silver name tag. "Well, Officer Young, I figure they would like to eat and they might not have any money and I have plenty of food."

Officer Young nodded. "The Chief wants to know if they get visitors."

Harry walked into the building. His eyes swept the room. The folding chairs were stacked along one wall. All except a dozen, which were arranged in a circle. A row of cots lined the other wall.

An area of the stage and floor were marked off with police tape. There was a chalk outline of a body on the floor.

The younger kids were playing. The rest of the family were talking or milling about.

Harry spotted Mrs. Reston sitting in one of the chairs and walked up to her.

"I'm Harry Thurgood. I own the Really Good Wood-Fired Coffee Shop and I brought you food. Have you had breakfast yet?"

The new widow stood, held out her hand, and said, "I'm Jerri Reston, and, no, we haven't eaten yet today."

Harry shook hands with her. "Then I came just in time. Let me bring in your breakfast and lunch."

"Samuel, Lofton, help Mr. Thurgood bring in the food he brought us."

At the mention of food, everyone stopped what they were doing and ran to the door.

"Thank you for your kindness, Mr. Thurgood."

"My pleasure, ma'am. And I'm very sorry for your loss."

"Thank you. But I'm not. A bad mistake has finally come to an end."

Her honesty surprised him. He said, "We all make mistakes. Don't always get a chance to undo them. Hope things work out well for you. Let me get the food."

He walked out to the SUV, opened the hatch, and handed out containers to the waiting hands. When the back of the vehicle was empty, he closed the hatch and walked back into the building, giving Officer Young a nod on the way.

Once inside, he grabbed a chair and set it by Mrs. Reston.

"Mind if I ask you a few questions?"

She studied his face for a moment, then asked, "Are you with the police?"

"No, I'm not. I just want to know what you need so I can help."

"Help? Why do you want to help us? We came here to con you out of your money."

"I know."

"You do?"

"I wasn't born last night, Mrs. Reston."

She smiled. "Call me Jerri. Please."

"Okay, Jerri. And I'm Harry, by the way. So, how can I help?"

She sighed. "I have no money. Purnell took it all when he ran off. If I had money, we could leave here."

"I don't think Chief Jager is going to allow that. At least not until you're cleared of murder."

Joetta handed her mother a wrapped paper plate. Jerri thanked her, took off the plastic wrap, picked up the sandwich, and took a bite. She chewed, and, after swallowing, said, "This is good. Thank you."

"Glad you like it."

"I suppose you're right. We're probably stuck here."

"For a time." Harry paused, then asked, "The police probably already asked—"

"Did I kill my husband? No, Mr. Thurgood, I didn't. He wasn't a nice man, but my children needed a father."

One of the girls, sitting two seats away, said, "Maybe not, Mama. Maybe we would've been better off without Papa a long time ago."

"Raylene, you stop that right now. Don't speak ill of the dead."

The daughter sitting next to Jerri stood up. "He was a bad man, Mama, and you just looked the other way." She ran out the door.

Harry said nothing. He did, though, think a visit from Mike Kurelek might be in order. Although the therapist might have his work cut out for him.

"Being a parent's a difficult job," Jerri said. "Damned if you do and damned if you don't. You have children, Mr. Thurgood?"

"No, I don't."

"You're possibly a very lucky man. Some days I think not havin' had all these children would have been a blessin'."

When Jerri didn't say anymore, Harry said, "The fellow who left…"

"Purnell Tully. He was the setup man. He was also the book-keeper. And he was also our Judas."

Harry nodded. "You said he left and took all of your money."

"My husband usually kept around eight hundred dollars on hand. For emergencies and to buy food and gas. It's gone. And I've looked everywhere. But it's gone. Just like Judas, Tully took the money and ran. He betrayed me." After a brief pause, she added, "Betrayed all of us."

Harry couldn't help but notice who it was Tully had actually betrayed. At least in Jerri Reston's mind.

"What about a bank account?"

"Purnell and my husband had access. The scoundrel's probably cleaned it out, too."

"Do you have a phone?"

"Yes."

"Let me give you my number. If you need anything, please call."

"You're so very kind, Mr. Thurgood."

"It's Harry. And it's my pleasure to be of help."

"Okay, Harry. Kindness and I are strangers. At least we've been for a very long time."

"Glad I can get you reacquainted."

"Thank you."

Harry wished her a good day and left. On the way back to Billy Bob's place, he couldn't help but think there were all manner of undercurrents going on in that family.

The question was, were any of them enough for one of them to resort to murder?

# 47

Reece Sovern was waiting in the Really Good when Harry Thurgood walked through the front door.

"Thurgood. Have a seat."

Sovern watched the coffee shop owner pull out the chair across from him and sit.

"Coffee?" Thurgood asked.

"Your coffee is too rich for my wallet."

"On the house."

"The Missus won't like it if I get spoiled. But okay."

Sovern watched with interest as Thurgood signaled for Estrelita to bring a cup of coffee.

*There's something about this guy,* he told himself. *He commands people effortlessly. Sure would like to find out where he's been and what he's done.*

When the coffee arrived and after Estrelita departed, the detective said, "The statue you gave your girlfriend is missing." He pushed his glasses up his nose, took a sip of coffee, and studied Thurgood's face.

"Say again?"

"Your girlfriend—"

Thurgood waved his hand. "Ember's not—"

"Save it, Thurgood. The whole town knows you have a thing for each other. The speculation is how much of a thing. What's important is that she's reported that ugly statue you gave her was stolen. And Father Lee thinks it's some long lost valuable relic."

"This is the first I've heard about it."

"Might be a good idea if you have a talk with your sweetheart about your relationship."

"You going into couple's counseling?"

"Hey. Just trying to help."

"Okay. Thanks. So why are you here?"

Sovern pushed his glasses so they were once again sitting on the bridge of his nose, rolled the cigar to the other side of his mouth, and took a sip of coffee. "Just want to know if you knew anything about the theft. Apparently, that visiting woman piano player is also a private dick and cautioned you about art. So says Jager. And then we find out you gave a valuable piece of art to your girlfriend. And now it's missing. Doesn't that strike you as strange?"

Thurgood stood. "All I can say, Reece, is you aren't going to find the statue here."

Sovern stood. "Okay, Thurgood. I have two murders on my hands, and now this. And *you* are right in the middle of all three."

"Coincidence?"

"Ha! Don't believe in coincidences."

Sovern turned around and left the shop. Standing on the sidewalk, he pitched his soggy stogie into the street and fished a new one out of his pocket. Cellophane removed and pocketed, he sank his teeth into the cigar.

"I know one thing," he murmured. "Thurgood's at the bottom of this. Maybe I should have another chat with Mary Lou Fight."

# 48

1:37 PM, SATURDAY, 14 OCTOBER

HARRY SAT AT HIS CORNER TABLE EATING A BUTTERMILK CAKE doughnut and drinking a cup of Columbian light roast.

He watched Father Lee Gorman enter and look around the shop. When the priest spotted him, he smiled and walked over to Harry's table.

"Hello, Harry. Mind if I join you?"

Harry held out his hand indicating the priest should sit. "Hello, Lee. Cup of coffee?"

Father Lee shook his head.

"So, what can I do for you?"

The priest cleared his throat. "I suppose you heard that the statue you gave to Ember was stolen."

"Reece Sovern was in here a couple minutes before you and gave me the third degree."

"Third degree? Why?"

"Thinks I had something to do with its disappearance."

"I see. Well, um, I think the statue is a valuable relic, and I was going to have it authenticated and, well, now it's gone." He cleared his throat. "I was wondering if you had any knowledge of its history."

"All I know is that it was a family heirloom; very, very old; and quite valuable."

"I see."

"Ember send you?"

"Huh? Oh, no. I came on my own. She knows nothing about the piece other than what you just said. I was hoping you knew more."

"Sorry, Lee, can't help you."

Father Lee stood, his face radiating disappointment. "Okay. Thanks. Have a good day."

Harry watched Lee Gorman leave. *That was a disaster. I wonder why Em would go behind my back? From here on out, Ember's on the no show, no tell list.*

———

Ember walked over to the park by the reservoir. *I should have left well enough alone,* she said to herself. *Now I've made a royal mess of things.*

She sat on a bench and followed a sailboat making its way down the length of the lake.

Someone sat on the opposite end of the bench. Ember smelled a subtle hint of perfume. She wasn't an expert, but she knew it wasn't something you'd find at the General Store.

She turned her head.

"Good afternoon, Reverend Cole"

"Good afternoon, Mrs. Hayden."

"Sorry to hear about the theft."

"Wow. News sure travels fast."

"That it does. Just don't know what's going on these days. Magnolia Bluff used to be such a quiet little town."

"I'm worried about what Harry's going to say."

"Ember, if I may? A little advice?"

"About what?"

"Men. They basically want two things."

"Two? I thought it was one."

Scarlett smiled and shook her head. "Two. Good food and sex. They'll say anything, give you anything, in order to get the sex. But if you really want the man, you win him through his stomach. The sex won't keep him. But good food will."

"So what does that mean?"

"You wear him out first, then cook him a good meal, and he won't even remember he gave you the statue."

"Yeah, but it was valuable."

"I hate to break it to you, honey, but it was just part of the mating dance. If that thing meant anything to Harry, he wouldn't have given it to you."

"I don't know."

"I do know. I don't know what your experience has been with men, but my suggestion to you is that you be cautious with Harry."

"What do you mean?"

"He's not the type of man to settle down. Even if you two get married, he'll have a roving eye. I know. From personal experience."

"I see."

"Well, I have to run." She touched Ember's arm. "If you need to talk…"

Ember nodded, and Scarlett left.

She turned her attention back to the lake. The sailboat was heading north now.

Ember considered Scarlett's advice. She was aware of the woman's reputation. The whole town was. If even half the gossip was true, Scarlett had been with a lot of men. So perhaps in her world what she said was true. But Ember knew Harry. And in her experience, he was a gem.

The sailboat disappeared behind the trees.

Even though no one was around, she whispered, "I'm willing

to bet you, Scarlett Hayden, I've had more men than you. Not something I'm proud of, and I, too, know a few things about men."

She stood. "I'd best tell Harry."

# 49

HARRY SHRUGGED. "THERE'S NOTHING TO FORGIVE."

"But—"

His upraised hand silenced her.

"Em, stuff happens in life. Murphy's Law?"

She nodded.

"I had an insurance policy on the statue."

"You did?"

"You bet I did. It may have been my family's white elephant gift, but that didn't mean I didn't recognize its value. So when I got it, I kept it. I hope you realize I didn't just fall off the turnip truck."

Ember giggled.

Harry continued. "If the statue isn't found, I'll file a claim."

"I guess that's some compensation."

"Ten million dollars worth."

"What?"

"And it's in your name."

Ember shook her head. "What did you say?"

"You'll get ten million dollars if the statue isn't recovered."

"But I don't want ten million dollars."

"Give it away then."

"Seriously?"

Harry nodded.

"So you're not mad at me?"

"Mad at you? No way. Crazy about you? You bet."

Ember blushed. "I don't know what to say."

"That's easy. Say, yes."

"But you don't know me."

"Em, I've known you for four years. And that's enough to tell me you are the woman I want to be my wife. The one to be my companion for all the days of the rest of my life."

"But—"

"No. A hundred and fifty years ago, people moved west to escape their pasts. We don't have that luxury today. Back then, there was an unwritten rule: you never asked anyone about their past.

"When a person moved out west, they became a new person. You judged that person by what they said and did, and if they kept their word. Because that told you everything you needed to know about the person.

"I know what I need to know about you. I want you to be my wife."

Ember thought for a moment. "It's like in the Bible: we're new creations in Christ."

"Yes, it is. We came here to Magnolia Bluff to get away from our pasts. We are, as it were, new creations."

"All right, Harry Thurgood, I'll marry you."

# 50

3:07 PM, SATURDAY, 14 OCTOBER

Joetta Reston did a three-sixty, taking in the room.

"What you lookin' at, Joetta?" Oralene asked her sister. "This place is a dump. I don't know how Mama could stand to come here with Purnell."

"Mama was desperate."

"And what about you?"

"Don't be goin' there, O. What's done is done."

"So what's goin' to come of us? And why do we have to stay in this place?"

"That woman, whose name is the same as this town, Mama said she arranged for us to stay here until the police find who killed Pa."

"You think one of us did it?" Oralene asked.

"Who else would want Pa dead?"

"Somebody he cheated."

"Possible, I suppose. Purnell was always good at keepin' those folk away."

"He was at that. Where do you think he went?"

Joetta clenched her fists. "I don't know. But if I find him, I'm gonna kill him."

Monika Crow took their picture. "It'll be in the next edition. Congratulations, you two."

Graham Huston chuckled. "Everyone in the county will know by then."

"Probably," Harry said.

Graham stroked his chin. "So you two are actually going to tie the knot?"

Ember looked at Harry and then back to Graham. "We are."

"Who's moving where?"

"Haven't decided any details yet, Graham."

"And you don't need to tell me when you do. The whole town will be talking about it within ten minutes. Although Monika will have the details in nine and have it in her gossip column for the few who aren't on the gossip line. Not sure why I bother to put out a newspaper."

"I'm glad you do. It keeps Neal's memory alive."

"You liked him, didn't you?" Graham said.

"I did. I miss him."

"Can't say anything bad about him. Gave me a job."

After a moment, Harry said, "Heard any scuttlebutt as to who would want Brother John dead?"

"Several hundred people from East Texas to Kansas to Missouri and down to Louisiana."

That's a lot of people over a pretty big area."

"But you know what they say: we're usually killed by our nearest and dearest."

"So the family, or that assistant of his?"

"Purnell Tully. Yes, the family or him. That's where my money's going. Makes the most sense. And why are you interested?"

"Sovern. He thinks I'm somehow involved in most every crime around here."

Graham laughed. "Always safe to pick on the outsider."

Harry nodded. "But he doesn't pick on you."

"I have sixty-four point type on my side."

Harry chuckled. "There is that. If you hear anything, you'll let me know?"

"Sure. Likewise?"

"You bet. Thanks, Graham. Catch you later. Bye Monika."

"Bye, you two," she said.

Standing on the sidewalk, Ember asked, "Now what?"

"I think we need to get close to that family. There are a lot of undercurrents there. And one of them just might give us a motive."

# 51

OLIVIA SET TWO LARGE PIZZAS ON THE TABLE. ONE A VEGGIE LOVERS, and the other a pepperoni.

"Anything else I can get you?" she asked.

Ember shook her head.

"Enjoy."

As Olivia headed back to the counter, Ember said, "Okay, girls, dig in."

Twelve-year-old Wendolyn grabbed a slice of pepperoni and began eating.

Raylene, as she reached for a slice of veggie, asked, "Why are you being so nice to us?"

Oralene gave her a look of disapproval, and Joetta said, "That's no way to talk, Raylene, when someone gives you somethin'."

"No one gives us anything, Jo, unless they want somethin' back. I'm just bein' up front. Let's be honest for once."

Joetta shook her head and took a slice of pizza.

"To answer your question, Raylene," Ember began, "you're in a strange town with no friends and the police are investigating the death of your father. I'm guessing you need a friend, and Mr. Thurgood and I help people who need help."

Raylene swallowed her bite of pizza. "Them words sound real good, Miss Reverend, but nobody helps anybody for free. They always want somethin' in return. So what do you want?"

Ember thought for a moment and then said, "Information."

"About what?" Joetta asked.

Raylene said, "Thank you for bein' honest."

Ember said, "You're welcome" to Raylene, then turned to Joetta, and said, "Mr. Thurgood and I are trying to help the police find who killed your father."

Joetta paused before taking a bite of pizza and asked, "Why?"

Oralene added, "Why do they need *your* help?"

Ember took a deep breath, let it out, and said, "Because the police inspector suspects Mr. Thurgood is somehow involved."

"So you're really only helpin' yourself, not us," Raylene said.

"No. We'd help you anyway. I became a minister because I wanted to help people. And Mr. Thurgood helps people because he's a good person."

"So what do you want to know?" Oralene asked.

"Did one of you kill your father?"

"Why would we tell you if we did?" Raylene asked.

"We could blame Mr. Tully," Oralene said. "He ain't here to defend himself."

"You could say Mr. Tully did it. The police have the Texas Rangers looking for him, and when he's found, he'll probably point the finger at one of you."

"He'd do that to save his skin," Raylene said.

"Not you," Wendolyn volunteered. "He likes you. Likes Mama, too." She took a bite of pizza.

Ember decided she might as well jump in with both feet. Nothing ventured, nothing gained.

"Did Mr. Tully have sex with you?" she asked.

Raylene laughed. "Everybody had sex with us, Miss Reverend."

Ember shook her head in disbelief.

"Not everybody, Raylene," Oralene said.

"But it was more than I wanted," Joetta said.

"This is terrible," Ember said. "When did this start?"

Joetta turned to Wendolyn. "Papa have any special prayer meetin's with you?"

The young girl removed the pizza slice from her mouth, shook her head, and put the slice back in.

"With Papa, about Wen's age," Joetta said. "Purnell just liked us older girls. And Mama."

"And anyone who was willin'," Oralene added.

"This is terrible," Ember said. "There's someone at the college you can talk to if you want. He can help."

Raylene laughed. "We have no money. Don't need another man tryin' to diddle my cooter."

"No, no. Mike isn't like that. And you don't need to worry about money."

Ember watched Raylene study her face. The girl then said, "Didn't know there were rich preachers."

"I'm not rich. But Mr. Thurgood and I will work something out with Dr. Kurelek. So keep it in mind."

Ember watched Joetta, Oralene, and Raylene glance at each other and slowly nod their heads. Wendolyn ate pizza.

*What's obvious to me,* Ember thought, *is that these girls were sexually abused for most of their lives and they're angry about it. Could one of them have finally snapped and killed her father?*

# 52

Harry hoped Em was getting some good information from the girls. He thought the boys might be willing to talk to him. Man to man, so to speak. So he and the Reston boys were at a different table on the other side of the pizza parlor.

Olivia dropped off the three pizzas, and after she left, the boys looked at Harry. He gave them a nod, and they dived in. All except John-John. He said a prayer first.

*Religious,* Harry said to himself. *Might be motive enough right there. Then, again, I'm biased.*

John-John looked at Harry when he was finished with his prayer. "You're not eating?" he asked.

Harry smiled. "I would never not eat Olivia's pizza. It's the best, this side of Italy. Hands down." And took a slice of the Meat Lovers Special.

"Thank you, Mr. Thurgood," Lofton said. "This is really good."

"You're welcome. If you want more when this is gone, just say the word."

"Why are you bein' nice to us?" John-John asked. "My father and Mr. Tully were con men, you know."

"I know," Harry said. "The police inspector thinks I'm

somehow involved. Long story there. So I'm helping you, number one, because you're in need; and, number two, because I'm also helping myself."

John-John nodded and took a bite of pizza.

"You in college?" Harry asked.

"No," John-John answered. "Pa thought college was a waste of time. And money."

"It can be," Harry said. "Why did you stay and help your father with his con game?"

"He used to be a good man," John-John replied.

Lofton shook his head. "You ask Jo, O, and Ray how good he was."

Harry watched the anger flit across John-John's face. *Anger over what? That Lofton contradicted him? Or that he exposed the lie?*

Lofton continued. "Pa was not a good man, John-John, and you know it. You got into plenty of fights with him. Why are you makin' up this story?"

Harry looked at John-John and said, "The police will eventually find out everything. So which of you switched the snakes in order to kill your father?"

Together Samuel and Elisha said, "Purnell Tully."

Lofton nodded.

John-John said, "I don't know."

"But it was someone in your group," Harry pressed.

Lofton shrugged. "No one could get to the snakes. Just us and Purnell."

"Unless it was the man who sold them to us," John-John said.

"Not likely," Lofton countered. "Why are you defendin' Purnell Tully? You punched him and threatened him."

"That true?" Harry asked.

Before John-John could answer, Samuel said, "It's true. I saw it."

"It's true," John-John said. "Told him to stay away from Ma."

Harry watched John-John lift his head and turn his dark, anger-filled eyes to meet his own. "Purnell Tully was bad, Mr.

Thurgood. Pa was bad. Everything was bad. And now God is making things right. He's called me to take over our ministry and preach His Word without sin. And I'm gonna do that."

He stood. "Excuse me. Thank you for the food." And the hulking young man walked out of the restaurant.

Harry took a slice of pizza. *I think the field of suspects just got brought down to a manageable size. Now we just have to figure out if it was the wife, the Judas, or one of the children.*

# 53

9:32 PM, SATURDAY, 14 OCTOBER

SCARLETT SET DOWN THE MARTINI AND PICKED UP HER PHONE.
"What on earth could Betty Lynn want at this time of the night?"

She pressed the button and said, "Hello."

After ten seconds, Scarlett said, "What did you say?"

When Betty Lynn repeated her words, a primal scream ripped from Scarlett's throat and she hurled the phone against the wall. It put a dent in the paneling and dropped to the carpeted floor.

She let out another scream and hurled the martini glass against the same wall. It shattered into a hundred pieces, spraying gin and vermouth across the dark paneling.

"No, no, no, no." She shook her head, and screamed as loud as she could, "No!". Then she dropped to the floor and her shoulders shook with the violence of her sobs.

After a time, she lifted her head and swiped the backs of her hands across her eyes.

To the empty room, she said, "I will kill you, Ember Cole. I will kill you, even if it's the last thing I do. I will kill you with the last breath I take."

Scarlett mustered all of her strength and screamed, "I hate you, Ember Cole! You are dead, dead, dead."

Then she lay prone on the floor and sobbed long into the night.

———

Reece Sovern pushed his glasses up his nose, shifted the cigar to the other side of his mouth, and entered the interrogation room.

Sitting at the table, in handcuffs, was Purnell Tully.

Reece sat opposite him. "You sure led our boys on a merry little chase. But the Rangers are better than the FBI, so you never had a chance. Welcome back to Magnolia Bluff."

When Tully didn't say anything, Reece tapped the button on the recorder, giving his name, Tully's name, the date, the time, and the location.

Tully looked up. "I would like a lawyer."

"Figures. Must be guilty if you are asking for a lawyer."

Tully said, "The law is very complicated. I would like a lawyer."

Reece said the interview session was over, shut off the recorder, and motioned for the police officer standing by the door to take Tully back to his cell.

When he was alone in the room, Reece muttered, "Lawyers. Sometimes I wish I was back in the thirties, so I could use a little force on these bastards. A little pain always gets people talking."

———

Harry sat in one of the tub chairs across from the sofa on which Ember sat. Wilbur lay next to her. They'd just finished exchanging the information and impressions each had gotten from the older Reston children.

Ember drank tea, and, when she set the cup down, said, "That family's a mess, Harry."

"Tell me about it."

"Incest. Adultery. Lying. Stealing. Cheating. I thought I'd sunk to the depths of depravity." A mirthless chuckle came from her lips. "The Reston family has reached lows I never dreamed of."

Harry puffed on his pipe. The subtle scent of Holiday pipe mixture incensed the room. "Certainly looks that way."

"You think one of them did it?"

"Without a doubt. John-John got religion somewhere along the line and is determined to end the sin in his family. Jearlene was having an affair with Tully, and I suppose she was hoping to run away with him. Joetta and Oralene were also with Tully, and it seems he was promising to take them away. Raylene may have been with Tully and was undoubtedly in special prayer meetings with her father."

Ember nodded. "Seems Tully was promising each of those women what they wanted to hear: an escape from the hell they were in."

"Exactly. Tully was playing a shell game with those women, and I do not know how he thought he could win. In addition, like Judas, he was embezzling money. It's a royal mess. Plenty of people with motive. But which one of them had the strongest motive?"

"Maybe several were working together."

"There's that, too. Tully and one of the daughters. Or Tully and Jearlene."

"Or the daughters to stop the potential abuse of Wendolyn."

"Possible. But why now? The abuse has been going on for years."

"It's Magnolia Bluff. It's where the murders happen."

"That's a bit farfetched, I think. There was probably some other catalyst than our geographical location."

"I don't know, Harry. We seem to be cursed."

"Perhaps. But it seems to me we'll find the motive to be much simpler. I wonder if Sovern has traced where the snakes came from. That might be a good place to start."

"It might be. But who had the most to gain from Brother John's death?"

"Ultimately, that is the question. We answer that, and we will have our killer."

"Or killers."

Harry nodded. "Or killers."

# 54

10:57 PM, SATURDAY, 14 OCTOBER

As Harry approached the street door to his apartment, that was next to the public door for the Really Good, he noticed a familiar car parked at the curb.

He shook his head. "What does *he* want at this hour of the night?"

Resigned to the fact he was going to have a conversation he most likely wouldn't like, Harry detoured to the car's driver's side and looked at the tinted window that was sliding down into the door.

"Evening, Reece. Don't you ever sleep?"

"Thurgood. No, I don't. Get in."

Harry shook his head, walked around the front of the car, and got in.

Sovern pushed his glasses up his nose, shifted the cigar to the other side of his mouth, and turned in his seat to face Harry.

"The Rangers picked up Purnell Tully over in Louisiana. Talked briefly with him a little while ago."

"Briefly? I can't imagine why he'd not want to chat."

"Not funny, Thurgood. Wants a lawyer. So he can cool his heels in the slam until we get around to finding him a do-gooder public defender."

"And you're telling me this, why?"

"Just in case he was your partner."

"Oh, for the love of God. I am not the guilty one in any of these cases you are investigating. And the longer you focus on me, the greater the chance the perpetrator is going to get away with it."

"You think so?"

"Look, Detective. I didn't kill Mary Lou's private eye. I didn't steal the statue I gave to Ember. And I certainly didn't kill Brother John. You're wasting time harassing me. Perhaps Lauderbach can do something about that."

"No need to get nasty, Thurgood. So you're innocent. If you say so. Then who killed the private dick if it wasn't you?"

"I have no idea. I wasn't there when it happened. And you can't put me there."

"You're right. I can't. But a jury might."

"I doubt it."

Sovern shrugged.

"And why would I steal the piece of art I gave to Ember?"

"I don't know. Just a stab in the dark. Insurance fraud? Oh, by the way, I guess congratulations are in order. So, congratulations. About time you made an honest woman of the Reverend."

"Thanks. And we haven't been making whoopee, either. Not that anyone believes it, or that it's even anyone's business. Now are we done here? Or do I have to call Stanton?"

"Get outta here."

Harry got out and watched Sovern drive away.

*The sooner Em and I find the culprits, the sooner I get him off my back.*

# 55

7:03 AM, SUNDAY, 15 OCTOBER

EMBER KNOCKED ON DOOR NUMBER TEN AT THE COZY CORNERS
Motel. The numbers were tarnished and didn't look much like
gold anymore.

She heard movement inside, the sliding of the deadbolt,
followed by the door opening the length of the chain.

"Oh, good morning, Reverend Cole."

"Good morning, Mrs. Reston."

"Jerri, please. I'd rather not hear… Jerri is fine. What can I do
for you?"

"Harry and I would like to take you and your children to
breakfast. And I'd like to invite you to worship at my church this
morning. No obligation. You can go elsewhere; or not at all, if you
prefer. The choice is yours, but I'd love to have you with us this
morning."

"That's awfully kind of you. You don't have to. Mr. Thurgood
gave us enough money…"

"You don't have to accept, of course. But you are strangers in
our town and now your lives are in an upheaval. We'd like to be
your friends. At least for the time you are here."

"Okay. If you can give us half an hour to get ready, I'll accept
your offer."

"Wonderful."

———

The Silver Spoon was doing a brisk business when they all walked in a little before eight. Ember was glad Harry had called ahead and asked Lorraine if she would reserve a couple tables or booths for them.

*Probably helps that he gives her free coffee,* Ember mused.

She and Jearlene had their own booth. Something she'd asked Harry to arrange with Lorraine, as well, because she had a feeling the dead evangelist's wife might be more forthcoming with information when talking alone with another woman.

After the waitress dropped off Jearlene's buttermilk biscuits and sausage gravy with an egg sunny side up, and Ember's hard fried egg and wheat toast sandwich, Ember asked, "Is it okay if I say grace?"

"Sure."

Ember reached out her hands, and after a moment's hesitation, Jearlene took hold of Ember's hands and closed her eyes.

Ember prayed, "Dear Lord, thank you for this wonderful day, the food You have blessed us with, and my new friend. Make us vessels of mercy to everyone we see today. In Jesus's name. Amen."

"Thank you, Reverend Cole, for calling me your friend."

"You're welcome, and, please, call me Ember."

Jerri Reston smiled. It was brief, but Ember felt it was genuine.

"What are you going to do when you're free to leave?"

Jerri swallowed her bite of biscuit. "I don't know. I'm so tired of traveling. I might decide to stay here."

"The Hill Country is beautiful, and Magnolia Bluff is a wonderful place to call home."

"Is there work?"

"Some. Like most small towns, I guess. If you can offer a service, you might be better off than trying to find a job."

Jerri nodded and ate biscuit and gravy. "You ever married?" she asked after swallowing her food.

"No. Harry and I just got engaged."

"Congratulations. Hope he's good to you."

"Wouldn't have said yes if I didn't think he would be."

A faint smile touched Jerri's lips. "Ever had your heart broken?"

"What girl hasn't?"

"Ain't that the truth."

"You all think Purnell Tully killed your husband. But he was kind of like the goose that laid the golden eggs. Brother John, that is. Your late husband was the magician that made the magic happen and brought in the money. Why would—"

"Why would Purnell kill him?" Jerri shrugged. "You'll have to ask him."

"Why didn't you take your children and run away?"

Jearlene put her fork down. "And where was I supposed to go? Didn't have any money. I was in prison. The bars just weren't visible."

"I see."

"Do you? I bet you had a nice, soft middle-class life and never had to do any hard work."

Jearlene stood. "Thank you for your kindness. But we don't need your help. We'll get by just as we always have."

She turned to a passing waitress. "Would you get to go boxes for my food and my children's, please?" Jerri pointed to the tables where her kids sat and then walked out of the cafe.

"I sure messed that up," Ember muttered. "Now what?"

# 56

## 9:13 AM, SUNDAY, 15 OCTOBER

Mary Lou Fight stood before the massive picture window that looked out onto Burnet Reservoir. Her mind, though, was focused on other things than admiring nature.

*The lothario and his strumpet are helping that family of hucksters. Figures. Thieves and charlatans always work together,* she told herself.

The good thing about this situation was that the police investigator was looking at Harry Thurgood for the murder of Hunter, and that religious huckster, as well as possible insurance fraud in the case of the strumpet's stolen statue.

"What I need is a way to make the coffee man look really bad in Reece Sovern's eyes," she whispered to herself. "The dandy likes to throw around money. Maybe that could be his undoing. Now, who can I rely on?"

Her mind ran over the names of the women in the Crimson Hat Society. Tiffany Graceson? No, wants too much attention. Carrie Ash? Too young. Katherine Hughes? She shook her head.

"I think Pearline Applewhite will do for this. She's always eager to please her queen."

Reece Sovern answered his ringing desk phone. He hoped it was a call from the medical examiner in Austin.

"Is this Reece Sovern?"

"It is."

"I'm Doctor Harrison Butts with the Medical Examiner's Office in Austin. Filling in for the regular medical examiner, who's on vacation. I have the report on your victim, John Reston."

"That's great, Doctor Butts. Can you give the short version?"

"Certainly. John Reston died from snake venom. He had eighteen bites and one hypodermic to the heart."

"Hypodermic?"

"Yes. A single, large-gauge needle. Pushed right through his clothing and a significant amount of tissue. Missed hitting bone. So my guess is that the person knew what he or she was doing."

"Unless they got lucky."

"Possible. That's for you to decide. I'll email the report to you later today. Just wanted you to know you have what looks to me to be another murder on your hands. And it wasn't a spur-of-the-moment killing, either. The syringe and needles were most likely purchased ahead of time. A large gauge like that is usually used for large animals. And the victim was an enormous man. I'm guessing some thought went into this."

"Thanks, Doc. Appreciate the call."

Reece put the handset on the cradle, and leaned back in his chair, gazing at the ceiling.

"Hypodermic. Well, I'll be damned. Somebody wanted to make sure the preacher man bit the dust. It's too bad I won't be able to pin this one on Thurgood. Too many witnesses agreeing with him he was nowhere near the victim when he went down."

Reece drew in a lungful of air and exhaled. The ceiling tiles told him nothing. But he didn't need them to. He already knew what he needed to do. He had to talk to Tully and the family. Again.

———

Harry could tell Ember was feeling badly. She sat behind the desk in her office, looking as though she had lost her last friend.

"You aren't responsible for her reaction, Em."

"I was too forward. I told her I was her friend and then I turn around and interrogate her. That isn't what friends do."

"You were trying to help, and she took it the wrong way."

"Sometimes I wonder if Mary Lou is right. I really shouldn't be a minister. I'm too great a sinner."

"Em, what's going on?" He got up and moved next to her chair. Then squatted next to her, putting his arms around her.

She slid to the floor, put her arms around him, and laid her head on his shoulder.

"You're a fabulous minister, Ember Cole. A woman of faith, and you care deeply about your congregation. But people who are broken sometimes don't want to be fixed, and I have a feeling Jerri Reston may be one of those people."

"You're probably right. You'd never think this is a really tough job."

"It is. And you don't even get to serve them booze."

"You are incorrigible, Mister. You know that?"

"I do."

"Thanks, Harry. Thanks for loving me. I will do my best to be a good wife for you."

"You will be."

"Now, I'd like some time alone before the service."

"Sure, Em."

They stood, he kissed her, and left.

Heading out of the building, he saw Caldwell Taylor. "Good morning, Cally."

She didn't bother to reply with words; instead, she favored him with a look that Harry guessed was supposed to make him shrivel up like a weed hit with Roundup.

He smiled back and continued on down the sidewalk.

Em had touched a raw nerve with Jearlene Reston. That much was obvious. He'd gotten very little out of the kids.

John-John didn't say more than a couple of words.

Lofton made small talk until silenced by a look from John-John.

The family was closing ranks, and that was going to make things difficult.

Harry started for home. "I think now is the time to divide and conquer."

## 57

## 10:11 AM, SUNDAY, 15 OCTOBER

From the windshield of the old bus that Brother John had converted into a motor home, Jearlene Reston saw the woman get out of the car and look around.

It was obvious the woman didn't buy her clothes at Walmart. And that car looked like something a movie star would drive. Jearlene wondered what she wanted.

When the woman's gaze turned to the bus, she waved and walked to the door.

Jearlene opened it and asked if she could help her.

"Are you Mrs. Reston?"

"I am."

"Then I can help you."

Jearlene cocked her head and said, "We don't need help."

"Do you want to leave here?"

"Yes."

"Then, courtesy of Harry Thurgood, I have thirteen Greyhound Bus tickets for you. Plus, five thousand dollars in cash."

"We don't need his help. We don't need anyone's help."

"You have five thousand dollars and a way to leave town?"

Jearlene looked the woman in the eye and then looked down. "No, we don't."

"Then take his gift and get out of town. Now that they've caught that Tully fellow, he's telling all sorts of stories about you. So you best leave now."

"And who are you?"

"My name is Estrelita and I work for Mr. Thurgood."

Jearlene eyed the woman. *I may have been born at night, but it wasn't last night. This woman hasn't worked a day in her life. But I know Purnell is doing whatever he can to save his neck. If I take the money and tickets, the police will think I'm guilty. If I stay here, they'll think I'm guilty because I'm not from here. And with Tully singing like a canary, even if his song is a crow's caw, I'm in hot water. Boiling hot water.*

She saw John-John leave his motel room. *And I have twelve children to think about. But what kind of life is runnin' and hidin'? The same kind I've been livin' for twenty-two years, ever since the bastard knocked me up.*

John-John stood next to the woman. "What's goin' on, Mama?"

"This woman is offering us a chance at freedom."

———

Harry was halfway back to his apartment when a familiar car pulled over to the curb.

"Now what the hell does Reece want?" he muttered.

The passenger window rolled down. "Get in, Thurgood."

Harry pursed his lips and got in the car.

"Morning, Reece. You accompanying me to Em's service this morning?"

"Didn't take you for the prayin' kind, Thurgood."

"I'm not. Just there to give her support."

"I see. Have to start callin' you the pastor's husband."

"Or her the coffee shop owner's wife."

"That's too long. Anyway, lovely morning."

"That it is."

"Remember last year when you said we'd be better off working together?"

"Louisa Middlebrook's murder. Yes, I remember saying that."

"Still feel that way?"

Harry studied the police investigator's face for about ten seconds before saying, "I do. I'm not the adversary."

"Good. You've been talkin' to these evangelist folk. I'm hopin' we can help each other."

Harry smiled. "I can possibly help you. I don't see how you are going to help me."

"Already have. Not looking at you for murder one in either murder case, and I'm thinkin' you have no need to commit insurance fraud."

"Well, thank you very much, Detective. I'm much obliged."

"Good. I like that. I'm goin' to capitalize on your indebtedness to help me solve a murder or two."

"When do we start?"

"Now would be good."

"Very well. Let me text Em."

# 58

HARRY FOUND HIMSELF SITTING ACROSS FROM A BEDRAGGLED-looking Purnell Tully and a young man who'd introduced himself as David Dreer. Tully's public defender.

"Where did you go to law school?" Harry asked the lawyer.

"Benjamin N. Cardozo School of Law. Yeshiva University in New York City."

"Long way from home. You don't wear a kippah?"

Dreer adjusted his gold wireframe glasses. "Not normally. Why do you ask?"

"That's an Orthodox school, isn't it?"

"It is. However, I'm Conservative."

Harry nodded and studied the young man. Dark hair, parted in the middle. Not long. Three-piece suit. Black. White shirt. Navy repp tie. He couldn't identify the young man's cologne, but the dark spice scent was definitely upscale.

He switched his gaze back to Tully. The man needed a shower, a shave, and a fresh change of clothes. Sovern and Jager were probably applying a little psychology to wear him down. Might not work now that he had Dreer helping him.

"You're a cop?" Tully asked.

"No. Just helping."

"Do you know anything about the law?" Dreer asked.

Harry nodded. "Don't run red lights, speed, or jaywalk. Don't kill people, maim them, or trespass. And don't play your music so loud it disturbs the neighbors."

A Mona Lisa smile touched Dreer's lips. "Are you the good cop, or the bad cop?"

"I'm the coffee shop owner looking for customers." He gave a business card to Dreer and one to Tully.

"This is highly unusual," Dreer said.

"This is Magnolia Bluff," Harry replied. He turned his head to Tully and said, "I will deliver if you can't make it to the shop."

"Gee, thanks." Tully's voice was laden with sarcasm.

Dreer shook his head. "Since I don't have all day, let's get started."

"You don't live in Magnolia Bluff, do you?" Harry asked the lawyer.

"Marble Falls. Does that make a difference?"

"Guess not. The law's probably the same here as there." Harry sat back in his chair and focused his attention on Tully.

After a moment or two, Harry asked, "Did you kill Brother John?"

"No."

"Were you having sex with his wife?"

"Yes."

"His daughters?"

"What about his daughters?"

"Were you having sex with them?"

Dreer held up his hand and whispered something to Tully, who shook his head. Dreer then nodded.

"Yes," Tully said. "The two oldest daughters."

"Were you embezzling money from Brother John?"

"How is this relevant?" Dreer asked.

"Motive. Steal money. Steal the wife, or a daughter. Start a new life."

"Don't answer that question," Dreer said.

Harry waved his hand. "Too late, Mr. Dreer. The police already know he was. I'm just asking to find out how Mr. Tully would answer."

Dreer glanced at Tully, then said, "I see. Go on."

"Everything was in chaos after the snakes bit Brother John. Did you happen to see who stuck the hypo into him?"

"Hypo?"

"Yes. A syringe. Someone stabbed Brother John with a syringe full of snake venom. Right into the heart. That's what killed him. Did you see who did it?"

"No, I didn't. As you said, it was chaos. A tangle of bodies trying to help him and capture the snakes."

"*You* didn't stab him, did you?"

Dreer held up his hand. "I'd like to talk more with my client."

"Good plan." Harry stood, and the police officer opened the door.

Harry walked out, followed by the police officer.

Reece Sovern was there and pulled Harry aside. Reece was smiling.

"You catch Tully's reaction to the hypo question?" Sovern asked.

"Yes. My guess is he knows who stabbed Reston with the hypo, or he did it himself."

"We're searching for syringe and needle purchases. We'll find out soon enough who bought them."

# 59

LANDON PACE, WITH HELP FROM MONIKA CROW, HAD WRITTEN A bang-up story for the Saturday edition of the *Chronicle*. Complete with pictures both he and Monika took.

Graham Huston had even put the story on the front page. Rob Carter wasn't too happy about that.

The newspaper editor merely shrugged. "Murder beats a crushing Bulldog victory any day of the week." Then added, "Quit complaining, Carter. You're on page two."

All Saturday, Landon monitored the Reston family. He was ticked he wouldn't get any more money or an in-kind payment now that the evangelist was dead. But there might be a heart-wrenching human-interest piece about the family that would bring a tear to the eye of the more sensitive folk in this backwater hick town. A story that would sell papers for Huston.

"Might get something out of that," he told himself.

He observed the family all day, and by evening had decided he'd see if he could talk to Joetta Reston. She was pretty and about his age and appeared to be the most approachable.

And being a preacher's kid, he might get lucky in more ways than one. Especially if she was anything like Paula back in high school, who'd taken the virginity of half the guys in the senior class. If the rumors were true, that is.

Then, just as he was about to make his move, that woman with the boobs showed up and started talking to Mrs. Reston. Then she gave the widow an envelope and a large satchel.

Now, all the kids were getting on the bus with bags and suitcases.

"Be my luck that they're leaving town," he muttered, watching them from his car.

A smile appeared on his face. "I can follow them and then call in their escape and be right there when the police take them off the bus. That ought to pimp anything Carter might come up with."

When the last kid was on the bus, he watched the exhaust belch from the tailpipe. He started his car, put it in drive, and said, "Here we go."

------

After the call to worship, and the opening hymn, the Reverend Ember Cole, wearing a white surplice over a black cassock, a green stole, and a clerical collar with long preaching bands, walked to the front of the platform.

She smiled, and said, "Most if not all of you have heard rumors about Harry Thurgood and me. I'm going to take a minute this morning to make sure what you may have heard is accurate, and put to rest the inaccurate.

"Harry Thurgood and I are going to marry. We're engaged. We were going to announce this together, but Reece Sovern requested his help on some police business.

"We have not had sex, nor are we going to until we are married. As Harry has said, 'Two people in love don't have to have sex in order to enjoy their love.'

"I intend to continue as your pastor. I love you and I love this town. Please stand and sing with me one of my favorite hymns. Betsy has the words up on the screen."

The organ began playing and Ember, with her clear and rich mezzo-soprano voice, started singing and the congregation, at least most of them, joined in.

> *Be Thou my Vision, O Lord of my heart;*
> *Naught be all else to me, save that Thou art.*
> *Thou my best Thought, by day or by night,*
> *Waking or sleeping, Thy presence my light.*
>
> *Be Thou my Wisdom, and Thou my true Word;*
> *I ever with Thee and Thou with me, Lord;*
> *Thou my great Father, I Thy true son;*
> *Thou in me dwelling, and I with Thee one.*
>
> *Be Thou my battle Shield, Sword for the fight;*
> *Be Thou my Dignity, Thou my Delight;*
> *Thou my soul's Shelter, Thou my high Tow'r:*
> *Raise Thou me heav'nward, O Pow'r of my pow'r.*
>
> *Riches I heed not, nor man's empty praise,*
> *Thou mine Inheritance, now and always:*
> *Thou and Thou only, first in my heart,*
> *High King of Heaven, my Treasure Thou art.*
>
> *High King of Heaven, my victory won,*
> *May I reach Heaven's joys, O bright Heav'n's Sun!*
> *Heart of my own heart, whatever befall,*
> *Still be my Vision, O Ruler of all.*

"Those words express my heart's desire," Ember said, "and I pray they express yours. Please be seated and let us pray."

———

Scarlett Hayden opened her eyes and immediately regretted doing so. The movement of her lids made her head protest in pain.

"Oh, God." She tried sitting up, but the merry-go-round was spinning too fast.

"I think I'm going to throw up." She tried getting out of bed, didn't make it, hung her head over the side, and heaved her guts out.

She rolled back onto the bed and pleaded with the God she didn't worship to make the room stop spinning. He was, though, and perhaps understandably so, somewhat reluctant to comply with her request.

"Oh, no, not again." She needed to get to the toilet.

Gritting her teeth, she rolled out of bed and hit the floor. Her arm and chest landing in her vomit.

She wanted to cuss a blue streak, but her head hurt too badly. Clamping her mouth shut and swallowing to keep her roiling stomach at bay, she crawled to the bathroom.

When she'd reached the toilet, she grabbed hold of the rim, pulled herself up, and hung her head over the bowl.

Her worship of the porcelain goddess began, and the sound of her retching filled the empty house.

# 60

LANDON PACE FOLLOWED THE BUS TO A PARKING LOT ON SOUTH Vandeventer Street, between Jackson and Pierce Streets.

There were three small businesses lining the lot. There was also a sign with a picture of a greyhound on it announcing that the lot was a Greyhound bus stop.

"Oh, this is choice," Landon said. "They're skipping town on the Greyhound. I wonder if that woman with the boobs has something to do with this?"

He watched one of the boys leave the bus and walk over to Nick's Convenience Mart. Dingy gray paint was peeling off the siding and duct tape was holding the glass in the door together.

*Business must not be too good, or Nick's a real cheap skate,* Landon thought.

Then he saw Joetta and one of her sisters, possibly Oralene (there were so many he had trouble keeping them all straight), leave the converted motorhome.

He got out of his car and walked over to them. "Hi. My name is Landon Pace. I was at the service when your father died. Please accept my condolences. I'm very sorry for your loss."

"Thank you for your kind words, Mr. Pace," Joetta said.

The sister cocked her head to the side, and said, "You lookin' for somethin'? I've seen your car by the motel. Are you with the police?"

The belligerence in the young woman's voice surprised him.

*Time to turn on the charm,* he told himself.

"No, I'm not," he said. "I'm with the county relief and assistance agency. We heard of your loss and would like to help."

"We have all the help we need, Mr. Pace," Joetta said. "We're leavin' on the noon bus and startin' a brand new life."

"Oh, I see. Will that be here in Texas? I might be able to reach out—"

"We don't need your help," Joetta's sister said. "Now maybe you need to be mindin' your own business and leave us alone."

"You don't need to be mean, O. He's just lookin' to help." Joetta turned to him. "Like my sister said, Mr. Pace, we're fine now."

"Okay. I won't be any trouble. May I ask where you're going to start your new life?"

"Chattanooga, Tennessee," Joetta said.

"Nice city." Although he had no idea if it was or not. "Visited a couple of times two, three years ago. You'll like it there. Nashville's not far. Might be able to get a recording deal. You have an exceptional voice."

Landon watched her blush and knew he'd scored a compliment. She was exceptionally pretty. Had he known she was this pretty, he might have been convinced to spend time with her instead of taking the cash Tully had offered.

"Well, I wish you luck." He reached into his pocket, took out his notebook and pen, wrote on a sheet of paper, tore it out, and handed it to her. "Once you get settled, call me. I can show you around town."

"Thanks. But I don't know you."

"Take it. We'll go together. Your sisters and brothers."

Still, she hesitated.

Landon stepped closer. "I don't bite. We've met. You know my name. I know yours. Joetta. It never hurts to have a friend."

Joetta took the paper. "Okay, Mr. Pace. I'll call when we get settled."

"Good luck, and safe travels. Until we meet again. And the name's Landon."

He gave the girls a smile and then walked back to his car.

Sitting behind the wheel, he was under no delusions that she'd call. "But it never hurts to leave a calling card."

The Greyhound bus pulled into the lot just after he drove out of the parking lot.

He pulled over, watched the family get on board in his rearview mirror, and when the bus pulled out, he turned around and followed it.

# 61

FATHER LEE, DOCTOR GERALD BETZENSTEIN, HARRY THURGOOD, and Ember Cole sat in a booth at the Corral 44. Father Lee and Doctor Betzenstein had joined Harry and Ember at Harry's invitation.

He knew they wanted to talk about the statue, so why not get the subject out of the way over a good meal of barbecue?

After the food arrived and the small talk had taken place, the Doctor asked, "Where did you get the statue, Harry?"

"As I told Em, the statue was in the family. Not sure how it came into our possession. Too many conflicting stories. Just that we've had the thing for a long time. Couple, maybe three generations. We used it as a white elephant gift at our Christmas parties. We'd pass the thing around, and you always hoped you didn't end up with it.

"One year, when I got it, I decided to keep it. I know a few things about art and thought the statue might actually have some value. I had it appraised by an auction house up north for insurance purposes and they valued her at seven to ten million dollars. But they couldn't tell me anything about the statue, other than that the piece was old. Middle Ages old.

"Then I gave it to Em. And now someone else has it."

Betzenstein said, "You don't sound upset at losing something worth seven to ten million dollars."

"Not much I can do about it, is there?"

"No, I guess not," the doctor agreed. "Still…"

Harry shrugged. "The statue will be difficult to get rid of. So whoever took it either wanted it for himself, or will find out the only thing of value is the silver."

"That's what I'm afraid of," Betzenstein said. "The person might destroy a priceless relic for a few scraps of silver."

"Worse has been done," Harry said. "So, Gerald, what do *you* think I had on my hands and gave to Em?"

"I think the statue is the lost *La Madone noire de la crypte*."

"That is an incredible thought. Well, I guess I was right: it is valuable."

"Yes, it is."

After a pause, the conversation drifted to small town life, art, and, inevitably, to the weather.

When the meal was over, Harry and Ember said goodbye to Lee and the doctor, and got into Harry's car.

"Did you see the sadness in Doctor Betzenstein's eyes?"

"Yes. He was very much upset about the statue."

"But you aren't."

"No. Well, yes, I am. But there's nothing I can do about it except collect the insurance. Well, you collect the insurance, since the policy is in your name."

"It is?"

Harry nodded.

"Why did you do that?"

"In case the thing got stolen."

Ember pursed her lips, then shrugged, and said, "I still can't believe something that ugly could be worth ten million dollars."

Harry chuckled. "To Lee and the doctor and millions of Roman Catholics, it's priceless. To you? You would have chucked it into the wastebasket. And that's why I said not to."

"That's true. I'm just sad they are so disappointed."

Harry shrugged. "It's just a guess at this point if that statue is in fact the lost Black Madonna. They'll get over it. What matters more, at least to my mind, is what are you going to do with the insurance money?"

"I don't know. I don't need the money. I don't even want the money. Tell me again how much you insured that ugly thing for?"

"Ten million dollars."

Ember chuckled. "You're right: I would have tossed it in the trash. And poor Lee and the doctor are just about in tears over the theft."

"Funny world we live in. Everything is in the eye of the beholder."

"Yes, it is." Ember paused, then added, "Including who lives and dies."

# 62

REECE SOVERN STOOD FACING ARNOLD AND BETTE WEISS, OWNERS OF the Cozy Corners Motel.

He was furious. The questioning of Tully hadn't gone well after Thurgood had left. That fancy pants lawyer kept telling the con man to not answer the question.

Then, not more than fifteen minutes ago, he finds out the Reston family has left town.

"Look, Reece," Arnold began, "I didn't know I was supposed to keep them locked up in their rooms."

"Nobody said we were supposed to be prison guards," Bette added.

Arnold continued, "The rent's been paid through the end of the month. They didn't destroy anything, and they left the keys in their rooms. Didn't know I was supposed to report every time they flushed the toilet. Next time, maybe you can provide some muscle to keep 'em here."

Reece took a deep breath to keep his blood pressure in check. "You happen to notice when they left?"

"Not sure," Bette said. She looked at Arnold.

He said, "About noon. Little before?"

Bette nodded. "That sounds about right."

"And they left in their bus?"

The couple nodded, and Bette said, "That's right."

Reece told them thanks and walked back to his car.

"Nuts," he muttered when he was behind the wheel. *Now we have to look for an orange bus with Brother John's name plastered all over it. At least it's orange, kind of difficult to hide that.*

He started the car, and was thinking how best to approach Jager about setting up a search for the missing family when the radio squawked his name.

"I'm here," Reece said.

"Reece, Winkler just reported finding the Reston family's empty bus at the Greyhound bus stop."

"Got it. I'm out."

He shook his head, smacked the steering wheel, and uttered a few choice cuss words before turning the car north and heading off to the bus stop.

# 63

## 4:11 PM, SUNDAY, 15 OCTOBER

EMBER SAT ON THE SOFA IN HER LIVING ROOM, BUT COULDN'T concentrate on the novel. She was still somewhat in shock over the news Harry had told her she would be a millionaire if the statue wasn't found. Miss Reed just couldn't compete with that.

Her eyes roamed the room. One wall contained her front door and picture window. Simple drapes and sheers were pulled back to allow the waning light to enter the room.

The fireplace dominated another wall. A third had a door to the dining room. All the walls were bare.

Her furniture was spare. The sofa faced the picture window. There was a tub chair and an end table on one end of the sofa. Facing the fireplace behind the sofa were two coastal-style wingback chairs, a low walnut stained coffee table was between the chairs.

The simple, spartan decor dominated every room in the house. Except for her bedroom. She had a simple, but very comfy bed; a cherry bentwood rocking chair; a small end table with an imitation Tiffany lamp; and a TV that she rarely watched. Hanging on the wall was a framed print of one of Albert Bierstadt's western paintings. Her bedroom was her favorite place to pray and meditate.

Wilbur was curled up next to her. She petted him and said, "What am I going to do with ten million dollars, Wilbur? I certainly don't need the money. I have everything I want. Well, at least when it comes to *things*. Harry said to invest some for the future, and give the rest away. Sounds like a good plan to me. But who should I give the money to? And what kind of investments should I make?"

Her teacup was empty, and she decided a refill was in order. She made her way to the kitchen, filled the teakettle with water, and put it on to boil. She removed another "Constant Comment" tea bag from its wrapper and put it in her cup.

When the water boiled, she poured it over the bag, placed the saucer over the cup, and let the bag steep.

"I can't even comprehend ten million dollars," she said to her cat, who had followed her into the kitchen. "Ten million! It's beyond understanding. All my adult life I've scraped by. Before I met Jesus, that bothered me. Never having enough to make ends meet."

She paused for a moment. "Well, that's not true. I had plenty of money in Vegas, I just over spent living a life of sin. But Jesus changed all that. I learned to make do with less and trust Him."

She smiled at the thought and started singing the song, "The Lord's my Shepherd, I'll not want."

When she finished the song, she took the tea bag out of the cup and returned to the living room, Wilbur following. Together, they sat on the sofa.

"Perhaps I'll give all the money away. I have Jesus. I don't need money."

Wilbur yawned.

———

Harry Thurgood sat in a booth at O'Gara's. On the only TV in the place, a football game was playing. But he didn't pay it any attention. He didn't like football.

Gill Simmons, the owner, was behind the bar. A fifty-something guy, who had enough rugged good looks to compete favorably with a bald rear tire.

His girlfriend, Fleur Beauchamp, made small talk and flirted with the four guys who were sitting at the bar.

Harry'd apparently given her enough signals he wasn't interested in company, and she'd finally left him alone.

In between bites of his burger, he nursed a gin rickey.

From what he'd heard, Fleur was from New Orleans and probably had a couple of years to go until she reached the big three-o. She was sufficiently attractive and had a bubbly enough personality that she could have her pick of any ranch hand or farmer's son in the county.

So what she was doing with Gill was a puzzle. To him. Not to them. Obviously. They seemed to get along just fine.

Harry's mind drifted back over the events of the past few days.

There was the guy who'd sat in his shop scrolling through his phone. He had disappeared as suddenly as he had appeared.

And there was Scarlett's warning that Mary Lou had hired someone to dig up dirt on him. Then the fellow ends up dead on his doorstep. Murdered.

His visit to Scarlett had done nothing but tease his mind into thinking perhaps it was she who had put three slugs into Sulzer.

Then there was the fiasco with Em and his gift. No wonder she owned a cat. Curiosity. Curiosity killed the cat, and satisfaction brought it back. Only in Em's case, there wasn't going to be any satisfaction. And she wouldn't be singing that she couldn't get any satisfaction, because ten million dollars is a mighty big distraction.

And now there was Brother John's murder. That shady-looking Purnell Tully was the likely culprit, but, in all honesty, the happy killer could have been the wife, or the older daughters, or the oldest boy. All were likely suspects. And they could even have worked in concert, as Em had suggested.

He swallowed the last bite of his burger and took a sip of his drink.

Harry studied the bar patrons, Gill, and Fleur.

*I bet none of those six people think they might be next. One way into this world, and ten million ways out. Yet most of us never think about the ten million ways to die. Heck, few of us think about living. We're too busy just existing.*

He downed the remainder of his rickey in two gulps, and, rather than invite the attention of Fleur, got up and walked over to the bar.

"Everything all right, Harry?" Gill asked, while he finished wiping a glass.

"I'm fine. Just meditating."

"You looking for a refill?"

"Change up. Brandy Manhattan?"

"Sure thing."

Gill began mixing the drink.

"You ever think about dying?" Harry asked.

The bartender placed the drink before Harry. "Why so morose? Heard you're going to make an honest woman out of that preacher."

Harry smiled. "Wasn't dishonest to begin with." He watched the incredulity slide over Gill's face.

"Don't tell me you and she…"

"That's exactly what I'm telling you. We haven't consummated our future marriage, nor have we been enjoying the honeymoon."

"Seriously?"

"Seriously."

"Well, I'll be damned. That'll probably go in the Guinness Book of World Records."

"Hardly. There's her position at the church to consider. So we watched our love grow without sex."

"Maybe that's why you're so morose."

"No. Just thinking about these murders."

"Ah. Well, they are disturbing. That's for sure. But I don't concern myself about them overly much. People die every day. But as long as I'm with Fleur, I just think about living. And you'll be doing the same once you and the preacher woman—"

Harry raised his hand. "Got it, Gill." He picked up the drink the bartender had placed before him, saluted, and walked back to his booth.

He sat and sipped the brown liquid. Maybe Em should use some of that money to buy a piece of land far from the madding crowd.

Someplace by a brook, with lots of forest around the house, the nearest neighbor five miles away, or even further, and the nearest town fifty miles in a direction no one wants to go.

He'd have to bring it up to her. No more church hassles. No more Mary Lou. No more gossip. And no more murders.

# 64

## 4:51 PM, SUNDAY, 15 OCTOBER

Landon Pace followed the bus into the Greyhound terminal in Houston. When he saw the Restons get off, along with all their luggage, he knew something was up.

He parked, got out of his car, and stayed a distance away so he could keep an eye on them. It helped that there were somewhere around three dozen people in the station, excluding the baker's dozen of Restons. He'd mingle and not be so easily noticed.

Jearlene was on her phone for the longest time. To Landon's eyes, it looked as though she made three calls right in a row. It wasn't, though, until the bus pulled out while the Reston family remained in the terminal, that Landon got the sinking feeling they weren't going to Chattanooga.

He raced back out to his car and drove to where the taxis and ride-share services picked up their fares.

*So, if I were ditching the bus,* he asked himself, *what would I do? I certainly wouldn't stay in Houston. I could take a different bus. I could fly. Did Amtrak service Houston? If so, the train was also a possibility.*

He asked Siri, and sure enough Amtrak did service Houston. Plus, the station was only two miles away.

*Flying is out,* he told himself. *Too many kids. Would cost a fortune.*

*A different bus or the train make the most sense. But which one and when?*

While he was musing on possibilities and likelihood, he watched two Uber vans pull up and the Reston family board them.

"I guess I'm about to find out."

He put the car in drive and pulled out after the vans.

———

Harry stepped out of O'Gara's and saw Reece Sovern's car parked at the curb.

The window rolled down and Sovern said, "Get in. I have a bone to pick with you."

Harry got in the car. "What is it this time, Reece?"

"Thirteen little birds have flown their cage all because someone bought Greyhound bus tickets for them."

"Are you talking about the Restons?"

"I am. So why did you do it, Harry? I thought we agreed to work together."

"Wait a minute. *You* think *I* bought bus tickets for the Restons?"

"Yep. To Chattanooga. Why?"

"I hate to burst your bubble, Reece, but it wasn't me."

"That's not what Greyhound says. The person purchasing the tickets online was one Harry Thurgood. They were then paid for, in cash, at the Walmart in Marble Falls."

"Greyhound said that?"

"Yep."

"All I can say is that it wasn't me."

"You've been helping them all along. Giving them food and money."

"The gossip around here is incredible. Yes, I've given them food and money. I was helping a family in distress. But I didn't buy them bus tickets."

"Says you."

"Come on, Reece. That's not my style. I would've rented cars for them. The Greyhound? I wouldn't put my worst enemy on the bus."

"So you're saying that someone bought the tickets in your name?"

"It would have to be, because I didn't do it. If they only reserved the tickets online, and then paid cash for them at Walmart, it seems to me they could put any name on them. Does the bus driver check names? Are names even on the ticket?"

"In theory, yes, ID is required. But in actuality it's rarely asked for. And if you get your ticket online, Greyhound says you can travel without ID."

"So it is possible someone used my name to get the tickets."

"And who would want to do that, Harry?"

"Don't look so smug, Reece. Mary Lou Fight, for one, thinking she can get me in trouble with you. Don't tell me you didn't think of that."

From the look on Reece's face, Harry would've wagered his new car that the detective hadn't.

Sovern pushed his glasses up his nose. "So you're saying Mary Lou bought those tickets using your name?"

"Probably not Mary Lou herself. You know she doesn't operate that way. She got one of the Hats to do it."

"You're on the up and up?"

"Cross my heart hope to die. Does that work for you?"

"Don't push it, Thurgood. I still have half a mind to bring you in and let you cool your heels in a cell."

"Lauderbach would have me out before you close the door."

"Lawyers. God, I hate them. Okay. I'll take your word for it. Talking to Mary Lou probably won't help."

"Not at all. But the security cameras at the Walmart might show who paid for the tickets. Just look for one of the Hats."

"Good thinking, Thurgood. I'll have Jager talk to Buck Blanton. Now get out of here."

"With pleasure. *Auf Wiedersehen.*"

Harry got out of the car and watched Reece drive off.

He pursed his lips and tilted his head in thought. After a moment, he shook his head and headed for home.

*I know one thing,* he said to himself. *I need to do something about Mary Lou Fight. And I need to do it sooner rather than later.*

# 65

IT SURPRISED REECE AT HOW QUICKLY SHERIFF BLANTON GOT HOLD OF the surveillance tapes from Walmart. He'd dropped them off himself just five minutes ago.

"Now, let's see who was doing the dirty work," he muttered, as he plugged the thumb drive into his computer. "Now I'll find out if Thurgood's telling the truth."

The file came up on Reece's screen, and he began playing the footage.

---

Landon Pace wasn't sure what to do. He'd followed the vans to a Marriott Hotel, and after parking his car, followed the family to the fifth floor. What surprised him is that they'd only taken three rooms.

*Mighty cozy accommodations*, he thought.

Landon hid in the stairwell, and keeping the door open a crack, he'd watched the family get settled.

But after twenty minutes had gone by and their doors remained closed, he started thinking.

*Do I get a room? Or should I wait in my car? I don't want to miss them when they leave.*

After a minute or two of weighing the options, he decided he'd wait in his car. That way, he could keep an eye on the doors, not be seen by them, and be able to follow them when they left.

Realizing he was hungry, he asked his phone to find the nearest pizza parlor.

*I shouldn't be gone long. I'll get the pizza, take a leak, and be ready for the night.*

An hour and a half later, he was back at the hotel. To make sure the Restons were still there, he walked into the lobby and up to the desk.

"I'm meeting some friends and I want to find out if they've checked in already. The Restons?"

The young woman manning the desk was a bit on the plain side, so Landon turned on the charm and flashed her a big smile, with a hint of suggestion to it.

She smiled back, and a bit of color touched her cheeks.

"They've checked in. Do you want me to ring them for you?"

"Not yet. I have to get a couple of birthday surprises from my car. I'll be back."

He gave her another big smile and left.

Back in his car, he ate pizza, drank Doctor Pepper, and monitored the hotel door.

———

A little over two hours into the footage, Reece spotted a face he recognized entering Walmart. Pearline Applewhite. He should've figured as much. Thurgood was right.

The rumor mill said that she'd become Mary Lou's right-hand woman after the Middlebrook murder. He couldn't help but notice that Pearline was a looker, and by the way she walked and dressed, she knew it.

Reece leaned back in his chair and closed his eyes. *There's plump, pleasing plump, and then Pearline Applewhite plump.*

He thought of his wife, took in a big lungful of air, and exhaled. "If only Hetta were more Pearline than plump," he muttered.

After a few moments, he shook his head, thanked the good Lord that Hetta was his wife and not Pearline, shut off his computer, and stood.

"Now to see what Pearline Applewhite has to say for herself."

# 66

EMBER WATCHED HARRY POUR THE BROWN LIQUID FROM THE HIP flask into the tumbler.

"What is that?" she asked.

"A Corpse Reviver Number One. Want to try?"

"I'll pass, thank you."

"You're not a drinker, are you?"

"Not anymore. I used to be. I used to drink a lot."

"Seriously?"

She nodded. "Drugs, too. Not every day. Mostly weekends. I hate to think how much crap went up my nose."

"I never would've suspected."

He took a sip of his drink and took out his pipe and began filling it with tobacco.

"That's the part of my life I wish didn't exist. But it does. I do my best to forget about it."

"Does Jesus help?"

"Yes. Prayer and singing gets my mind off of the past."

"You don't mind if I...?" He held up his glass and pipe.

"No. Go ahead. I'm not tempted anymore."

"Were, are you in AA?"

"No. Just Jesus and willpower. I don't think any of those so called social sins," she made air quotes around social sins, "are sins. Mostly, they are just a waste of time and money, in my opinion. But if you enjoy a drink, or a smoke, I'm not going to stop you." A mischievous smile appeared on her lips. "I still love you in spite of your evil habits."

Harry lit his pipe. "I'm so very glad about that. I'll stop if it bothers you."

"No, I don't want that. You are who you are and I love who you are. As long as you're good to me, and love me, I'm okay."

She watched him set the drink and pipe down and move from the chair to the sofa and sit next to her.

He put his arms around her and she let him pull her to him.

"Em, I will always love you and be good to you."

"Even if I was a very bad person in my past?"

"Did you kill somebody?"

She giggled. "No. I guess I wasn't that bad." She grew serious. "But I was a bad girl. And I'm so sorry..." She stifled a sob. "I'm sorry, Harry."

"Em, whatever you did, you have to forgive yourself and move on."

She pulled away and nodded. "I'm sorry."

"It's okay. Don't worry."

"Harry, may I ask you to sit in the chair?"

"Sure." He moved back to where he'd been sitting before.

"It's not that I don't want you next to me or holding me, because I do. And right now, I want to take you into my bedroom and let you make love to me."

"Should I go?"

"No. But to be safe, a little distance will help."

He smiled. "Anything to help."

"Thank you, my love." She took a breath. "So Mary Lou tried to get you in trouble with Reece?"

He nodded, lit his pipe, and said, "That's what it looks like. Using one of her minions is my guess. There is something seriously wrong with that woman."

"In my opinion, she has megalomania, which would also make her a narcissist."

"You been taking classes from Mike?"

"No. Pastoral care and Clinical Pastoral Education in seminary."

"I see."

"The fact that the Restons ran isn't going to put them in a good light, is it?"

Harry took a sip of his drink and puffed on his pipe. "No, it isn't."

"Do you think they're guilty?"

"The most logical approach is to assume this is an in house affair. Tully, one of the older girls, the oldest boy, or Jearlene."

"And the hypo would confirm that."

"Exactly. Tully is proving difficult to crack because of that hotshot young lawyer from the Public Defender's Office."

"What would Tully's motive be?"

Harry puffed on his pipe. "I don't see one. If he was a Judas, and was padding his pockets, he has no reason to kill Brother John. Why kill the guy who's bringing in the bucks? Just leave when you have enough. Or when you get caught."

Em considered for a moment. "Wouldn't Brother John bring charges?"

"No. John Reston was a scoundrel. Tully probably had plenty to come right back at him. So no, I don't think there would be any lawsuits. Reston might kill Tully, but I don't see it the other way around. Both are, were, conmen. Conmen aren't killers. At least not usually."

"So that leaves the family."

Harry puffed on his pipe. "Yes. From what we have pieced together at this point, they seem the most likely in my book."

"Jearlene Reston was not happy in her marriage and the evidence indicates she was having an affair with Purnell Tully, hoping he'd take her away."

"That's how it looks. Too bad she couldn't see that would never happen."

"It also looks like there's the possibility of incest, and we know the older girls were having sex with Tully."

"So plenty of motive for Jearlene to kill her husband and for the kids to kill their father." Harry finished his drink.

"What about John-John?"

"There seems to be a lot going on in that boy's head. He's taken a turn towards a serious faith. He sees himself, at least I think he does, as the head of the family because his father was not a good father."

"So he might have killed his father to protect his mother and sisters."

Harry nodded. "Very possible. As well as serve the judgement of God upon a sinner."

"That's scary."

"It is."

"Now we just have to get some evidence."

"That's where we're at." Harry stood.

"You're leaving?"

"Yes. Because if I don't, I'll be carrying you to your bedroom to make mad, passionate love to you."

A big smile appeared on Em's face. She stood, crossed to where Harry was standing, hugged him, and kissed him.

"I'm blessed, Harry Thurgood. Thank you for your patience and thank you for loving me."

With arms around each other, they walked to the door.

"Goodnight, my princess."

Ember let him press his lips against hers for only a few seconds, then she gently pushed him away.

She giggled. "I'm so horny, Mister. Git yourself on home before ah commit some terrible sin."

Harry laughed. "Can't have a sinning parson. Goodnight, my love."

Ember watched him walk down the sidewalk. He gave her a

wave, which she returned, and when he was out of sight, closed and locked the door.

She made herself a cup of tea and took it to her bedroom.

Sitting in her rocking chair, Em let the little bits of information drift in her mind. Was one of them the key? Or was the key in a fact they had yet to uncover?

# 67

REECE SOVERN RANG THE DOORBELL TWICE, AND WHEN NO ONE CAME to the door, he started pounding on it. That action got a response.

The lights by the door came on and the voice coming through the speaker said, "What do you want?"

Reece pressed the button, and said, "This is Reece Sovern of the Magnolia Bluff Police Department and I need to speak with Mrs. Applewhite."

"Can't this wait until morning?"

"If it could, I wouldn't be ringing your doorbell and pounding on your door when you didn't answer the doorbell."

The door opened, and Reece was looking at what he guessed to be a forty-something year old male dressed in a burgundy robe. What looked to be a velvet burgundy robe. He looked at the man's feet. He was wearing pajamas under the robe and dark brown slippers covered his bare feet.

"I'm going to talk to your superiors about this."

The cigar shifted to the other side of Reece's mouth and he stepped past the man into the foyer of the Applewhite home.

From the top of the stairs, a female voice said, "What is it, Cy? What's going on?"

"Mrs. Applewhite?" Reece called out.

A woman came into view on the stairs. "I'm Mrs. Applewhite."

Even wearing a robe and no makeup, Pearline Applewhite was a wonderful sight to behold. Reece cast a glance at the man standing slightly behind him. *Lucky devil.*

"Mrs. Applewhite, I'm Reece Sovern. Magnolia Bluff Police Department. I need to talk with you about the purchase of Greyhound bus tickets."

"I don't know what you're talking about, Mr. Sovern."

"We can do this here, or I can take you down to the station and talk with you in a very uncomfortable and probably somewhat smelly interview room. Which do you prefer?"

"Don't say anything, Pearline. I'm going to call our lawyer."

"You call your lawyer, Mr. Applewhite, and I'm going to arrest your wife right now and put her in a cell. Is that what you want?"

"We're entitled to legal representation."

Not for the first time, Reece wondered what it would be like to be so loaded to have lawyers on speed dial.

"Look, Mr. and Mrs. Applewhite, I merely want to ask some questions to try to clear up a few things. We can do it the easy way, all friendly like, or we can do it the hard way. Your choice."

Reece watched the Applewhites look at each other and, by their facial expressions, he guessed some form of communication passed between them. Much like what passed between him and Hetta.

"I'll talk to you, Mr. Sovern," Pearline said.

"But we'll call a halt if she could get in trouble," her husband added.

The cigar moved to the other side of his mouth, and Reece said, "I wouldn't be here if things were all lily white."

The husband started to speak, and Reece's upraised hand stopped him. "We're going to play nice, or I might toss you in a cell for obstructing a police investigation. Now let's get this over with."

The husband nodded. "Very well."

Reece turn to Pearline, who was still standing on the stairs, although she'd moved halfway down the staircase. "Why did you buy Greyhound bus tickets for the Restons in Harry Thurgood's name?"

"I did no—"

"Mrs. Applewhite, don't lie. I have video from Walmart and confirmation from Greyhound of the ticket purchases, and Thurgood said he didn't do it."

"He's lying."

"Fine. That's the line you want to take? We'll do this the hard way. Good night."

Reece shouldered his way past the husband and was halfway down the walk to his car when he heard Pearline's voice asking him to stop.

He turned around. "Yes?"

"I did it. I bought those tickets."

"Why?"

"Because Mrs. Fight told me to."

"Do you do everything she tells you to do?"

"If I want to stay in the society."

Reece shook his head. *Goddamn rich people*, he thought. "Why in Thurgood's name?" he asked.

"Because Mrs. Fight wants to ruin him."

"Tell me something I don't know."

"That's all I know. Please, don't tell Mary Lou. Because—"

"Oh, for crying out loud."

Reece turned around and walked to his car.

When he was behind the wheel, he let out a huge lungful of air.

"I'm too young to retire, and I can't quit. So I guess I have to solve this damn case."

He started the car, put it in drive, and headed for home.

*Hetta's definitely no Pearline when it comes to the looks department, but at least she's a good woman and the best wife a man could want.*

## 68

HARRY THURGOOD WALKED THROUGH THE DOOR OF THE SILVER Spoon, and the conversation stopped. He smiled at that.

"My God, Thurgood," Graham Huston said, "a little early for you, isn't it?"

"Very funny, Huston. I own a coffee shop and it doesn't run on banker's hours."

"Well, take off that jazz musician's hat and that fancy coat of yours and join us," Huston said.

Harry took off his brown pork pie and dark brown car coat. He was wearing a rich chocolate brown custom-made Alex Trevino three-piece suit. His eyes took in the men sitting with Huston. By their dress, Harry figured almost all were farmers or ranchers. He didn't know any of them, except for the retired vet, Jack Rice, Dr. Mike Kurelek, and, of course, Graham Huston.

Huston asked, "Have you gotten Sovern off your back yet?"

Harry pulled up a chair and sat at the table. "He's asked me to help him. Don't know if that means he's off my back or not. Probably more in line with the enemy of enemy approach."

"You're probably right on that," Huston said, and drank coffee.

One old fellow asked, "So who did it, and why?"

Harry chuckled. "Which crime?"

"Any of them. All of them."

"Don't know."

Lorraine Dillard, owner of the Silver Spoon, walked over to the table with a coffeepot in one hand and a mug in the other. "You didn't bring your own coffee, so I assume you'll want a cup of mine."

"Coffee's fine, Lorraine. A little cream and a doughnut?"

Lorraine poured coffee and said, "Cream and a doughnut coming right up."

"So, Harry, what do you make of that itinerant evangelist's death?" Huston asked.

Harry smiled. "What do *you* know about it, Graham?"

With a twinkle in his eye, Huston said, "Not enough to solve it."

"Not what I asked," Harry replied.

Huston laughed. "Fishing, are you?"

"I like fish," Harry said.

That set the table to laughing.

Lorraine put the doughnut and a little pitcher of cream in front of Harry.

She looked at the men and said, "You boys are just havin' too much fun."

"Harry's fishin' and ain't got no pole," one of the men said.

"I have a feeling that Harry's fishing style doesn't need a pole," Lorraine replied. "Noodlin's more his style. Am I right?"

Harry saw the smile on her face and the wink she gave him.

"That's how it appears," Harry answered.

"A man who can get his hands dirty has my respect," she said, and winked again before leaving.

"To answer your question, Harry," Huston began, but turned his attention to the person who had just entered the diner.

"Stanton, what are you doing here?" the newspaperman asked.

Stanton Mirabeau Lauderbach strode to the table. Harry

noticed his suit was every bit a custom make as his own. He'd have to ask the lawyer who his tailor was.

Lauderbach said, "I suspect I'm here for the same reason you are, Graham. Get some coffee, a bit of breakfast, and a whole lot of gossip."

"Then grab yourself a chair and have a sit," Huston said.

"Thanks. I will." Lauderbach grabbed a chair and squeezed into the circle around the table.

Jack Rice said, "We just might have to rent a convention hall."

The old guy sitting two seats away said, "Or get here earlier."

"That's up to Lorraine," Kurelek said.

Lorraine set coffee, a plate of biscuits and sausage gravy, and a plate piled high with bacon before the lawyer.

Lauderbach gave Huston a grin. "You see, I'm here more often than you think, Graham. Thanks Lorraine."

"Welcome, Stanton," she said, and added, "I'm not coming in any earlier for you fellas. Maybe you need to sell tickets." She turned around and went back to her prep work for the day.

Graham drank coffee, then said, "So, Harry, to get back to what I was saying before, I don't think the police have a clue regarding Brother John's death."

Lauderbach swallowed bacon, then said, "To be fair, that new hot shot lawyer out of the Public Defender's Office is good and seems to be on a crusade of some kind. He's giving Sovern and Jager a good run for their money. Almost made Buck lose that grin."

Huston raised his eyebrows. "That's saying a whole mouthful right there."

"And the Reston family has skipped town," Harry said, drank coffee, and added, "Courtesy of Mary Lou. She also tied my name to it, so I'd be in Dutch with Sovern."

"How so?" Huston asked.

"One of the Hats bought Greyhound tickets online in my name and then paid cash for them at Walmart."

"That woman has it in for you," Lauderbach said. "Want to press charges?"

"Can we tie it back to Mary Lou?" Harry asked.

"If the Hat gives her up," Lauderbach said, and deposited biscuit and gravy in his mouth.

"I'll think about it," Harry said.

"Any idea where the family is?" Huston asked.

Harry shook his head. "Reece is still working on that. The destination is Chattanooga, but he thinks they might get off before then to throw the police off their trail."

Huston nodded. "Makes sense. They're con artists. Probably plenty of dodges of their sleeves."

"The Rangers tracked down that Tully fellow," Lauderbach said. "They'll track down the family."

"In your opinion, Harry, who do you think did it?" Huston asked.

"Probably one of the family. Lots of bad stuff going on there."

"How so?"

"I suspect infidelity, incest, and underage sex."

One fellow said, "Shoot, half the county is probably having underage sex. It's all kids think about these days."

"No more dolls and model cars," another man added.

"Ain't that the truth," Huston said.

Harry slid a folded bill under the raised rim of the plate that had held his doughnut and stood. "Well, gentlemen, duty calls. Catch you all later."

He put on his hat and coat, waved to Lorraine, and headed for the door.

Once on the sidewalk, he looked towards the courthouse. *Too little justice there.*

He turned and walked down the street to the Really Good. "One thing's for certain," he whispered to himself, "Reece needs to find that family and go to work on them."

# 69

FROM A DISTANCE, LANDON PACE FOLLOWED THE RESTON FAMILY into the Amtrak station.

*So they are switching things up,* he thought. *I'm going to have to call this in. I'm not getting on the train with them.*

He watched Mrs. Reston buy tickets and decided he would call Graham Huston once he learned what train they were on. And then he'd be done.

Back to Magnolia Bluff and whatever boring assignment Huston gave him. Although, if he played his cards right, he might get a bit of the limelight. After all, who else knew where the family was?

"You know," he said to himself, "maybe I should call the police. And *then* call Huston. That way, the police will know who is responsible for the tip."

He smiled. "Yeah. I like that: call the police, *then* tell Huston."

―――――

Reece Sovern was tired. He hadn't gotten more than five hours of sleep. He stifled a yawn and drank coffee.

*God. Who made this? Used crankcase oil would taste better.*

He set the cup down, grabbed his hat and coat, and muttered, "Think I'll go to the Spoon. Get some breakfast with my coffee."

The phone rang. He picked up the receiver. "Reece Sovern."

"Mr. Sovern, are you investigating the murder of the traveling evangelist known as Brother John?"

"I am. Who are you?"

"My name is Landon Pace. I'm a reporter with the *Magnolia Bluff Chronicle*."

"Okay. I don't have anything for you."

"That's fine, because I have something for you."

"Spill it. I was just going out my door on important business."

"The Reston family is at the Houston Amtrak station. I followed them to the station."

"Are they still there?"

"They are. Mrs. Reston bought tickets. I'll call back as soon as I find out what train they're on."

"I'll give you my cell number. Call as soon as you learn something."

"Yes, sir."

Reece gave Landon Pace his cell phone number and hung up.

"Oh, this is good. It's about time we got a break on this case."

He walked down the hall and poked his head into Jager's office, but the chief wasn't there.

Deciding this wasn't something he should sit on, he called his boss's cell to pass on the information.

Jager was ecstatic on hearing the news, and Reece was thinking coffee and breakfast were going to be tasting mighty fine this morning.

# 70

THE COPS WERE EVERYWHERE, AND LANDON PACE WATCHED THEM take the Reston family into custody.

Mrs. Reston's reaction surprised him. She didn't fight or resist arrest. She simply started singing, and then the family joined in.

> *When peace like a river attendeth my way,*
> *When sorrows like sea billows roll,*
> *Whatever my lot, Thou hast taught me to say*
> *It is well, it is well with my soul.*

The look on Mrs. Reston's face was so peaceful. And Landon noticed the same peaceful look on the face of Joetta. It was a look of happiness. As if they were glad they were being arrested.

And Landon wondered what it was that they had that he didn't.

After they put the last child into the police vans, he watched the vehicles drive off.

And as the vehicles disappeared from sight, so did the peaceful visage of Joetta Reston's face.

Landon said to himself, *Now it's off to the Houston police station. This story is going to clinch it for me.*

With a big smile on his face, he walked out to his car.

———

Graham Huston and Billy Bob Baskin entered the Really Good. Caroline McCluskey and Magnolia Nadine Roane entered right after them. Ember was already seated at the table.

"Jager won't be joining us," Huston said. "He's on his way to Houston, with Sovern, to pick up the Reston family. My ace intern, Landon Pace, is the one responsible. He followed them all the way to Houston and the Amtrak station."

"Amtrak?" Magnolia Nadine said.

"Apparently they were going to try to throw off the police by taking the train to California," Huston explained.

"Didn't they realize they'd eventually be caught?" Caroline asked.

"Con artists never think they're going to be caught," Harry said. He was standing behind the counter, helping Estrelita assemble a tray of pastries.

"But they get caught eventually," Caroline said.

Harry chuckled. "And they try to con their way out of police custody."

"You sure know a lot about con artists," Huston said.

"There are lots of them in the art world and I dabble in art," Harry responded.

"I didn't know art was that shady," Magnolia Nadine said.

"If it can be faked, the con artist will be there," Harry said.

"I guess we'll be getting to the bottom of this case soon," Reverend Billy Bob said.

Ember shook her head. "The family was all ready closing ranks when Harry and I talked to them."

Harry and Estrelita brought over coffee carafes and mugs. While Estrelita went back to retrieve the pastries, Harry poured coffee for everyone.

"I hear congratulations are in order," Caroline said.

"You know, Harry, since everyone from here to Dallas will have heard about the engagement by Tuesday, I might as well run something else in that space," Huston said.

"Don't you dare!" Ember said, her voice half an octave higher than usual.

"I guess she told you, Graham," Caroline said. "Anyway, congratulations you two. Have you set a date?"

"Not yet," Ember said.

"I don't think there's any need to wait," Harry said, "but I'll leave that to the bride-to-be."

"Do you know who you want to officiate at the service?" Billy Bob asked.

"Not yet," Ember said.

"I'd be perfectly happy if Wylie would do it right now," Harry said.

Ember shook her head. "Wylie may be a nice man, and a fabulous justice of the peace, but he's *not* doing my wedding."

Laughter rippled across the table.

"I guess she told you, Harry," Huston said.

"You said it was your intern who followed the Reston's bus to Houston?" Harry asked.

Huston nodded. "Yep. A go-getter, that one. He's giving Carter a run for his money."

"Which one killed that man?" Magnolia Nadine asked.

"My guess is one of the family," Harry said. "Although Reece thinks the one he has in custody, Purnell Tully is the likely culprit."

Huston chuckled. "If Reece is of that opinion, then the one who did it is probably my mother."

"He's not that bad," Ember said.

"You are a forgiving soul, Ember Cole," Billy Bob said.

Graham took out a pen and opened his notebook. "At the Spoon, Harry, and just now, you said you suspected the family. Want to elaborate on that?"

"Em and I talked some with the family. I also questioned

Purnell Tully. In my opinion, Tully is out. He was getting rich embezzling money. Why kill the guy making you rich? Even if he got caught by Brother John, my impression is that he wasn't worried about the consequences. He had enough dirt on John Reston, at least that's what I suspect, that Reston wouldn't go after him. So why should Tully kill the man? Brother John wasn't a threat. So I think Tully is off the hook."

"So you're saying his wife or kids killed him?" Billy Bob asked.

"Yes," Harry answered. "His wife because she wanted to run away with her lover. The older girls for the same reason, or to stop the incest that was going on. Or at least I think was going on.

"The oldest son, to get rid of the sin he saw his father committing. And therefore purify the family. All just guesses at this point, since I have no proof. But those are the roads I'd start driving down in order to get a confession."

"What about the snakes?" Huston asked.

Harry nodded. "You could work it from that end, too. Find who switched the snakes and you will probably have your killer."

"That might be the easier way to proceed," Huston said.

"I think so," Harry said. "Especially with the family closing ranks."

"What has happened to our town?" Magnolia Nadine said. "Nothing but murders and kidnappings. When is it going to end?"

"Those are questions which have no answers," Billy Bob said.

"Except prayer," Ember added.

"Yes, prayer," Billy Bob agreed. "God moves in a mysterious way His wonders to perform."

"What the late Brother John showed us is that people are thirsty for the Word of God," Ember said. "If we all lived our faith and shared our faith, evil would be defeated. Greater is He Who is in us than he who is in the world. If Christians seriously practiced their faith and spread the Lord's kingdom to every corner of every neighborhood, we'd bring about our Lord's glorious millennial reign, and have peace forever and ever."

Billy Bob smiled. "I don't want to get into an eschatological debate, but, yes, I think a good part of the problem is that all of us would rather do things our way instead of the Lord's way. People, so it seems, at least some people, would rather kill than pray and wait upon the Lord."

Ember nodded. "As a society, we suffer from an increasing narcissism. It's all about what everyone can do for me. What government can do for me. What the church can do for me. Social media is a platform for me. Come, see how great and important I am."

There was a pause, as though everyone was digesting the words of the two ministers.

After a moment or two, Harry said, "That may be the solution."

"What do you mean?" Huston asked.

"There was a British criminologist in the first half of the twentieth century."

Huston nodded. "F. Tennyson Jesse."

"Yes. She noted that all criminals have big egos. But murderers are the most egotistical of all. Perhaps we need to discover which one of that group has the biggest ego. Because, in all likelihood, that person will be our killer."

# 71

5:11 AM, TUESDAY, 17 OCTOBER

"What the hell is this?" Police Chief Tommy Jager said. "Harry Thurgood at the Spoon?"

"He was here yesterday," Graham Huston said.

"What's going on, Thurgood?" Jager said. "You getting ideas on how to run that coffee shop of yours from Lorraine?"

Sniggers and guffaws rippled through the group sitting around the table.

Harry hung his hat and coat on the tree by the door and joined the men sitting around the table.

"Business is fine, Tommy. Didn't know you cared."

"Actually, I do, Thurgood. A thriving downtown helps cut down on crime."

"The doors are open and I intend to keep them open."

"Good to hear. So what brings you out so early in the morning?"

"Like Lorraine, here, I run a business. Can't afford to sleep till noon. Before I started my day, I just wanted to catch up on the scuttlebutt. Anything new on the Reston case?"

"You'll be hearing from Sovern soon enough. I'll tell you this, though, that family sang the entire four hours it took to get back to town here."

Someone in the group said, "Sang?"

"Yeah. Religious songs. Just about drove Sovern and me crazy."

Sheriff Buck, grin on his lips and mirth in his eyes, said, "Get an itch to trust Jesus?"

Jager snorted. "Not hardly."

Buck said, "They needed to sing louder."

Guffaws and chuckles rolled across the table.

Harry said, "Be thankful they have good voices."

"I suppose so," Jager said.

Harry turned to Graham Huston. "Is your intern's story going to make it for today's paper?"

"You bet. Made him work all night on it."

Jager said, "If it wasn't for your intern, Huston, the Rangers would be chasing them down someplace west of El Paso."

"Or be waiting for an empty bus in Chattanooga," Sheriff Blanton added.

"So what will happen to them now?" Harry asked.

"Lots of questions," Jager said.

"More questions than Carter has pills," Buck added.

Harry pointed at Mike Kurelek. "Might I suggest you have Mike present when you're doing the questioning?"

"Why?" Jager asked.

Huston chuckled. "Because Harry thinks the one with the biggest ego is the most likely suspect."

Jager glanced at Dr. Kurelek and scratched his head; and Sheriff Blanton settled back in his chair, a puzzled look in his eyes.

"Okay," Jager said, "I'll bite. Why?"

Harry cleared his throat. "There was a British criminologist, Mrs. F. Tennyson Jesse, who said that all criminals are egotists, but murderers have the biggest egos of them all."

Buck Blanton said, "Huh."

Jager said, "Are you serious? Whatever happened to facts?"

"Do you have any?" Harry asked.

"We're working on it, Thurgood," Jager said. "A good investigation takes time. Unless you're an advocate of lynching."

"I'm not. I am just throwing out Mrs. Jesse's opinion as a line to follow. To help sort the evidence."

"I'll keep it in mind."

"Sounds good, Chief." Harry stood. "Well, gentlemen, you all have a good day. Got to go. I have a business to run."

When Harry was on the sidewalk, heading back to the coffee shop, he thought of all the players in the traveling salvation show.

*Which ones have big egos?* he asked himself.

He thought of all the men and then ran down his mental list of the women.

When he reached the Really Good, he unlocked the door, and entered. When he turned around to lock the door, he saw Reece Sovern waving at him from the middle of the green.

He opened the door and waited for the detective to arrive.

"What can I do for you, Reece?"

"You and your wife like to play detective. Get her up, grab your hat, and get down to the station. You can watch the interviews."

"I'm not married."

"Okay. Your common law partner, then."

"We aren't living together, holding forth to the community that we're married, nor enjoying connubial bliss."

"Connubial?" Sovern shook his head, then added, "Says you. Anyway, if you want to play detective, shake a leg and get down to the station."

"Half an hour be okay?"

"Yesterday would be better." He turned around and walked off toward the police station.

Harry closed the door, got out his phone, and told it to call Em.

# 72

## 6:37 AM, TUESDAY, 17 OCTOBER

STANDING ALONGSIDE HARRY IN THE OBSERVATION ROOM, WATCHING the close circuit monitors, was Dr. Mike Kurelek, the psychologist from the college, and Ember Cole.

Mike said, "Reece said something about looking for the person with the biggest ego. Do you want to refresh my memory?"

Harry repeated what he'd said at the Spoon about Mrs. F. Tennyson Jesse and her opinion.

Mike's response was, "Hm. Interesting."

Sitting on a chair on one side of a battleship gray table was Jerri Reston. Officer Hans Winkler was standing in a corner by the door.

Mike looked at his watch. "I hope Reece doesn't play the waiting game with each one."

Ember nodded. "If he does, we'll be here all day."

"And all night," Harry added.

As if on cue, Reece Sovern entered the room. He sat and turned on the recorder. He mentioned the date, time, and who he was interviewing. Then his attention was focused on Mrs. Reston.

"Why did you attempt to run away with your family?"

Jerri Reston's face was blank, other than the smile on her lips.

"You can choose to cooperate or not, Mrs. Reston, but we are collecting evidence. Even as we are talking here. So the truth will eventually come out."

Jerri Reston stared at Sovern's face, smile still in place, and said nothing.

"Okay. Did you kill your husband?"

Jerri Reston opened her mouth and began singing.

> *Jesus, lover of my soul,*
> *Let me to thy bosom fly*
> *While the nearer waters roll,*
> *While the tempest still is high.*
> *Hide me, O my Savior, hide,*
> *Till the storm of life is past;*
> *Safe into the haven guide.*
> *O receive my soul at last!*

Sovern, a disgusted look on his face, gave the time, and said the interview was terminated.

Jerri Reston continued singing.

> *Other refuge have I none,*
> *Hangs my helpless soul on thee;*
> *Leave, ah! Leave me not alone,*
> *Still support and comfort me.*

To Winkler, Sovern said, "Get her out of here."

Hans nodded and moved next to Mrs. Reston.

She stood and belted out the next lines so half the station could hear them.

> *All my trust on thee is stayed,*
> *All my help from thee I bring;*
> *Cover my defenseless head*
> *With the shadow of thy wing.*

Winkler escorted her out. Sovern could hear her voice echoing down the halls as Hans took her back to her cell.

He shook his head, stood, looked up at one of the cameras, and said, "You better start praying, Reverend, we get some cooperation, or we're going to be here until Ralph Jensen's cows come home." Then he walked out of the room.

Ember giggled. Mike and Harry, puzzlement on their faces, looked at her.

"It's a local joke," she said. "Ralph Jensen didn't have cows."

"Okay," Mike said.

Harry ran his hand through his hair. "Aren't there lots of farmers who don't have cows?"

"There are," Ember answered. "It's just a saying. There is no Ralph Jensen."

Harry smiled. "Like Ned Ludd."

"Who?" Mike asked.

"Ned Ludd is the legendary figure who supposedly founded the Luddites. Possibly derived from a fictional account of a knitter's son who, in defiance of his father, destroyed the needles for the knitting frames in Nottingham, England. So whenever frames were sabotaged, the people blamed Ned Ludd."

"Interesting," Mike said.

Ember laughed. "Harry reads the encyclopedia for fun."

Mike, a smirk on his lips, said, "I see that."

"Ha, ha. You two want anything?" Harry asked. "There's a vending machine in the cafeteria."

Mike shook his head.

"I'm good," Ember said.

"I'm going to see—"

The door opened, and in walked Joetta Reston, followed first by Officer Winkler and then Investigator Sovern.

Joetta sat down, Sovern sat across from her, and Winkler stood by the door.

Sovern leaned back in his chair. The cigar moved from the left corner of his mouth to the right.

Joetta folded her hands and bowed her head.

"Are you willing to talk to me?" Sovern asked.

Softly, Joetta began singing.

> *When peace like a river attendeth my way,*
> *When sorrows like sea billows roll,*

"Get her out of here," Sovern said.

Winkler escorted Joetta back to her cell, the walls ringing with her sweet voice.

> *Whatever my lot, Thou hast taught me to say*
> *It is well, it is well, with my soul.*

Sovern took the cigar out of his mouth, held it up before his eyes, then hurled it across the room.

# 73

9:17 AM, TUESDAY, 17 OCTOBER

HARRY, EMBER, AND MIKE KURELEK WERE BACK IN THE OBSERVATION room. On the monitors, they saw Jearlene Reston, Reece Sovern, and a man sitting next to the detective.

"Who's the new guy?" Ember asked.

"Beats me," Harry and Mike said at the same time.

Sovern began speaking. "Now before you start singing, Mrs. Reston, I want you to listen to what Assistant District Attorney Chuck Dillon has to say."

"Reece is bringing in the big guns," Mike said.

"Looks like it," Harry added.

"Mrs. Reston, as Mr. Sovern noted, my name is Chuck Dillon and I'm an attorney with the District Attorney's Office."

When she didn't say anything, Dillon continued. "You're not in a good situation. You are the only parent your twelve children now have, eight of whom are minors under Texas law."

Jearlene's face, which had been pointed toward the table, lifted, and her eyes focused on the face of the assistant district attorney.

Dillon waited for her to say something. When she didn't, he said, "You are being held as a material witness. As such, we can more or less hold you in jail as long as we want."

"Is that true?" Ember asked.

Harry shrugged, and Mike said, "I think there are limits."

Jearlene had said nothing in response to Dillon, so he continued with his speech. "And because you can't take care of your children while you are in jail, Mr. Sovern can remove them from your custody and turn them over to the Department of Family and Protective Services."

"Oh, God," Mike said.

Dillon looked at a sheet of paper. "Let's see. That would be your daughters Raylene, Wendolyn, and Mary Jean."

Jearlene spoke. "You can't separate a mama from her children."

A big smile appeared on the assistant district attorney's face. "Oh, yes, we can. And we will, unless you start answering our questions."

"That is downright dirty," Ember said.

"Welcome to the American legal system in action," Harry said.

Jearlene had started to stand up when Officer Winkler stepped to her side and asked her to sit.

"You can't take my babies," Jerri Reston said.

Chuck Dillon, smile gone, ignored her statement, and said, "Let's see, yes, you have five boys under the age of eighteen. Samuel, Elisha, Jeb, Sinclair, and Jacob. Mr. Sovern will be turning those eight children—"

"What do you want to know?"

A grin spread across Dillon's face. Harry noted from the gleam of his teeth the guy had a great dentist. He might have to ask him who he or she was.

Dillon said, "That's more like it, Mrs. Reston."

Sovern started the recorder.

The assistant DA said, "First things first. Did you kill your husband?"

"No."

"Do you know who did?"

"God."

Dillon looked at Sovern, who shrugged. The assistant DA turned his attention back to Jerri Reston. "How did God kill your husband?"

"Snake poison."

"And you didn't, by chance, help God, did you?" Dillon asked.

"I prayed and the Lord God Almighty heard my prayer and struck down my husband, a sinner, with the bringer of sin."

Harry noticed Mike was glued to the monitor that had the clearest and fullest view of Jerri Reston's face.

"But you're saying you didn't kill your husband, is that correct?" Sovern asked.

"Yes, sir, that is what I'm saying. I prayed, and the Lord heard my prayer. The prayer of a sinner. But who's hand it was, I have no idea. We never used rattlers that had poison in them. But that night, the snakes had poison."

Dillon, with that grin on his face, said, "Your husband didn't die from snake bites."

"Why, he surely did. I saw it with my own eyes."

"It seems, Mrs. Reston, the Lord had a little help. Someone stabbed him with a syringe filled with snake venom. That's what killed him."

"A syringe? I don't believe it."

"Believe it or not, it's true. We are checking, Mrs. Reston. We'll find the person who bought the syringe and the needles. Are you sure you have nothing to tell us? Perhaps who helped the Lord answer your prayer?"

"If you're meaning I killed my husband or someone else in my family killed him, then you can't tell a barn door from a fence gate. I wanted to be free from the man, but I'm no Jael. I'm too much the sinner to do the Lord's work. If what you're sayin' is true, I know nothing about that. All I know is I prayed and he died. The Lord truly is merciful to us sinners."

"Oh, what I'm saying is very true, Mrs. Reston," Dillon said. "So if you didn't kill your husband, then that leaves Mr. Tully or one of your children. It certainly would make sense for Purnell Tully to kill him. He's your lover, isn't he?"

"Was. He ran off and left me. I was a fool to believe his lies."

"Perhaps. But it certainly makes sense for Mr. Tully to have killed your husband. Doesn't it?"

"Purnell Tully is a lyin', cheatin', snake in the grass. He might kill a pesky mosquito, but another man? Ha! He'd rather con him than kill him."

"Is that so? Want to explain why he was carrying a pistol with a silencer?"

"I know nothing about that."

"That will be all for now, Mrs. Reston."

"I get to keep my babies?"

"While you're in jail, a Child Protection officer will take care of their needs."

"But I talked. I did what you asked me to do."

Dillon favored her with that smarmy smile of his.

"God," Ember said. "I'd love to kick him in the nuts."

"Right now, Mrs. Reston," Dillon said, "since you seem to have the Lord's ear, if I were you, I'd be praying that we find who killed your husband, if it wasn't you. Because if we don't find someone else with a motive, we're going to be charging you with murder."

## 74

9:18 PM, TUESDAY, 17 OCTOBER

OLIVIA SET A PEPPERONI, MUSHROOM, AND BLACK OLIVE PIZZA ON THE table, said, "Enjoy," and left.

Mike Kurelek studied the pizza for a moment, shook his head, and said, "How does Olivia know what we want?"

Harry sipped wine and shrugged.

"She's gifted," Ember said.

"It's amazing and kind of spooky at the same time," Mike said.

"All I know is that it saves me time, and that's a good thing." Harry picked up a slice and took a bite.

Ember drank wine, set the glass down, and asked Mike, "So what's the verdict, Doc?"

"Doc, eh? Well, Rev, that family is a disaster."

"That we know," Harry said. "But which one is the likely suspect?"

"Who has the biggest ego?"

Harry nodded.

"The one who has the biggest ego of any of them is the assistant DA."

"That guy is something else," Harry said.

Ember stopped the pizza slice for entering her mouth. "He's

evil. He's manipulative and conniving." She let the pizza continue its journey.

Harry sipped wine and set the glass down. "Jerri Reston. Yea, or nay."

Mike shook his head. "I'd say no." He ate a bite of pizza.

"What about the girls?" Harry asked.

"I wouldn't rate any of them high on your ego scale," Mike said. "Raylene knows she is stunningly beautiful and I imagine uses that to her advantage. Although, I don't think she's vain. It's more along the lines of mesmerizing the men into giving her what she asks for."

"Isn't that being manipulative?" Ember asked.

"To a degree," Mike answered. "Joetta, being the oldest, acts like a second mother, and probably earned that position by helping with all the children.

"The one, though, that I'm most interested in is Oralene. She has the brains and knows how to use them. She has an excellent command of language and displays cunning, and I'd wager is quite conniving. And she's the only one who could go toe to toe with Dillon."

"Could she have killed her father?" Ember asked.

"It's possible," Mike answered. "But I can't say she did for sure."

"Okay," Harry began, "we have one. How about the boys?"

"The boys possess an interesting dynamic. The three youngest, the ten, nine, and five-year-olds, look to John-John as a father figure. Samuel and Elisha, the fifteen- and fourteen-year-olds, are like twins. They respect John-John, but definitely have their own minds. And quite honestly, have plenty of ego."

"That leaves the two oldest," Harry said.

"Yes. John-John, who is twenty, has plenty of ego. From what I gather, he's a younger version of his father, but has a very strong puritanical streak. He said it himself: he's Elisha, and the mantle has fallen to him.

"Lofton is two years younger than John-John. He sees himself as his brother's companion. Ego is low."

"So that leaves us with Oralene, John–John, and possibly Samuel and Elisha." Harry stroked his chin. "I didn't have the younger boys on my list, and was up in the air over Oralene."

"What about Purnell Tully?" Ember asked.

"He's a complex fellow," Mike said. "Plenty of ego there, but I wouldn't say it's his dominant trait. He's the consummate con artist. Always looking for the next hustle. In my opinion, he'd con you, not kill you."

"So it's just as you said, Harry," Ember began, "it's a family affair."

# 75

## 8:07 AM, WEDNESDAY, 18 OCTOBER

REECE SOVERN SLAMMED HIS OFFICE DOOR, TOOK THE CIGAR OUT OF his mouth, and hurled it against the far wall.

The soggy stogie made a wet thwack, hung there on the wall for a moment, before it dropped to the floor.

He fell into his chair, opened the bottom desk drawer on the right, and took out a tumbler and the bottle of Glen Rose pot distilled single malt whiskey.

At a hundred bucks a bottle, this was special occasion whiskey; made right here in the Hill Country.

*And this is no special occasion. If I could get away with it, I'd go right now to his office and shoot Judge Jones right between the eyes.*

He put the bottle and glass back in the drawer and pushed it closed.

A great big sigh escaped from his lips. He shook his head and leaned back in his chair.

Nothing I can do for the moment except keep a tail on him, Sovern thought. What in the world was Judge Jones thinking? It was that doggone hot shot public defense lawyer. God, I hate lawyers.

Reece sat up. "What's done is done," he muttered.

He took the cellophane off of a brilliant emerald green corona and stuck the stogie in his mouth.

There was a knock on the door.

"Come in."

The door opened and Idalee Freeman, one of the secretaries, poked her head in.

"Mr. Sovern, Chief Jager would like a word with you in his office."

"Thanks."

The door closed and Reece wondered what Tommy wanted this early in the morning.

He took the stogie out of his mouth, said, "Only one way to find out," stuck the cigar back in, and walked down the hall to the chief's office.

"Hey, Reece, grab a seat. More bad news, I'm afraid."

"You're kidding."

"Wish I was."

Reece sat.

"Just got a call from the DA's office. Ham Hamilton has decided we don't have any reason to hold the Reston family and has told us to release them, with a warning to not leave town."

"A lot of good that did last time. I thought this guy had been a tough on crime police chief in Houston."

"Maybe his decision is what they think tough on crime in Houston is all about."

Reece shook his head. "No wonder this country's going to hell in a handbasket. They're material witnesses. They fled. They should at least go before a judge and have bail set."

"You won't find me disagreeing with you. I don't make the rules."

"I know. Just letting off steam. Now all of them are out. Tully and the family. We don't have enough manpower to watch all of them."

"No, we don't. So, until I'm told otherwise, I've ordered that they have to wear monitors."

"Good idea, Tommy."

"Figured you'd like that. That's all I have. I've assigned two office staff to be on monitor duty at all times. But hopefully, the family and Tully will play nice this time."

"Hopefully. That's it?"

"It is. Keep on them. Maybe being in the open air they'll get tired of singing."

"Yeah, that was really getting on my nerves. Okay. Thanks, Chief."

Reece walked out of Jager's office and down the hall to his own office. He grabbed his hat and coat and left the building, stepping outside into the gray morning.

*Smells like rain,* he thought. *Wonder where they'll be spending the night?*

———

Harry wasn't sure she'd answer her phone. Five before nine was a bit early for Scarlett.

After five rings, he heard, "You have a lot of nerve calling me, Mr. Thurgood."

He thought, *Criminy. What did I do now?* To Scarlet, he said, "I know it's early—"

"That's not what I'm talking about."

"Why are you angry with me?"

"You know how I feel about you. You could at least have told me in person. But no. I had to first find out from my friend, Betty Lynn, and then read it in the newspaper. I thought we were at least friends. Is this how you treat your friends, Harry Thurgood? Because if it is, it explains why you don't have any."

The phone was dead silent.

"Are you there?" he asked.

"I'm here, and I am waiting for an answer."

"I'm sorry, Scarlett. You're right. I should have said something. I didn't, and I'm sorry."

"So what the hell do you want, Mr. Thurgood?"

"Do you have any cabins available?"

"You're calling *me* for *that*? Call the goddamn office."

The phone was silent. Harry looked at it and saw that Scarlett had ended the call.

He shook his head. *You are in Dutch now. She is hopping mad. Hell hath no fury like a woman scorned.*

Harry took in a huge lungful of air and let it slowly escape. He thought of that song: "Blowin' in the wind."

He turned around and watched Miguel working in the kitchen. He was hand grinding something. It looked like spices.

"How long have you been married, Miguel?"

"Ten years, Mr. Thurgood. Why do you ask?"

"Did you date other women before you got married?"

"Araceli and I had a big fight once. Before we were married. She didn't talk to me for two weeks. So I went out with Zaneta. Jesus, Joseph, and Mary. You would have thought I'd committed adultery. But at least Ari was talking to me again."

Miguel looked up from his work. "And we got married two months after that. You having trouble with Reverend Ember?"

"No. Scarlett Hayden."

"Ah. She has the hots for you, that one. She'd be a good mistress. Maybe. But not a good wife. Stay with Reverend Ember."

"Oh, I am. Scarlett's upset because I didn't tell her about Em's and my engagement."

"With that one, Miss Scarlett, that is, you will have a better chance of not being burned alive jumping into the crater of Popocatépetl. She is the serpent in the Garden of Eden. On second thought, she would not make a good mistress. She's a she-devil. A demon. She will burn you with the fire of hell."

"Scarlett knew I was with Em. I told her nothing was going to happen between us, so why is she mad at me?"

"It is a trick to get your sympathy. Stay away from that one, Mr. Thurgood. She will destroy the good Reverend and she will torture you to the day you die for betraying her. Even though you didn't."

"I'll remember that. Thanks."

"No problem."

Harry turned around and looked at the empty coffee shop.

Ember had called earlier to tell him what one of her parishioners, who works in the city hall, had told her: the Reston family was being released from jail and probably needed a place to stay.

Maybe I should just let Em handle it. On the other hand...

# 76

JOETTA WAS SITTING ON A BENCH IN THE PARK BY THE RESERVOIR NEXT to her mother. Her sister, Oralene, was sitting on the other side of their mother.

Her brother, Lofton, was sitting on the ground picking blades of grass, while John-John was pacing back and forth.

Not far from the bench, Raylene was watching her two younger sisters play finger games with string. Closer to the shore, Samuel and Elijah were playing kickball with their younger brothers.

"Is there any money left from what Mr. Thurgood gave us?" John-John asked.

"There's four hundred and thirty-eight dollars and forty-two cents," Joetta said. "I counted it when we got out of jail to make sure no one took any."

"So we have some money, but not much," Lofton said, "and they're makin' us stay in this town. What are we gonna do, Ma?"

"I don't know," Jerri Reston said.

"That preacher woman said she'd try to help us," Oralene said. "Too bad the motel won't let us stay there. I think we could sue for discrimination."

"That's not gonna help us for tonight," John-John said. "And it's lookin' more like rain now than when we got out of jail."

Joetta took a deep breath, and said, "Which one of us killed Pa?"

Her mother's head snapped in her direction. "Why Joetta Lynn, what on earth made you say a thing like that?"

"Because it's true, Mama," Joetta shot back. "And you know it."

John-John stopped pacing. "Pa was bad. A very bad man. He disgraced the Lord, and the Lord has made him answer for his sin."

"That may be, John-John," Joetta said, "but one of us was the Lord's instrument of death and I'd like for that person to confess *their* sin."

"Maybe it wasn't a sin," Lofton said. "If one of us killed Pa, then that person might have been possessed by the Angel of Death. Besides, how do we know *you* didn't kill Pa, Jo? Huh?"

"Enough," Jerri Reston said. "I don't want to hear any more frivolous talk. Do you hear me?"

"We have company," John-John said.

Joetta, Oralene, and Mrs. Reston turned around to see who was coming to join them.

"That's Mr. Thurgood," Oralene said.

"Wonder what he wants?" Jerri said.

"He's been nice to us, Mama," Joetta countered.

"Only means he wants something," Jerri replied.

"Hello, ladies and gentlemen," Harry Thurgood said. He took off his pork pie, gave a short bow, and put the hat back on his head.

"Hello, Mr. Thurgood," Jerri Reston said. "I don't think we have anymore answers for you. Any new ones, at least."

He smiled at her. "I'm not looking for answers to questions I'm not asking."

"So why are you here?" John-John asked.

"Because I have an answer to *your* housing dilemma."

"How much is it going to cost us?" John-John asked.

"We don't want charity, Mr. Thurgood," Jerri said.

"Fair enough," Harry replied. "How about this: consider what I'm about to give you — should you want it — a loan. Fair enough?"

"We don't have jobs. You know that. How are we going to pay you back?" Joetta was surprised at her mother's belligerent tone of voice.

"I don't need the money right now. You can pay me back when you get jobs. Will that work?"

"How do you know we are going to stay?" Jerri asked.

"I don't. But you need shelter until all of this is over. I can provide that for you. Pay me back when you can. Better than sleeping in the rain, don't you think?"

"Sounds like a good deal, Mama," Joetta said. "Maybe this is the Lord blessing us."

"Do you want to see the place?" Harry asked. "I rented a five bedroom house for you on Pepperwood Drive, which is on the eastside of town. It's a month-to-month lease. So no long-term commitment. What do you say?"

"You already rented the house?" Jerri said. "But I haven't said yes."

Harry smiled. "I'm an optimist. Shall we go see it?"

"Very well," Jerri Reston said. "We've run out of options."

"Good. I think you'll like the place. Let me text Reverend Cole for our rides, and we'll be on our way."

# 77

## 12:14 PM, WEDNESDAY, 18 OCTOBER

HARRY THURGOOD LET EM AND ONE OF HER PARISHIONERS GET THE Restons settled in their new digs. Em was also going to help the older Reston children find jobs, and maybe even some work Jerri Reston could do at home.

*Meanwhile,* he said to himself, *I need to find out what Reece knows about that syringe.*

Harry walked downtown, stopped at the coffee shop to make sure Jack Bonhoffer, his floor manager, had everything under control, and then continued on to the police station.

Reece Sovern, though, wasn't there, and the desk officer didn't know where he was.

Harry headed back towards the coffee shop. He was in the middle of the green when a very familiar car pulled over to the curb in front of the shop.

The driver's side front window slid down, and Reece Sovern said, "Been looking for you, Thurgood. Get in."

Harry got into Sovern's car and said, "Don't you ever use the word 'please'?"

"Not if I don't have to."

"Okay, now that we got that cleared up, what do you want?"

"Heard you rented a house for the Reston family."

"Seriously? You heard that already?"

"Yeah. Unfortunately, I never hear anything that helps me put perps behind bars. So what I want to know is why are you and your woman so interested in these people?"

"Don't you want to catch a murderer?"

"Of course. You sure it's one of them?"

"Has to be. It's either Tully or the family. Tully isn't talking and you haven't gotten any proof to show he did it. Right?"

"Keep talkin'."

"Since you haven't, that leaves the family. With the family, there's a variety of motives. They all had the means, and they all had the opportunity. It's just a matter of finding out which one actually did it."

"Have it all worked out, do you?"

"You've talked to them. What do *you* think?"

Reece pushed his glasses up his nose. "I'm pretty much tracking with you. Jager's working with Buck to see if we can find any evidence in the county. And both are working with the Rangers to find any evidence from other towns in Texas, or the neighboring states."

"Did you find out if they bought any snake venom, or where they purchased the syringe and needle?"

"The only ones with credit cards are Tully and the deceased. Neither used a credit card to make hypo purchases. So it was bought with cash. And you can get them just about anywhere. Phineas Henry didn't sell one to anyone in the family, or to Tully, and no one else working at the pharmacy admitted they did. In case you were wondering."

"I was. Thanks. Fingerprints?"

"None usable."

"Snake poison?"

"No purchases we've been able to trace so far. And we haven't been able to find out where they got the rattlers that still had their poison sacs."

"Probably more cash transactions. So that means the psychological route is the only one that's left."

The corona rolled from one corner Reece's mouth to the other. "I thought that's why you had Kurelek observing. The one with the biggest ego."

"It was."

"And according to his report, I saw nothing that's going to give me a reason to slap cuffs on anybody."

"All that means is we need to keep poking and prodding until we uncover the right rock. We have to play Porfiry Petrovich to their Raskolnikov."

"What the heck are you saying? Who's Por whatever, and that other guy?"

"The police inspector and the murderer in *Crime and Punishment*."

Sovern waved his hand. "Whatever, Thurgood. Go play Sigmund Freud. Meanwhile, I'll play Dick Tracy."

"Good choice, Reece. You even have the fedora."

"Very funny. Now that you and the missus got the Reston's a house, are you going to hire Lauderbach to defend them?"

"Geez Louise, Reece. You do realize we're playing on the same team, right?"

"So you say. Sometimes, I'm not so sure. After all, you're a Yankee. Now get out of here. I got work to do."

"With pleasure. Hope you have a better day, Mr. Tracy."

"Very funny, Sigmund. Wait." Sovern reached into his pocket and took out a cigar. "You need one of these. Freud didn't smoke a pipe."

"I'll pass. Ciao."

Sovern shook his head. "Yankee."

Harry got out and watched the police investigator drive off. His phone dinged, and he took it out of his pocket. The text was from Graham Houston. It read: "Stop by when you get a chance."

Harry looked across East Main, the Green, and West Main to the *Chronicle* building. "I guess I know where I'm going next," he murmured.

# 78

1:38 PM, WEDNESDAY, 18 OCTOBER

HARRY FOUND GRAHAM HUSTON AT HIS DESK AT THE BACK OF THE newspaper's diminutive office.

He said hello to Monika, who was at her command post by the front door, and continued on to the old beat-up desk Graham had inherited.

"Hi, Graham. What's the word?"

"Hello, Harry. Have a seat." Harry sat, and Graham continued. "Landon Pace, my intern, has taken a genuine interest in the Restons, so I'm letting him stay on the story."

"What's he doing?"

"He is on his way back from Zwolle, Louisiana. He was interviewing eyewitnesses to a fight between Purnell Tully and the oldest Reston boy. While there, he ran across rumors about some of the cheerleaders having private prayer meetings with Brother John."

"I can just imagine what those meetings were like."

"Probably not a lot of praying going on, unless 'Oh, God' counts."

"Exactly."

"Just wanted to keep you in the loop."

"I appreciate that, Graham. Do you know where Tully's staying at present?"

"At the Cozy Corners. Sovern has a man watching him. Plus, Jager put trackers on all of them."

"I'm aware of the trackers."

"I'll let you know when Pace gets back."

"Sounds good. Thanks, Graham."

"Don't mention it."

Harry left the *Chronicle* office and headed back towards the Really Good.

Crossing the green, he saw Fergus sitting on a bench. He detoured and joined him.

"Did you attend any of Brother John's meetings?"

"Didn't need to, Mr. Thurgood. There was nothing he could tell me I don't already know."

"I see. Guess I have to agree with you there."

"He liked the young ones, he did."

"How do you know that?"

"Ain't blind, nor deaf, yet." He paused, drank from the bottle in the paper bag, and continued. "Heard Chrissy Hansen talking to Maybelle Lungkwitz. What these kids do nowadays. Make a drill sergeant blush."

"That it would. So Chrissy was at Brother John's meetings?"

"Nah. Was only interested in his laying on of hands. And the way those girls were giggling, I don't think she was healed from the flu."

"Interesting. Do you know who killed Brother John?"

"Heard it was the Angel of the Lord. But it might have been two archangels."

"Huh. Didn't catch the names by chance, did you?"

"The parables are given to the outsiders, so they won't believe. Only the chosen are told the true meaning."

"That is usually the case."

"And you know what?"

"What?"

"I don't think we're the chosen."

"Probably not."

"But you keep knocking and the door might be opened. You got the Reverend on your side. I only got MD Twenty-Twenty."

"If you need something to eat, knock on my door anytime."

"Thank you, Mr. Thurgood. I'll be doing that. Good luck with your knocking. You'll be needing it."

Harry watched Fergus get up and shuffle off down the green, swaying in counterpoint to the breeze.

*Angel of the Lord, or two archangels. He heard something. That's for sure. But what do those clues mean?*

## 79

## 1:38 PM, WEDNESDAY, 18 OCTOBER

"THAT IS AN AWFUL LOT OF FURNITURE, REVEREND COLE," JEARLENE Reston said. "I don't know how we can pay Mr. Thurgood back."

"Don't worry about it. Do what you can, when you can. And please, call me Ember. I'd like us to be friends."

Jearlene looked down at the shorter woman. "I'm not used to callin' a parson by their Christian name. Doesn't seem right somehow."

"I don't want you feeling uncomfortable. How about Rev Em? People call me that. Especially the kids."

Jearlene smiled. "Rev Em. I suppose I could do that." The smile disappeared. "So, Rev Em, why do you want to be my friend?"

"Don't you want one?"

"I do. What are you lookin' for in return?"

"Your friendship."

"That's all?"

"Yes. I also wanted to help you. But being friends comes first."

Jearlene looked back at the house and the men who were moving in the furniture.

She took Ember's hand in hers and looked down at the minister. When Ember's eyes met hers, Jearlene smiled, gave her a hand squeeze, and said, "Thank you."

———

John-John looked at the knife display. The sheer number the hardware store carried surprised him. Kitchen knives, fillet knives, pocket knives, multi-tools, bush knives, daggers, stilettos, and combat knives. He wasn't aware all these different knives even existed.

"Looking for anything in particular, son?"

John-John looked at the older man and shook his head. "No, sir. Just looking."

"That's fine. Just give a holler if you need any help."

"Thank you, sir."

The man walked away, but John-John felt he was keeping an eye on him.

*This probably isn't such a good idea,* John-John thought.

Nevertheless, his eyes roamed the assortment of knives until he saw it. That was the one he wanted. The label called it a boning knife. It had a six-inch blade, and the black resin, ergonomic handle, was five and a half inches long.

"Uh, Mister?"

The man returned. "Yes, son?"

"How much is that one?"

"It's a hundred and twenty dollars. Made by Cutco right here in the US and worth every penny."

"That's… Uh, I don't have that much."

"I have this six-inch, extra-wide blade Victorinox boning knife for twenty-five dollars. Swiss made, good quality, and a real bargain."

"Okay. I'll take that one. I'd also like a camping axe."

"I have a Pittsburgh axe with a fiberglass handle. Sturdy. Lightweight. Fiberglass absorbs impact shock better than wood. Easier on the hands. Ten bucks."

John-John nodded.

"Follow me," the man said.

John-John followed the man to where the axes were on display and took the tool from the man when he handed it to him.

It was indeed lightweight, and John-John thought it would work just fine.

"Okay, sir, I'll take it."

"I don't recognize you. Are you new in town?"

"Yes. But I'm just camping. By the reservoir. My axe handle broke, and I lost my knife fishing."

"Rotten luck. Well, you got some excellent replacements."

The man rung up the items, John-John paid him, and left the store.

He started walking back to the house. Going through his mind were the words, *Now he's gonna pay.*

# 80

Reece Sovern had just picked up Oralene Reston and put her in the backseat of his car. In the front passenger seat sat Harry Thurgood.

"All right, Thurgood," Reece said, "ask your questions."

"Oralene, the police know someone in your family killed your father."

The young woman looked at her hands. They were folded in her lap.

"Do you want to tell me who did it?"

Her eyes continued to study her hands.

"We know your father did some bad things. Did he do them to you?"

Oralene continued to study her hands.

"Very well. You don't have to talk. But I want you to understand that most murder cases are built on circumstantial evidence. Do you know what that is?"

Oralene continued to look at her hands and said nothing.

"Circumstantial evidence is what is used when there are no eyewitnesses to a crime. In this case, murder. Circumstantial evidence is indirect evidence. It proves nothing by itself. What it does, when there's enough of it, is lead to a logical conclusion.

"In the case of your father's death, there is a lot of circumstantial evidence. And it is leading the police and the district attorney to believe your mother killed your father. Do you want to see her go to jail?"

Oralene lifted her face and her eyes bored into Harry's. "She didn't kill Pa. God did."

Harry looked at Reece and shook his head. Reece got out, opened the back car door, and said, "You can go back to the house."

Oralene got out of the car, crossed the street, and walked up the walk to her new home.

Reece got back into the driver's seat. "I'd have to say that was a bust. Pretty good lie, though."

"We aren't going to budge them."

"Tell me something I don't know."

"Do you mind dropping me off at the general store?"

"Not a problem. Heading back that way myself. So what's next? In your opinion."

"Can't tell you."

"Don't tell me you're playing cowboy."

"Okay, I won't."

"You better not be doin' something to get *your* butt in the wringer."

"What you don't know can't hurt you or me."

"Seems I've heard that one before."

Reece started the car, put it in drive, and headed north.

———

Harry noted the clock said the time was ten before six. He emptied the bag of things he bought at the general store onto the kitchen table. Paper, envelopes, stamps, tape, and surgical gloves.

To the pile, he added yesterday's *Chronicle*, a knife, and a pair of tweezers.

Em had a committee meeting and would probably get out late. She'd text when the meeting was over and meet him at Olivia's.

He wanted to be done by then so he could drop the envelopes in the mailbox at the post office.

"Let's get started," he said to himself.

He wrote a few lines on a sheet of paper, read it over, and told himself it would do.

Then, putting on a pair of surgical gloves, he wiped every-thing to remove fingerprints, picked up the knife, and began cutting words and letters out of the newspaper.

# 81

---

## 9:01 AM, THURSDAY, 19 OCTOBER

HARRY AND ESTRELITA HAD PUT PLATES OF PASTRIES AND CARAFES OF coffee on the tables just in time.

Graham Huston, Tammy Jager, Caroline McCluskey, Magnolia Nadine Roane, Billy Bob Baskin, and Ember Cole arrived seconds later.

"Anything happening on the murder of that evangelist?" Huston asked.

Chief Jager turned to Harry. "Anything happening?"

Huston started laughing. "Might have to get Harry a badge."

Shaking his head, Harry said, "Don't want one. I enjoy being my own boss."

"You just want to meddle, Thurgood," Jager said. "Haven't talked with Sovern, yet, this morning. Family still not cooperating?"

"No. They've closed ranks," Harry said.

"That's going to make it tough," Jager said.

"What it means is you're going to have to do a little work," Huston said.

"I think Harry's right," Ember said.

Huston nodded sagely. "Of course you would."

Ember shot him a frosty look. "Women don't lose their brains when they take up with a man. That saying, 'the woman behind the man', explains why so many men are successful."

"Bravo!" Caroline and Magnolia Nadine chorused.

Billy Bob poked Huston in the ribs with his elbow. "You just set off a landmine."

"Don't I know it," Huston replied.

"Not a landmine," Magnolia Nadine said. "It's a burning ember."

"Good one, Nadine," Jager said, and before she could protest the shortening of her name, the Chief hurried on. "So what is it that Harry's right about, Ember?"

"It's a family affair," she answered. "Only I think we are looking for more than one person. Several of them got together and decided to kill Brother John."

Jager sat back in his chair and stroked his chin while staring off into space.

The group watched him, and for a moment the only sounds came from Miguel moving pots in the kitchen. Then Jager sat forward.

"You might be on to something there, Rev," the chief said. "So who do you think are the conspirators?"

"From what Mike Kurelek said, we can probably eliminate Jearlene Reston and her daughter Joetta."

"Why?" Jager asked.

"Jearlene doesn't have enough ego," Harry said.

"And Joetta is like the second mother in the family," Ember added.

"Okay. Go on," Jager said.

Ember continued. "Raylene is clearly aware of her beauty, but isn't overly vain or egotistical. She knows she can use it to get what she wants, so she does."

"How can that be?" Huston asked.

Harry answered, "Kind of like a strong man. He uses his strength when he needs to. Doesn't brag about it. Just knows he has it and uses when needed."

Huston's face was skeptical. "Not many of those types around."

"Didn't say there was," Harry replied. "Just saying how Raylene acts. It's possible the ego and vanity will come later. They have all lived, in a way, very sheltered lives. Always moving. Never in one place for very long. Closed group."

"I suppose," Huston conceded.

"You didn't say anything about the other girls," Jager said.

"Mike ruled out the youngest two," Ember said. "But he has lots of reservations about Oralene. She's the brainy one, and she knows it. She's also pretty, which has made her a bit vain. But the key for us is that she's highly intelligent and knows she is. And she uses her brains."

"So there may be some ego there," Jager said.

"Right," Ember replied.

"Boys can have a lot of ego," Jager said. "What about the boys?"

"The oldest, John-John, is a definite possibility," Ember answered. "Along with the middle ones, Samuel and Elisha."

"Lofton is a follower," Harry added. "Sort of idolizes his older brother, John-John."

"So he might do what John-John tells him to do," Jager said. "He might also be the weak link. Followers often are."

Billy Bob nodded, "Good point, Chief. When the pressure comes, most followers fall away."

Jager's phone chirped. He took it out of his pocket and looked at it. "Gotta go, folks. Duty calls."

He stood, thought a moment, and said, "Harry and Ember, you two might want to join me."

## 82

10:11 AM, THURSDAY, 19 OCTOBER

EMBER WAS RETCHING OUTSIDE THE DOOR. HARRY LOOKED AT THE corpse of Purnell Tully and wondered who could do such a thing.

Wylie Garrison, the Justice of the Peace, and by default the coroner, pronounced Tully to be indeed no longer living.

"Good to know he's not faking it," Jager said, and then excused himself.

Sovern looked at Harry. "Pretty gruesome."

"I'd say there was some anger here," Harry replied.

"Plenty of anger," Sovern amended. "I mean, what the hell? Pull down the guy's pants, cut off his equipment, and shove it into his mouth? What's that all about?"

Purnell Tully's body was lying on the floor of the small hotel room. The blood pool was no longer getting larger.

"I'm not an expert," Wylie said, making a futile attempt to straighten his wire-framed spectacles on his small nose, "but given where the axe, or possibly a hatchet, struck him in the chest, it had to be someone of some size, who could generate sufficient force in a short distance to drive the blade right through the sternum."

"Jesus," Sovern muttered, pushing his glasses up his nose.

"You think he died right away?" Harry asked.

"Probably," Wylie said. "This cut here?" He pulled the shirt apart. "The axe split the sternum and probably cut into the top right side of the heart. To do that required a lot of strength. The heart probably quit beating right after that. But the ME will give you all the details. My job is to tell you if he's dead or not. And in my opinion, legally, we can say he's dead."

Sovern nodded. "Thanks, Wylie."

"Good day, gentlemen," Wylie said, and left.

"My guess," Sovern said, the cigar rolling to the other side of his mouth, "is that the perp—"

"Or perps," Harry said.

"Or perps, were let in by Tully and then they attacked him."

"Could be," Harry said.

"How do you see it?"

"More or less as you do. The perps knock on the door, Tully opens, they push their way in, and in the process bury the axe into his chest. You can tell he was expecting trouble. That pistol with the suppressor attached, lying over there over there by the chair, was probably dropped when they rushed him. And who goes around with a silenced forty-five anyway?"

"Someone expecting trouble and wants to keep the solution quiet."

"My thoughts exactly."

"So why didn't he shoot the perps?"

"My guess? It was because whoever knocked on his door, he recognized. Maybe he thought he could talk his way out of what- ever was ticking them off."

"In other word, you're sayin' it was the Reston kids."

Harry nodded. "Barring anyone else he might have ticked off, yes, I believe it was the Reston kids."

Sovern took in a huge lungful of air and exhaled. The cigar rolled over to the other side of his mouth. He pushed his glasses up his nose. "Makes sense."

"I think Tully saw the kids through the peephole, relaxed his guard, figuring they were here to talk, and when he opened the door, they rushed him. He was either knocked to the floor and hit with the axe, or they impale him while bursting into the room and he falls to the floor as a result."

"Then they cut off his parts and shove them into his mouth while he's dying or after he's dead."

"Sounds right to me."

"Must be some kind of message, don't you think?"

"I do. He's not going to be having sex anymore with whoever the perps didn't want him to."

"You think that's it?"

"I do. It seems to me the Reston boys came here and killed him for having sex with their mother and possibly their sisters."

"Jesus."

"I don't think he's going to help us on this one."

"Very funny, Thurgood. You aren't too religious, from what I see. How are you going to get on with the parson? You'll be hearing Jesus twenty-four seven. And it won't be just in bed."

"Ha. Ha." Harry shrugged. "Perhaps she'll be the one to save my soul."

"I think that's Jesus's job. She just brings the message."

"Maybe she'll convince me."

"Let me give you some advice, Thurgood. Just nod your head and keep your trap shut. Makes for a very peaceful marriage."

"I'll keep that in mind, Reece."

"Make sure you do." He took the cigar out of his mouth. "The Reston boys, eh?"

"John-John, Lofton, Samuel, and Elisha. That's where my money is."

Sovern nodded. "Now to see if we can get them to crack. Although we do have a problem."

"What's that?"

"The monitors show they didn't leave the house."

# 83

## 11:51 AM, THURSDAY, 19 OCTOBER

HARRY AND REECE SOVERN SAT ON ONE SIDE OF THE BATTLESHIP GRAY table. Lofton Reston sat on the other. Sovern pressed the button on the recorder. "Reece Sovern and Harry Thurgood interviewing Lofton Reston regarding the murder of Purnell Tully. Time is eleven fifty-one a.m. Also present is Officer Tom Prettyman."

Lofton began singing. Sovern stopped the recording, leaned across the table until he was inches from the boy's face, and yelled, "Shut up!"

Lofton's eyes got as big as saucers and the song stuck in his throat.

The police investigator sat down. "Now, if you so much as start humming, I'm going to arrest you for obstructing justice and will keep you here in a stinking cell for all eternity as a material witness. Do you understand?"

Lofton nodded.

"You will answer my questions and no monkey business. Because if you don't answer them, I will send Thurgood and Officer Prettyman out of here and I will beat you with a rubber hose until you do answer them. Are we clear?"

"You can't do that," Lofton said.

"Just try me," Sovern replied.

Harry watched Lofton gulp and nod his head.

Sovern pressed the record button. "Now where were you from nine p.m. last night until nine this morning?"

"At home."

"Liar!" Sovern yelled.

Lofton flinched, and Harry thought he saw tears forming in the boy's eyes.

The police investigator continued. "You foiled the monitor and took a walk to visit Tully. Didn't you?"

The Reston boy studied the table.

Harry, his voice soft and soothing, said, "We know you were at the hotel. We found a shoe print. And we're pretty sure it will match your shoe."

Lofton looked up. "A shoe print?"

Harry nodded.

"I, I wanted some money. I, um, I knew Tully stole our money, and I wanted some."

"Why?" Harry asked.

"For Mama. So she could buy food for the kids."

"When was this? Your visit to Tully for money," Harry asked.

"I don't know. After dark."

"Who was with you?" Sovern asked.

"I was by myself."

"So you expect me to believe you walked down to the hotel sometime last night to ask Tully for money?" The police investigator crossed his arms over his chest.

"Yes, sir."

"What did Tully say?" Sovern asked.

"He didn't answer the door."

Harry leaned forward. "Why were you really there, Lofton?"

"I told you."

Harry sat back. "Now I know for a fact you, your family, had plenty of money. I'd given your mother five thousand dollars."

"You did?"

"Yes. And I was going to give her more until you all got jobs."

"Oh. I didn't know."

Harry shook his head. "I find that difficult to believe, Mr. Reston. I think your family discusses everything together."

"Mama, Jo, O, and John-John. They handle everything."

"Who are 'Jo' and 'O'?" Sovern asked.

"Joetta and Oralene," Lofton answered.

"How much money did Tully give you?" Sovern asked.

"He didn't answer the door, and I went home."

"You're lying," Sovern said.

"No, I'm not. I'm not lying."

Sovern chuckled. "Too bad the good Lord doesn't strike down liars like He did in the old days. You'd give fried chicken a run for the money."

Lofton looked at the table.

The police investigator said the interview was over and gave the time, shut off the recorder, turned his head towards Prettyman, and said, "Take him to his cell."

Harry watched the officer handcuff the boy and take him away.

"That was very creative, Thurgood. A shoe print. Really threw him there. Made a fast recovery, though. But that was clever on your part."

"Thanks."

"Did you really give them five grand?"

"No, it was less than that. Wanted to get his reaction."

Sovern nodded. "So now what? The weak link didn't crack."

"Leave him sit for a while."

"I can do that."

"Maybe he'll feel differently about talking after some very bad food for lunch."

Sovern smiled. "You are Mr. Wicked. Huh. We might get along after all."

"Just looking for results. Although I have my limits."

"Good to know. I'm sure the parson will appreciate that you have limits, too."

Harry let the comment about Em slide. "Do we need someone present to talk to Samuel and Elisha?"

"Kids are tricky. Technically, yes, I can talk to them. But they don't have to talk to me. Or they can demand their parent and/or their lawyer be present. Gotta be tricky with kids. But *you* don't have any restrictions. Or the missus. You and the parson could talk to them because you're just a couple of do-gooders trying to help."

"Okay. I'll see what Em and I can do. That leaves Joetta, Oralene, and John-John."

"I don't think we'll get anywhere with them." Sovern shrugged. "We can try, if you want."

"Why don't we just leave it with Lofton for now. See if we can get him to crack. Em and I will talk to the younger kids and see if we can get anything out of them."

"Sounds like a plan. Good luck."

# 84

EMBER AND ORALENE WERE SITTING IN A BOOTH IN THE BACK CORNER of Olivia's pizzeria. They'd no sooner sat down than Olivia was at their table with two glasses of iced tea.

"Your pizzas will be ready in five minutes," Olivia informed them, smiled, and left.

"Did you call in the order?" Oralene asked.

"No. She just knows. She has a gift."

"It's a trick. Pa and Tully—"

Ember was shaking her head. "No. Olivia truly has a gift. Change your order."

"But I didn't order—"

"In your mind, tell her you changed your mind and you want a different pizza."

Oralene's face had the look of a skeptic. "Do I need to do something?"

"No. Just picture in your mind your new pizza."

"Okay. I did."

Olivia showed up with a mushroom, black olive, and pepperoni pizza, and put it in front of Ember. "There you go, Reverend." To Oralene, she said, "Your new pizza is going to take a few more minutes."

"Box the other one, would you please, Olivia? We'll take it with us."

"Sure thing, Reverend. Enjoy." To Oralene she said, "And I'll be back with yours in a minute."

Olivia left, and Oralene said, "Is she a prophetess?"

"I have no idea. She has a gift. I don't even know if she goes to church or uses it outside of her business here."

"Maybe she's filled with the spirit and don't know it. Although, I suspect it's a trick."

Olivia came back with Oralene's hamburger and sausage pizza. "There you go, young lady. And there's no trick. I just know some things." She turned to Ember. "Do you know her middle name?"

"No. Do you even have a middle name, Oralene?"

"I do. I never use it."

"Why not?" Olivia asked. "Jean's a fine name."

Oralene's eyes got as big as saucers.

Olivia smiled. "Enjoy your pizza, O," she said over her shoulder as she left.

"You told her," Oralene said.

"Nope. Did not."

"How could she?"

"She has a gift. Eat your pizza before it gets cold."

The two ate in silence for a couple of minutes. Ember focused on her pizza and tea. She didn't want to make her guest feel uncomfortable.

Oralene, though, would take a bite of pizza and then look out the window. Finally, she spoke. "No one is gonna talk, you know. No matter how nice you treat us, none of us will talk to you. This is a family affair. And you ain't family."

Ember set her pizza slice down. "Okay, I'm not family. But I want to be your friend."

"People see us as dumb because we haven't gone to school. But I'm smart. I took one of those IQ tests. I scored one hundred and seventy-two. That makes me a genius. But Pa didn't want us goin' to college. Said there was nothin' to learn there. Just the ways of the heathen. The godly don't go to school."

"Your father was wrong. Some very godly people do go to school. Would you like to go?"

"Don't have money."

"You could get a scholarship."

"You talkin' free money?"

Ember nodded.

"I'm a genius. I don't need school."

"If people don't see you as a genius, they won't think you are one. A degree with honors would convince them you were a genius."

Oralene picked up a slice of pizza, took a bite, chewed, swallowed, and put the slice on her plate.

"There's lots of geniuses who are rich and never went to school. Now that Pa's gone, I will become rich. I'll make the Reston Family Singers millionaires."

Ember asked herself, *How do I say this? Should I even ask? No, I'll wait.* Out loud, she said, "If you went to school, what would you like to be?"

"They don't give a degree in what I want to be."

"What's that?"

"A great person."

---

After reassuring Jearlene that the police would let Lofton out and that he would be home soon, Harry took Elisha with him to the coffee shop to taste test a few new ice cream flavors.

He'd had to stiff arm Samuel, promising he'd get his chance tomorrow.

Harry and Elisha were sitting at Harry's table. Three dishes of ice cream were in front of the young boy.

"What do you want to be when you get older?" Harry asked.

"You mean like a job?" The spoon went in and then came out of his mouth. "This one's really good."

"I'll make a note of that. Chocolate, peppermint, with a dash of espresso. Noted. Yes, what job would you like to do?"

"Sam and me, we're gonna be boxers."

"Really? Do you practice now?"

"Not too much. Pa wasn't for it. He said violence begets violence. But he's gone now. So Sam and me can become boxers. We're gonna make a lot of money, too."

*It won't be me who bursts his bubble,* Harry thought. *Then again, who knows? Maybe they'll be a couple of the lucky ones.*

"You sure you wouldn't want to run a coffee shop like this?"

"Do you make any money?"

"Not really."

"Maybe you should sell more ice cream. This one's really good, too, Mr. Thurgood."

"I'll make a note of that. Who would've thought ice cream might save my coffee shop?

"What are you going to do now that your father is gone?"

"John-John says you need the true gospel here. He wants to start a church. Sam and me might help him. Until we get rich boxing."

"I see. There are lots of churches here. Which means lots of competition."

"John-John has the gift. Like Pa."

The three bowls were empty.

"May I have some more, Mr. Thurgood?"

"Tell you what. I'll let you take home enough so everyone in your family can have some. Would five gallons be enough?"

The boy's eyes bugged out. "Gee, Mr. Thurgood, that would be amazing. But I have to tell you something."

"What?"

"This isn't going to get us to talk."

"Is that what you think I'm doing? Bribing you?"

"You're not?"

"No, I'm not. And I am very sorry you think that."

"But Oralene said—"

Harry held up his hand. "I'm sorry your family holds that opinion regarding my generosity. And because I don't want to be seen as bribing you, I'm going to have to cancel the ice cream. Sorry. Let's go. I'll take you home now."

"Wait a minute, Mr. Thurgood."

"No. Sorry. I don't want to be accused of bribing. I'm a generous man. But I have my limits. And I think I've reached mine with your family."

"I'm sorry. I didn't mean—"

"C'mon. Let's take you home."

"You aren't gonna take the house away, are you?"

"I don't know. That's a topic for another day."

The boy continued to protest, but Harry just guided him out to the car. All the while, he thought, *Divide and conquer. Get them fighting among themselves. I'd like to be a fly on the wall when they get the letters.*

After dropping Elisha off at the house, Harry sent Reece Sovern a text.

The message read:

*Release Lofton and send him home. Am working on divide and conquer, so we don't want them to have a reason to unite. Let's get them fighting among themselves.*

In a minute, back came a thumbs up emoticon.

# 85

## 1:18 PM, THURSDAY, 19 OCTOBER

THERE WAS A KNOCK ON THE DOOR, AND JOETTA ANSWERED. SHE SAW an old man, a man about her late father's age. He was wearing a uniform; and a bag was at his waist, the strap going around the shoulder opposite the bag.

"Hi," he said. "I'm Hayward. I deliver the mail. No one told us this house was occupied." He looked at the envelopes. "Are you the Reston family?"

"Yes. I'm Joetta. We have mail?"

"You do. There are eight letters here for y'all. Nice to meet you, Joetta." He handed her the letters, turned, and left.

Joetta closed the door and looked at the names on the envelopes.

The return address was in Zwolle. But there was no name. With a frown on her face, she took the letters into the living room where her mother was sitting, enjoying a brief break and an iced tea.

"Mama, someone sent us letters."

"Who would do that?"

"There's no name. Just an address in Zwolle."

"Zwolle?"

"That's what's on the envelope. Here's yours."

Joetta sat, put the other letters in her lap, and tore open her letter.

A gasp came from Jearlene Reston. "What does your letter say, Jo?"

Joetta read the letter silently, then out loud:

> *I know you did it.*
> *An eye for an eye.*
> *A tooth for a tooth.*
> *A life for a life.*
> *Now you must die!*

"Mine says the same thing," Jearlene said.

"What does it mean, Mama?"

"Someone's trying to scare us."

"But Mama, one of us did kill Pa."

"Joetta, don't say such a thing."

"It's true, Mama. And now one of us killed Purnell Tully."

And once the words were out of Joetta's mouth, she started sobbing.

She stood, the letters falling to the floor, went to her mother, dropped to her knees, and put her head in her mother's lap.

"Oh, Mama, I've sinned terrible. I've got Purnell's baby in me and now he's dead. What am I going to do?"

Jearlene Reston bit her lip, swiped the tears from her eyes, and slid off the chair to sit on the floor next to her daughter, and hugged her.

"It's gonna be all right, baby girl. It's gonna be all right."

———

Lofton opened the front door and walked into the entryway. He heard someone crying deep heart wrenching sobs. He walked to the living room, saw his mother and sister, and the letters on the floor.

"Mama? What's going on? Did someone else die?"

"It's okay, Lofton. I'm so glad you're home, honey. Go to the kitchen. I'll be with you in a minute."

"Did we get mail?"

"You leave them alone."

Lofton walked over to the letters on the floor, scooped them up, saw his name on one of the envelopes, and separated it from the others.

Jearlene Reston's voice was sharp. "Put those down this instant, young man."

"But I got a letter, Mama."

Joetta turned her face to him. "It's no letter you want to see, Lof. Just put them down."

*What's going on here?* Lofton asked himself. *Something weird is going on.*

He set the letters down on the seat of the chair Joetta had been sitting in, shoved his down between the cushion and the chair arm, and walked out to the kitchen.

*Must be something real bad in those letters for Mama to use that tone of voice. Real bad. And what's up with Jo and Mama sittin' on the floor cryin'? Do they know what we done?*

———

Jearlene made Joetta lie down on her bed and take a nap.

"You'll feel better and then we can talk."

"Okay, Mama. I'm so sorry."

"Shush. Just sleep. Jesus forgives us sinners. Don't ever forget that."

"Okay, Mama."

Jearlene stroked her oldest baby's hair and soon the young woman was asleep.

*You poor thing,* Jearlene thought. *That two-timin' scalawag... Best for you he is dead. He wouldn't be a fit father, no way, no how.*

Jearlene stood and went out to the kitchen. She saw Lofton stuff a sheet of paper into his pocket.

"You read that letter, didn't you?"

Her son hesitated, then said, "Yes, Mama."

"Just because you're eighteen doesn't mean you can disobey your mama. What's gotten into you?"

"I'm sorry, Mama. I never got no mail before, and…"

"And what? We don't know anybody except for people who want money we don't have."

"Somebody knows, Mama."

"Knows what?"

"Knows that we killed Pa."

"Don't be talkin' nonsense."

"It's true, Mama. That's why I was at the police station. They know."

"What do they know?" Jearlene grab Lofton's shirt and pulled her son so he was inches away from her face. "What did you do?"

"Tears started streaming down Lofton's face."

Jearlene screamed, "What did you do?"

"We killed them, Mama. Pa and Tully."

# 86

ELISHA SLAMMED THE FRONT DOOR CLOSED AND YELLED, "Where's O?"

Samuel came running down the stairs. "O's not home, yet. Somethin's going on."

"Well, Mr. Thurgood is mad at us. He was goin' to give us lots of ice cream and then he said, no, he wasn't — and he might take the house away."

"What?"

"You heard me, Sam. We might not be livin' here."

"What did you say to him?"

"I just told him that bein' nice to us wasn't gonna work. Then he got all mad and—"

"You know somethin'? You really are damn dumb."

"Don't you go swearin' at me, you pig poop." And Elisha landed a right hook to the side of Samuel's head.

Samuel staggered and fell to one knee. Elisha landed another blow and laid his brother out flat on the floor.

From the kitchen, Elisha heard his mama scream, "Get out of my sight! Get out! Get out!"

Seconds later Lofton ran past him and Samuel, and on out the front door, leaving it wide-open.

Elisha said to himself. *Somethin' not good is goin' on. Somethin' not good at all. In fact, it's really bad. Mama never yells like that.*

As he was looking down the hall toward the kitchen, a Mack truck hit his head. He fell against the wall and slid down until he was on his knees. The pain was excruciating and he couldn't see straight.

He heard, "You give me a headache, I'm givin' you one back."

Elisha shook his head, took Samuel's hand, and stood up.

"Lord God Almighty, Samuel. You coulda killed me."

"You didn't hit me with a feather, you big gorilla. Geez Louise."

"We're even?"

"I hope so. Look, Elisha, somethin's goin' on."

"You hear Mama screamin' and see Lof run outta here?"

"I did. I have a feelin' the beans got spilled."

"Oh, man. We're fat fryin' in the skillet, we are. Where's O?"

"She's with that preacher woman."

"Still?"

"Guess so. Maybe we should wait outside and catch her before anyone else does."

"You meanin' Mama."

"Maybe you do have brains after all."

"I'm gonna—"

"Save it. Let's wait for O."

———

Oralene got out of Ember's car carrying a pizza box. She said goodbye to the minister and started up the walk to the house. Sitting on the front step were her brothers Samuel and Elisha.

"Why are you two out here?"

"Waitin' for you," Samuel said.

"What for?"

"Because we've got big trouble, O," Samuel said. "We think Lofton spilled the beans to Mama."

Oralene didn't move a muscle. She didn't know what to do. But she had to do something. And fast. "Where is Lofton now?"

"Don't know," Elisha said. "Mama was screamin' for him to get out of her sight, and he ran out of the house. But we don't know where he went."

"Where's John-John?"

"Don't know," the brothers chorused.

Oralene hurled the pizza box to the ground. "Why must I be surrounded by idiots?"

"Now, O," Samuel started protesting.

"Shut up. You two good for nothin' lazy dogs go find John-John. And fast. We gotta fix this. On second thought, you boys are worthless. *I* have to fix this. Now git and find John-John."

Oralene watched her brothers leave. *Now I have to find a story that will convince Mama all is well.*

She entered the house humming the chorus: "It is well with my soul."

# 87

Harry was sitting in Ember's car, which was in the parking lot of the park by the reservoir.

"You had a pleasant chat with Oralene?" he asked.

"I did. Did you get anywhere with Elisha?"

"Yes. I should serve more ice cream."

"Very productive meeting."

"If the kid wasn't bent on being the next Oleksander Usyk, he'd make a brilliant businessman."

"Who's Olek whoever?"

"Ukranian boxer. Best in the world."

"Oh. Okay. Well, back to the case. I think Oralene is behind the murders. She's our Moriarty."

"Lightning strikes. Tell me more."

"She has ego. She has brains. She has the desire to be great and doesn't want anything to stand in her way."

"Productive lunch, I'd say."

"Very. Now what do we do?"

"I think we wait. Today may be the day things come to a head."

"What do you mean?"

"Intuition."

"Right, Mister. You have things on the stove cooking and you don't want to say what they are."

"Perhaps. Then again, it might simply be a little old feeling."

"Look. Over there. Aren't those two of the Reston boys?"

"Yes. Samuel and Elisha. Who are they talking to?"

"Don't know."

Harry and Ember watched the seated figure stand.

"That's John-John," Harry said.

"The two younger ones are sure animated."

"Something is up."

"All three are running back toward town."

"I have a feeling the crap hit the fan."

Harry's phone started ringing. He took it out of his pocket and glanced at the screen. "It's Sovern."

"I think you're right," Ember said. "The dam broke."

"Hi, Reece. I have you on speaker."

"You and the missus might want to come down to the station. Big development."

"We're on our way."

The call ended, and Harry put the phone back in his pocket.

"Missus? This town. The people are incorrigible."

"You might want to consider buying a nice place on a lot far, far away. Then it would be just you and me."

"Ember started the car. "Don't tempt me."

"Just think: no Mary Lou."

"You're tempting me."

"I know."

"You're incorrigible, too." She leaned over, gave him a kiss, and put the car in drive.

## 88

3:46 PM, THURSDAY, 19 OCTOBER

HARRY AND EMBER WERE WATCHING THE CLOSED CIRCUIT MONITORS for Interrogation Room Two. Seated on one side of the battleship gray table was Lofton Reston. Seated on the other side were Reece Sovern and Assistant DA Chuck Dillon.

Sovern was in his slightly worn navy blue suit. The collar of his white shirt was open. There was no tie. He had a green corona stuck in his mouth. His glasses were perched on the end of his nose.

Dillon's dark hair was perfectly coiffed. His charcoal gray, three–piece suit exquisitely tailored. But not, Harry noted, custom-made. His shirt was white, collar crisply starched. His tie, a light gray and red repp.

"That guy's running for office some day," Ember said.

"Probably."

Sovern turned on the recorder. Stated the date, time, place, and parties present.

After which, Dillon spoke. "Mr. Sovern tells me you are here to confess to killing your father, John Reston, and Purnell Tully, your father's business associate. Is that correct?"

"Yes, sir."

"I also understand you refused your right to have an attorney."

"I don't have any money."

"The court will appoint an attorney for you."

"That's all right. I did it. I don't need a lawyer."

"Like hell he doesn't," Harry said. He took his phone out of his pocket and told it to call "Stanton". After a couple of rings, Harry heard, "Lauderbach".

"Stanton. Harry. Police station. Interrogation Room Two. Lofton Reston. Same arrangement as before."

"On my way."

Call ended, Harry slipped the phone back into his pocket.

"Same arrangement as before?" Ember said. "What does that mean?"

"Stanton and I have an arrangement".

"I see."

Harry pointed to the monitor. Dillon was speaking.

"For the record, let it be noted that, after giving Mr. Lofton Reston his Miranda warning and explaining that he has the right to consult with an attorney, Mr. Reston has waived his right to an attorney."

Sovern asked, "Do you understand and agree with what Mr. Dillon just said?"

"I do," Lofton answered.

"Now tell us, Mr. Reston, how did you kill your father?"

"I found a man who hunts rattlers."

"What is his name?"

"Do I have to?"

"We need to verify he sold snakes to you."

There was a knock at the door, and Officer Winkler opened it a crack, spoke to someone, and then let the person in.

Through the doorway strode Stanton Mirabeau Lauderbach. He was wearing a custom-made, charcoal gray pinstripe, three-piece suit, with a shirt that was freshly starched and brilliantly white. His tie was red with charcoal gray dots, and the shoes on his feet were black wingtips, that were so highly polished they sparkled in the light. His full head of lustrous, dark hair had been styled to perfection.

"Sorry I'm late," he said.

Sovern threw his soggy cigar across the room, looked at one of the closed circuit cameras, and mouthed the words, "We're gonna talk."

Chuck Dillon's face registered disgust. He said, "What are *you* doing here?"

Lauderbach smiled, set his attaché case on the table, and said, "I am this young man's attorney."

"He waived his right to an attorney," Dillon said.

"Did you fully explain what that means in a murder case?" Lauderbach countered.

"Probably not to your satisfaction," Dillon said.

"Well, then, it is a good thing I am here. Isn't it? Now, gentlemen, let me talk to my client. If, after we are done, he still refuses the help of an attorney, then you may continue."

"Fat chance of that happening," Sovern said, while turning off the recorder.

Sovern and Dillon exited the room, and Sovern stormed down to the viewing room, yanked open the door, and yelled, "Whose side are you on, Thurgood?"

Harry raised his eyebrows and said, "Justice."

"Get the hell out of here," Sovern yelled. "You're *persona non grata*. You, too, Reverend. Get out before I find some reason to arrest you. Both of you."

Harry and Ember walked out of the police station.

Once outside, Ember said, "That didn't go so well."

"Not for us. Hopefully, Stanton will convince Lofton that he needs an attorney. And I have every reason to believe he will. Stanton is very persuasive."

"You don't believe he did it?"

"What I think is that you are right, Em. This is a family affair. Oralene, the mastermind. Her brothers doing her bidding and the dirty work. Lofton is guilty. Guilty of something. Accessory? Conspiracy? Possibly murder? Doesn't matter. He didn't do it alone and he shouldn't have to pay the price for all of them."

"But how are we going to get the rest of them to confess?"

"That, my lovely wife-to-be, is an excellent question. To which I have no answer, as of this moment. But I think one may be coming. Coming very soon."

# 89

## 7:32 PM, THURSDAY, 19 OCTOBER

SEATED ON THE SOFA WERE FOUR OF HER CHILDREN. JEARLENE RESTON stood before them, studying their faces. They were the picture of innocence, but she did not have a good feeling in her heart. There was something wrong. Something wicked. And it had come to her babies.

"If I'm understanding you, Oralene, you're tellin' me that Lofton misunderstood what you all were talkin' about and then killed his father and Purnell Tully. Is that what I'm hearin'?"

"Yes, Mama. We were all talkin' and sayin' how Pa had gone astray. Was maybe even demon possessed, and that was what was making him sin against the Lord. And how Purnell Tully was just like Judas. Stealin' from us and goin' to betray us. Us, Mama, the servants of the Lord Jesus Christ."

John-John added, "I tried to stop Lofton's thinkin', Mama. Because I knew it was goin' down a bad road. A very bad road. And I told him so. But he didn't want to hear it. I know he thought he was doin' good. But I told him, 'You can't be doin' good by doin' bad. It don't work that way.' But he kept tellin' me no. 'The Lord's tellin' me to stop them,' he kept sayin'. And I told him maybe it wasn't the Lord, but a devil that was talkin' to him. But he kept tellin' me no."

Jearlene took in a deep breath and exhaled. "So my baby boy killed his father and Purnell because he thought the Lord was tellin' him to do it?"

"Yes, Mama," John-John said. "That's what he told me."

"We're just as shocked as you, Mama," Oralene said. "But what's done is done. We can't bring the dead back to life. And even though I think Lofton may have received the word of the Lord, no judge will see it. Pa was right: there is much wickedness in high places in this land."

Jearlene sat in the wingback by the fireplace. "Please leave. I need to pray. Make sure the little ones are doin' all right."

Oralene stood. "We will, Mama. We'll take good care of our family."

———

Mary Lou Fight put the phone down. Using her walker, she made her way out to the patio and sat. The air was cool, but comfortable. She sat in her chair and looked out over Burnet Reservoir. The fading light made the water look like ink. Dark. A slight sheen to the ripples.

*Hunter was good, but clearly he had his limits. Hopefully, the new detective will be better.*

She took her phone out of her dress pocket, typed the word "tea", and sent the text to Gabriella, her maid. The phone went back into the pocket.

*Now that the strumpet and her lounge lizard are going to get married, I will be able to kill two birds with one stone.*

The door to the patio opened, and Gabriella set the tray of tea items on the table next to Mary Lou's chair.

"Thank you, Gabriela."

"Is there anything else, Mrs. Fight?"

"Did you listen to the podcast?"

"Yes, Mrs. Fight."

"What did you think?"

"Mrs. Applewhite did a very wonderful job, Mrs. Fight."

"That's good to know. Thank you, Gabriela. That will be all for now."

"Yes, ma'am."

Gabriella withdrew, and Mary Lou was left alone with her thoughts.

She poured herself a cup of tea, drank some, and held the cup and saucer in her lap.

*It will be good to be rid of that ghastly podcast. Not my style. More Pearline's type of activity.*

She drank tea and returned the cup and saucer to her lap.

*Yes, Hunter had his limits. Although I doubt Armes International will do everything I want. But we'll see. Money is a powerful motivator for most people.*

Dusk was turning into night. Mary Lou liked the dark, the night. She felt safe in the dark. Safe from spying eyes.

Pearline's call had been a bit of very good news. News that the detective from Armes International might be able to use.

*It's good that Reece Sovern and that rakehell aren't working together any longer. It's good that the roué is being isolated.*

Mary Lou drank tea.

"Everything takes time. Everything in its season. And a watchful eye to know when the season has come."

She smiled and drank tea.

## 90

9:03 AM, FRIDAY, 20 OCTOBER

ESTRELITA SET TWO INSULATED CARAFES OF COFFEE ON THE TABLE AND returned to her position behind the counter. Harry set a plate of tarts and a plate of cream cheese and fruit-filled Czech kolaches on the table and sat in an empty seat.

"Where's your better half, Thurgood?" Graham Huston asked.

Actually, everyone was curious as to where Ember was. It was just Huston who asked.

"She's at a meeting. Sends her regrets."

"How very formal," Magnolia Nadine said.

"That's just Harry talking," Caroline McCluskey said.

Jager chewed and swallowed a bite of tart. "Sovern is royally pissed with you, Thurgood. And I have to say I can't blame him."

"What did you do, Harry?" Huston asked.

"I didn't do anything."

"Like hell you didn't," Jager countered. "Are you going to sit there and tell us you didn't call Lauderbach?"

"From the sound of it, if I said no, you wouldn't believe me anyway."

Jager chuckled. "Come on, Thurgood, look at it from our point of view. Sovern and the assistant DA are going to get this kid's confession after he waves his right to an attorney. Now you and

Ember are watching the interview. And suddenly Lauderbach shows up, claiming to be the kid's lawyer. And we all know Stanton is *your* attorney. I mean, two plus two does equal four."

"Okay, let's say I did call Stanton," Harry began, "what do you and the DA have against an American citizen exercising his or her right to legal counsel? The legal system is very complex. It takes knowledge to navigate it. That kid probably doesn't understand the ramifications of anything he has said or might say."

"And we all know that the police do like to take shortcuts," Magnolia Nadine said.

"Whoa. Who's side are *you* on Nadine?" Jager said.

"Not yours if you don't start using my full name."

Huston laughed. "You're on the slippery slope, Tommy. Might be best to stop while you're ahead."

Jager stood. "Thanks for the coffee and apple tart, Thurgood."

"Those aren't apple tarts," Harry said.

"They're not? Sure taste like apple."

"They're jujube tarts."

"What the hell is a jujube?" Huston asked.

"Yeah. You trying to poison us, Thurgood?" Jager added.

"Geez. I'm not even from around here, and I know what they are. So does Miguel."

"Enlighten us," Reverend Billy Bob Baskin said.

"The jujube is an Asian shrub or small tree. The fresh fruit has an apple-like taste, and the dried fruit tastes like a date. They're grown right here in the Hill Country. I got mine from Elder Smythe."

"On that note, people, I'm out of here. Thanks to Thurgood, I have to go find evidence so the DA doesn't have a coronary."

When the police chief was out the door, Huston said, "Apparently, Lauderbach got the Reston kid to change his mind about confessing to murder. Sovern arrested him on charges of murder, obstructing justice, and concealing evidence."

"Interesting," Harry said.

"But you already knew that, didn't you?" Huston said.

"I'm not saying one word," Harry replied.

Huston leaned back in his chair, folded his arms across his chest and said, "Guilty as charged."

"So what?" Billy Bob said. "Isn't the kid entitled to a fair hearing? I agree, Harry, the law is too complicated. You need a lawyer present every time you open your mouth, pick up a pen, touch a keyboard, get in your car, turn on the light switch..."

Caroline laughed. "We get your point, Billy Bob. Let's hope this is the end of our latest round of murders."

"Amen to that," Magnolia Nadine said.

———

In a booth, in a back corner of the Silver Spoon, Ember Cole was having breakfast with Oralene Reston.

The young woman cut into her stack of flapjacks and put the large forkful into her mouth. Ember smiled at the look on her face. It was classic died-and-gone-to-heaven.

After Oralene swallowed the big bite of pancake, she said, "It's a shame our family will have to bear. A son killin' his own pa."

Ember put her fork down. "I'm going to be open and honest here, Oralene, woman to woman. You, not your brother, should be in that cell right now."

"I don't know at all what you mean."

"Of course you do. You planned the whole thing and got your brothers to carry it out."

"What 'whole thing' are you talkin' about?" Ember noticed a decided edge had crept into her tone of voice.

"You planned the murder of your father and Mr. Tully. You got your brothers to carry it out. I just can't figure out the reason you wanted them dead."

"You're so high and mighty. What do rich people know about bein' poor? And then to be a woman on top of it all? All you're good for is lettin' a man have his fun and makin' babies. Men don't know nothin' about love. They don't care about love. Just want some bones to jump. I've seen Pa with my sisters. He had Jo, and me, and Raylene, and was eyin' Wen. Enough is enough. And we wasn't even enough for him. He had to have every pretty little thing that come down the road.

"What a fool Mama was to stay with him. A complete and utter fool."

"I think you're being a bit hard on your mother."

"Look at you talkin'. All educated and earnin' a nice big paycheck every week. Don't talk to me. Mama shouldn't have let him do that to us. But no, she was too busy spreadin' her legs for Purnell Tully to care about what Pa was doin' to her own daughters."

"So you killed him."

"I did no such thing. It was the Lord. He answered my prayer and struck down the sinners."

"You killed them. You. And you're letting your brother take the blame. What happened to you and your sisters was horrible. Horrible. But there are laws for that. Why didn't you talk to someone?"

"I did. I talked to the Lord. I asked him to make me great. To show me the way. And He did. He showed me my oppressors. And then He struck them down. For me. He did it for me. So I could be great."

"But what about Lofton?"

"Don't you know your Bible, Miss Preacher Woman? The sins of Israel are cast onto the scapegoat and it is let loose to carry away those sins. Lofton is our scapegoat. When he vanishes into the wilderness, our sin goes with him. And we will be free."

# 91

## 2:07 PM, FRIDAY, 20 OCTOBER

THE REALLY GOOD WAS EMPTY. HARRY WAS SITTING AT HIS TABLE, drinking coffee, eating a jujube tart, and looking over his accounts.

Winter would give him plenty of time to plan the expansion into Really Good ice cream and frozen custard.

In the meantime, he needed to improve business. He had to at least appear to the IRS he was breaking even.

The door chime roused him from his marketing contemplation. He glanced toward the sound and then looked again.

Walking towards his table was Goody Preminger. A very wide-brimmed pastel blue fedora was on her head. Her dark chocolate hair was pulled over her left shoulder and fell to her waist. She wore a simple white blouse and pastel blue slacks. Against the cool air, she wore a heavy cardigan sweater that was almost mid-thigh.

*She's quite the looker*, Harry thought. *A genteel version of Scarlett.*

"Good afternoon, Mr. Thurgood. Mind if I sit?"

Before he said yes, she was sitting across from him.

"We meet again, Mrs. Preminger. How do you do?"

"Yes, we do; and I am doing well, thank you. Is it always this quiet?"

"No, not always."

"I don't pay attention to idle gossip, but I have heard that you are struggling to make a go of the shop."

"Business has been rough, I will admit. Would you like a cup of coffee?"

"Yes, please. But only if you allow me to pay."

"Very well. What would you like? Colombian light roast? Or a medium Sumatran?"

"You pick."

Harry got up, went behind the counter, poured coffee into a mug, and placed it on a tray. He put a tart on a plate and set it on the tray along with sugar, milk, and cream.

He returned to the table and set the items before his guest.

"A tart? Did you make this?"

"Miguel. He's a culinary wizard."

She took a sip of coffee, raised her eyebrows, and said, "Definitely not from the grocery store."

Harry smiled. "I should hope not."

She sampled the tart and nodded her approval.

"How are you getting adjusted to being back home?" he asked.

"My days are busy, but not very fulfilling. And that's the reason I'm here."

"Enlighten me."

"I have a lot of money. Old money. I'm a Braxton, although that probably doesn't mean anything to you. But it does mean something to the people of Magnolia Bluff."

"Makes sense."

"As I said, my days are full, but the time spent... Well, let's say I think it could be better spent. So, I'm proposing a partnership. I'd like to buy into your coffee shop. With my connections, business will be booming in no time."

"I have to confess, I didn't see that coming."

Goody smiled. "My being here will be good for you. Let's be partners, Harry. What do you say?"

## 92

### 3:31 PM, FRIDAY, 20 OCTOBER

SCARLETT HAYDEN STILL WASN'T SURE IF SHE WAS DOING THE RIGHT thing, but she had to do something. And that something was to see Mike Kurelek, the psychologist and psychotherapist at Burnet College.

Now, sitting in his office, she was having a few doubts. But just a few.

She didn't remember a thing from the past three days, but then being in a constant state of drunkenness will do that to a person.

Very early this morning, she'd stopped mid-pour and put the gin bottle down. She walked to her bedroom, took the pistol out of her nightstand drawer, and sat on the edge of her bed for the longest time holding the gun in her lap.

She wasn't sure how long she'd sat there, but she knew probably an hour had gone by, judging from where the sunlight was coming in through the window.

The gun promised relief. Freedom from her sorrows. Freedom from all the troubles in her life. But most of all, freedom from being unwanted.

She hadn't had a shower for three days. "God, I stink," she muttered.

Putting the gun on the nightstand, she stood, stripped off her clothes, and took a long, hot shower.

When she was done, she put on her favorite negligee, lay down on the bed, and picked up the pistol. She racked the slide, lay back so her head was on the pillow, and put the muzzle of the gun against her skin. Just behind her chin, in the soft part of her flesh.

She took a deep breath, tossed the gun aside, and sat up.

"Scarlett Hayden, you idiot. You will not kill yourself over a man. Get your act together."

She then put the pistol back in the nightstand drawer, went out to the living room, and phoned Dr. Kurelek for an emergency appointment.

Mike was looking at her. It was one of those "assessing" looks. He sat in an overstuffed chair across from her. She was on the sofa, her feet tucked up under her.

His voice was soothing. "Whenever you're ready. No hurry. Take your time."

"Are you a mandatory reporter?"

"If you tell me you are going to hurt yourself, or someone else, yes, I have to report that."

"What about the past?"

"If you tell me you killed someone ten years ago, or last week, that's in the past. That's between you and me."

"Okay. Here goes. I love Harry Thurgood. He's all I can think about. It's been that way for well over a year now. Probably more like two."

"You're aware he's engaged."

"In this town? How could I not be?"

"True."

"Well, he's the man I love and even though he doesn't want me, I want him. Call it a mothering instinct, call it protecting the one you love, whatever you want to call it, I've been watching over him. Protecting him from Mary Lou Fight. I'll do anything to save him from that woman. He doesn't realize how dangerous she is."

"I might disagree with you there. Harry wasn't born last night."

"That's what he said. But I *know* Mary Lou. If she's out to get someone, she will. Nothing will stop her. And she's out to get Harry. And I will do anything to save him. Anything."

"What do you mean by that?"

"Exactly what the words mean. I'll do anything to protect him. Anything. Whatever it takes."

"And have you?"

Scarlett nodded. She looked at the floor, cleared her throat, then looked Mike in the eyes. "Yes. I have."

"What did you do to help Harry?"

"I killed two men to save him."

# 93

HARRY WATCHED GRAHAM HUSTON SPOON CHILI INTO HIS MOUTH, while he took a bite of his doughnut.

"Don't you gain weight eating those things?" Huston asked.

Harry shook his head. "High metabolism."

"We should all be so lucky."

Huston swallowed another spoon of chili and Harry sipped coffee.

"The Restons," Huston began.

"What about them?"

"You and I both know the kids collectively committed murder."

"Orchestrated by Oralene."

"Right. But the DA is only pursuing Lofton Reston. What about the others?"

Harry shrugged. "If my gambit works, Sovern and Jager will be very happy campers. If it doesn't, then some folks are getting away with murder."

"Care to enlighten me? About your gambit?"

"If it works, you get the exclusive."

Huston laughed. "I'm the only paper in town."

Harry shrugged. "Still makes it exclusive."

"I guess it does." Huston spooned more chili. When he swallowed, he said, "Let's say they get away with it. Lofton's thrown under the bus and the rest walk free."

"It's happened before."

"That it has. What if they stay here?"

"Good question. And I have no answer."

"I think my intern has developed quite an interest in Joetta Reston."

"Has he now? Interesting. He's not from around here, is he?"

"No. Virginia."

"Perhaps he'll take her back home."

"I kind of doubt that. Family has money. And, well, you know…"

"Joetta's good looking and very sweet, but she ain't got no breeding."

Huston laughed. "Exactly."

"Joetta, though, is innocent as near as I can tell. She wasn't in on the conspiracy. If she stays in town, her problem will be guilt by association. And if she hooks up with your intern, that might cause him problems."

Huston shrugged. "In this town, everyone is guilty by association."

Harry laughed.

"Which leaves the rest of the family," Huston said. "The rumor mongers are already weaving stories that the Restons are axe-wielding psychopaths."

"No doubt they are. But you and I know the Reston family are strangers here, and the good citizens of Magnolia Bluff care about strangers as much as they care about mosquitoes in winter."

Huston chuckled. "Harsh, but true. Still, if they stay, I wonder how successful Em will be in getting them jobs."

"If they want to work, they'll get work, eventually. I plan on hiring Elisha and possibly Samuel come summer to run my new ice cream venture."

"Not concerned you might find an axe in your chest?"

"I'm not their father, and I didn't have sex with their mother or sisters. I think I'm safe."

"I'll keep that in mind. Just in case I have to write your obit."

"You do that."

"What about the murder of that private detective?"

"Talk to Reece about that. I have no idea who might have wanted him dead enough to make him dead. I didn't know him. Had no reason to kill him. So I didn't. And you can quote me on that."

"I will, if I have a slow news day."

Huston finished his chili and cornbread, stood, and asked, "How much do I owe you?"

Harry stood. "Nothing."

"No wonder you have cash flow issues."

"Where did you hear that?"

"Word on the street."

"Can't believe everything you hear on the street."

"No, you can't. But it makes good articles for the paper."

"I suppose so." Harry paused a moment before continuing. "Graham, you and I are strangers in a strange land. We don't really fit in here. Here in Magnolia Bluff, that is. Yet here we are and here we stay. I consider you my friend. And friends help each other. Word on the street is that your paper is about as profitable as my coffee shop. My pockets are deep enough to sustain the shop. And to help friends. I got this one covered. You buy our next meal together."

"You said that the last time I was here."

"Did I? Huh. Don't remember that."

"Harry, there's nothing wrong with that head of yours. You remember. And thanks. I appreciate the gesture. Thanks, too, for considering me your friend."

"It's a pleasure to know you."

"Have a good evening."

"You, too, Graham."

Harry locked the door after Graham was gone. He poured himself a fresh cup of coffee and grabbed another doughnut.

*We're all strangers in a strange land. Most of us don't think so, but we are. If we all thought so, maybe we'd be kinder to each other. Maybe.*

# 94

HARRY DESCENDED THE STEPS INTO THE STORM CELLAR, WHICH WAS ten feet underground. Although "storm" was probably a euphemism. The cellar was designed to support six people for ten months following a nuclear attack. He had it built after he purchased the house.

This morning, he'd gotten up early to retrieve the statue from the temporary hiding place where he'd hid it after taking it from Ember's office.

His goal was to reach Arlington Heights, an exclusive Fort Worth neighborhood, by half-past noon and be back in Magnolia Bluff in time to have dinner with Em.

The drive north had been pleasant. The sky was clear, the sun bright, and the air warm and dry.

He'd phoned ahead so the Clarks knew he would be making a visit.

The storm cellar was a large circular affair. Surrounding the common area, bathroom, and kitchenette, were three bedrooms, a room for food storage, and one for survival equipment.

There was also a secret chamber and safe, only accessible through a hidden door at the back of the room containing the survival equipment. And only Harry knew of its existence.

He said goodbye to *La Madone noire de la crypte*, kissed the statue, let his eyes take in the two dozen other works of art, and then closed and locked the safe.

The secret chamber had a small desk and chair, a single bed, and a rocker recliner. Two lamps provided illumination.

As he closed the door to the chamber and pressed the button so the false wall slid into place to hide the access door, he whispered to himself, "About as safe as she will ever get."

He left the equipment room, crossed the common area, shut off the lights, and mounted the stairs. Once in the sunlight, he closed and locked the ground-level doors.

Walking up to the house, he could smell meat cooking for the dinner Mrs. Clark was preparing.

*That smells so good,* he said to himself.

He climbed the half-dozen steps to the back door and entered Mrs. Clark's kitchen. She was at the sink, washing a head of lettuce.

"If you don't have to be leaving right away, Mr. Grantly, we'll be having our dinner in about fifteen minutes, just as soon as Reggie gets back, and we'd love to have you join us. Nothing fancy. Just a pot roast."

"Your dinner smells heavenly, Mrs. Clark. I'd be delighted to join you."

"Have a seat in the living room. I'll call when we're ready to eat."

Harry moved from the kitchen to the living room, sat on the sofa, and looked around the room. The Clarks had simple, homey tastes. This was a room a person felt comfortable in. At home in.

The couple seemed happy with their new identities and lives. And he was glad he had helped them out.

To them, he was simply Mr. Grantly. He was pretty sure they knew the name was a cover. After all, in some worlds, everyone's name was a cover. It was safer that way.

Homes in Arlington Heights were pricey; but the neighborhood's virtually non-existent crime rate justified the high property values in Harry's mind.

Maybe this is what he and Em should do. Get new identities, move to a nice quiet neighborhood like this one, and live out their lives in peace and quiet.

*I doubt Em will go for it. She is on a mission to do good in the world. And I guess I am, too, since I want to be with her until death parts us.*

*Then again, Em might see things differently when she gets the insurance money for the stolen statue. You can do a lot with ten million dollars.*

"Mr. Grantly, Reggie just got home. We're ready to eat."

Harry stood. *Yeah, this would be a very nice life.*

———

Two hours later, Harry was on the road heading back to Magnolia Bluff. Kirsten Flagstad was belting out Brünhilde's battle cry from *Die Walküre* on the Alfa's sound system, when the phone rang.

"Unknown number," Harry muttered. He silenced the phone, so he could finish listening to the Wagner aria.

When the phone chimed to indicate a message had been left, he got curious.

He played back the message. "Hello, Mr. Thurgood. This is Gerald Betzenstein. We briefly discussed the missing Black Madonna. I just wanted to let you know that Saint John's university, here in Collegeville, Minnesota, the school I teach at, has hired a private investigator to look into the statue's disappearance. If you have any questions, do give me a call back. Goodbye."

Harry slapped the steering wheel. "Great. Just what I need. Thanks, Betzenstein."

He took in a deep breath and exhaled his frustration. "Let them look. That statue, as far as the world is concerned, is gone with the wind."

## 95

8:47 PM, SATURDAY, 21 OCTOBER

EMBER HAD ONLY GOTTEN THE HALF-RACK OF RIBS, BUT EVEN THAT was too much for her to finish.

"I'll have to take this home," she said.

"The Corral Forty-Four gives you a lot of food for the money," Harry said.

"Yes, it does."

"Do you want to go home and have coffee?" he asked.

"Speaking of home..."

Harry held up his hand. From out of a pocket came a small box. He opened it and held it before Ember.

"What do you think?" he asked. "Do you like it?"

In the box was a gold ring. The center stone was a large ruby. Surrounding the ruby were tiny white, yellow, and black diamonds, and two fair-sized emeralds were on either side of the ruby and diamonds.

"Oh, Harry, I love it. But I don't know. It must have cost a fortune."

"If it did, so what? You're worth it. You still want to be my wife? Will you marry me?"

"Yes, I still want to be your wife. And, yes, I will marry you. Thank you for loving me. Will it fit?"

"Let's see."

He took the ring out of the box and slipped it on her finger.

"How did you know my size?"

"Lucky guess."

She took his hand, smiled at him, and said, "Come on. Let's get out of here."

"Sounds good to me."

Harry flagged the waitress, asked for a to-go box, and the bill.

When the waitress returned, Ember put her food in the box while Harry paid the bill. Then they walked out to his car and got in.

"You know," she began, "I've been thinking about the Restons all day. You've made me so happy, and I just wonder what's going to happen to them. Their world is falling apart."

"I don't know. It seems that to keep things together as much as possible, they're willing to throw Lofton to the wolves."

"It seems that way. Although, he decided to let Stanton represent him. Maybe that's his way of rebelling against the family."

"Might be. I guess time will tell."

Ember nodded. "Sorry. Didn't mean to rain on our parade."

"You didn't." He leaned over and gave her a quick kiss before starting the car. "Your place, or mine?"

"Mine. Hot mulled cider. One kiss goodnight. And then off you go to your own bed."

"Glad to see someone's wearing the pants in this family."

"And what's that supposed to mean, Mister?"

"Nothing."

"Yeah, right."

And they both started laughing.

————

He watched Harry Thurgood's car drive out of the parking lot. After a minute, he activated the GPS tracking device, and once he got a signal, followed the red Alfa Romeo.

# EPILOGUE

THE LOFTON RESTON CASE WAS THE FIRST ONE STANTON MIRABEAU
Lauderbach did not win in over twenty-five years. He didn't lose
either. The jury was hung, and Judge Rutherford B. Jones declared
a mistrial. The District Attorney decided not to pursue a retrial.

The Reston family decided to stay in Magnolia Bluff in spite of
the initial hue and cry against them. Jerri Reston was quoted in
the *Chronicle* as saying, "We are thankful for the good people who
have tried to make us feel at home and provided for us in our
hour of need."

Part of her comment may have been in response to Harry
hiring private security for them in the month following the trial.

The gambit he engineered didn't work. There were no confes-
sions of murder by the Reston children. And after the hung jury,
the town eventually lost interest in pursuing justice for a couple of
strangers who happened to meet their end within the city limits.

Harry was philosophical about the failure of his gambit. "We
are all killers, and have destroyed our families, friends, and the
strangers we meet many times over. A few of us are more efficient
and don't need to do a repeat performance. We get it right the first
time. There are ten million ways to die and every day one of them
chooses us."

During the week, John-John and Lofton Reston work on a farm outside of town. On Sundays, though, John-John preaches the Word of God at the Flaming Light Gospel Tabernacle, which he started in order to bring the true gospel to Magnolia Bluff. The services are held in the building across from the Piggly-Wiggly, and each Sunday a couple dozen believers hear the rightly divided word of truth.

Besides the preaching of the young Brother John, you can hear the heavenly voices of the Reston Family Singers. And if you like what you hear, you can, for a buck a song, download their music from the Reston Family Singers's website.

The younger Reston children are in school and seem to be adjusting to the change quite well.

Joetta got a job at the General Store, and Oralene is a teller in training at the First National Bank.

Jearlene Reston, with Ember's help, found a position that allows her to work from home.

Monika Crow's gossip column, "Monika Hears", has become quite a popular *Chronicle* feature in the wake of the trial. And Monika hears quite a few interesting things.

Monika's heard that Joetta Reston was seen in the company of Landon Pace at various college functions, a couple barn dances, the Halloween hayride, and that she makes a most beautiful mother-to-be.

Monika's also heard that Harry and Ember are planning on a spring wedding, but hasn't heard where the couple will go for their honeymoon.

However, all is not bliss in Magnolia Bluff. Just a few weeks ago, Harry and Ember received quite a big shock when one afternoon Mary Lou Fight and her Crimson Hat brigade entered the Really Good. The shock wasn't because of the Hats themselves; it was due to who Harry and Ember saw wearing one of those crimson hats. The person was none other than Oralene Reston.

Magnolia Bluff. A small town. A quiet town. A town with murder waiting in the wings.

# AFTERWORD

I hope you enjoyed *Ten Million Ways to Die*. If you did, please leave a review where you bought the book and on your favorite social media sites. Your review is like word of mouth advertising. And it is pure gold.

Become one of my VIP Readers. You'll get a free copy of my *Vampire House and Other Early Cases of Justinia Wright, P.I.* (it's an introduction into the exciting world of Private Detective Tina Wright and her brother Harry), a monthly email announcing other goodies from my pen, as well as curated content. And you'll be the first to know about the next release in the Magnolia Bluff Crime Chronicles!

Sign up today for your free book at BookFunnel! Just scan the QR code!

*Afterword*

# ABOUT MAGNOLIA BLUFF

"A multi-author crime novel series, you say? What is that?"

That's the question I got when I proposed the idea to my fellow Underground Authors back in 2021.

We'd just collaborated on a short story anthology, and I was interested in taking the idea of collaboration to the next level.

A multi-author series is what happens when a group of authors decides to write a series of novels. In the case of the Magnolia Bluff Crime Chronicles, the Underground Authors decided to create a fictional town that would be the common denominator for each of the books in the series.

Each author would have his or her characters, perhaps use some of the characters the other authors created, but all of the action would take place in the beautiful little Texas Hill Country town of Magnolia Bluff.

We now have a dozen authors showing us a dozen different sides of the town.

There's humor, dark dilemmas, suspense, romance, thrills and spills — all told through a dozen voices giving us a whole lot of good storytelling. The kind that will keep you up past your bedtime, or make you miss your bus stop.

Stay tuned. There's lots happening in Magnolia Bluff. And you don't want to miss any of it.

Magnolia Bluff. A small town. A quiet town. A town with murder waiting in the wings.

# COMING TO MAGNOLIA BLUFF IN NOVEMBER

The next installment in the ongoing Magnolia Bluff Crime Chronicles is Kelly Marshall's *Bye Baby Bye*.

Madison Jackson came back from Mexico suffering from trauma and pregnant.

A year later, and Maddy has a beautiful baby girl, Anna, and life is finally getting back to normal.

But this is Magnolia Bluff. A small town. A quiet town. A town with mayhem waiting in the wings.

And mayhem has struck. Maddy's little Anna is missing. Kidnapped from her crib.

Read the first two chapters here and watch for the book in late November. Enjoy!

**Bye Baby Bye**
by
Kelly Marshall

## CHAPTER ONE

I gently closed the door to my room and crept down the hall. Anna had slept through the night! What a gift. She awakens at two most mornings, and often refuses a bottle. So, it isn't hunger that arouses her. I wondered if she had bad dreams. What kind of nightmares could an infant have?

As much as I missed sleeping though the night, I cherished those sweet moments when I'd pick her up and cuddle her while her fussy snuffles quieted as I rocked her back and forth. She smells of formula and baby powder; her skin is soft as silk. Those gentle moments are a slice of heaven.

I turned the knob and eased open the door. I listened for the gentle intake of her breathing, but the dark room was eerily silent. My bare foot stepped on a rubber toy. I flinched at the squeak that filled the room like a bullhorn. Anna still didn't arouse.

I reached into the crib to touch her sleeping form. I felt only her fleece blankets. I patted the mattress, and my hands still didn't connect with my daughter. "Anna?" I whispered. My frantic fingers groped the perimeter of the crib. My heart slammed against my rib cage as my louder insistent voice called her name one more time.

I spun around, raced back across the room, and flipped the light switch. Light blinded my vision for a moment. I retraced my steps and gaped at the empty crib. I stupidly repeated her name. "Anna! Anna"—as if my shrieking would manifest my child.

Maybe Dad had her. Had she awakened in the middle of the night, and he rocked her to sleep? I hurried out of the nursery, down the hall, into a darkened living room. "Dad! Dad!"

I heard his bedroom door open.

"Do you have Anna?" I shouted.

The hall light flipped on, illuminating my dad—hair poking in all directions, rubbing his barely-open eyes. "What's this?"

"Anna's not in her crib. Do you have her?"

His stunned expression told me the terrible answer. I grabbed the back of the couch to steady me. "Dad, she's gone. Her crib is empty."

Dad spun on his heel and disappeared into his bedroom. I heard him on the phone talking to 911 dispatch. He reappeared. "Don't go back to her room, Maddie. The army's on the way. I know you know this, but we don't want to disturb any evidence. Do you have socks on?"

I shook my head no, rounded the sofa and collapsed on the cushions. "I can't just sit here, Dad. Jesus."

He looked at me with pained eyes, his jaw balled into a tight knot. "Let's start there." He crossed himself, dropped his head, and said, "Jesus, we need you now. Right now. Help us find the low-belly son-of-a-bitch who's taken our Anna."

**CHAPTER TWO**

The house seemed like a three-ring circus. Although I knew everyone was doing their job, the hustle and bustle of the forensic team shuffling between the rooms in their paper shoes irritated me. Chief Jager's battery of questions drove me nuts. I knew he was doing his job, but I wanted to scream in his face, "Go find Anna!"

The kidnapper hadn't left a note. My baby was just gone. The nanny cam had been turned off in her room. If Anna had whimpered or cried, I wouldn't have heard her. How frightened she must have been to awaken in strange arms! I had made my share of enemies as a police officer, but who would have had the guts and the know-how to break into a police officer's house and escape with her child? I could think of only one person and that individual was currently imprisoned. Because of his cartel connections, Anna's father and my-still legal husband, Jose Miranda, was incarcerated in the nation's most secure facility, officially titled ADMAX Florence United States Penitentiary, also known as Supermax.

I watched Jager's lips move, but since he didn't have answers for me, my mind stopped listening to him. I interrupted his yammering. "What you need to do is to make sure Jose Miranda is still at Supermax."

Jager scowled. I know you're upset, Madison, but what you need to do is let us do our work. We haven't received any notifications that Miranda has been relocated from Florence."

"Have you checked?"

Tommy ran fingers through his thick hair. "Madison…"

He didn't get to finish his sentence. I felt Dad's fingers on my shoulders kneading my knotted muscles. His prying fingers hurt, but it helped to release some pressure. "Maddie, they are doing what they can at this point. Let them get started. Besides, I've already called my old pal Dick Richards with the Rangers. He's helicoptering in from Austin and should be here shortly."

Jager squared his broad shoulders and yelled, "You did what? I'm running this investigation, Grant." All other conversations in the room hushed. Everyone turned to watch the power play out between Dad and Tommy.

The chief blushed. "How dare you usurp my authority."

Dad took his hands off my shoulders and turned to Magnolia Bluff's Chief of Police. "Nobody's questioning your authority, Tom. But you must admit this looks like an act of revenge against a police officer. We need all hands-on deck. An innocent child's life is at stake. And that innocent child is my one and only grandchild. The Rangers are doing this as a personal favor to me. I'd think you'd welcome their assistance. The next few hours are critical." He glanced at me. "For all of us."

Tommy glanced at me as well. "Point taken. Have them check in with me first when they arrive."

Dad nodded. "Of course. I'd like to call Supermax. Madison is right. Jose Miranda is the one person who has the motive and the money to pull something like this off. I'd like to start there."

Tommy hooked his thumbs in his gun belt. "You're retired, Grant. I'm the lead law enforcement officer on the case. Best I call them."

"Sure. Let me know how I can help. We have years of experience in this room. We all want to see a good ending to this."

Tommy nodded. Dad turned to me. "I know this sounds impossible for you right now, but if you can, sit down, try to do some deep breathing."

I peered into Dad's eyes. They registered the fear I felt in my gut. Cartels were known for their ruthless behavior. Public news and police intel were loaded with ghastly stories of the slaying of entire families including infants so that the cartels could exact their revenge. Just acknowledging that fact sent my stomach into a pitch and roll. I fled to my personal bathroom. I made it just in time to flip up the toilet lid and vomit the remnants of last night's snack. After flushing the commode and washing my hands, I dropped the seat, sat down, and cradled my face in my hands. I sobbed until every ounce of energy had drained from my body.

Grateful that I didn't have to face everyone, I zombie-walked in the dark to my bedroom and fell onto my California King. I began a mantra I had learned years ago. The simple "om" tickled my lips as I repeated the word over and over, but it did the trick. My mind stepped back from the edge of madness.

Visions of my child played across my mental screen. A natural beauty, Anna inherited her father's olive skin tone, huge brown eyes, and dark hair. She was the only reason I could be grateful to Jose—our child filled my life with immeasurable joy. Between work and motherhood, my schedule maxed out every day. Every minute was dedicated to the pursuit of my role as a mother or my job as a police officer. But the pleasure of my new lifestyle outpaced any exhaustion I felt.

I couldn't measure the time that had passed, but my heart returned to its natural rhythm and my brain ceased its scrambled thoughts.

The door creaked open, and a sliver of light beamed into the room. I recognized Dad's silhouette. His whispered voice followed. "Maddie, are you awake?"

I croaked my reply.

He moved across the room and sat at the edge of my bed. "They're gone for the moment. "I hope to God Jager doesn't think he's going to do this investigation by himself. Dick arrived, and I asked him to keep everything on the down low. He's tight with the new chief of the Rangers, David Hargrove. Richards will run cover for me and give me any discovery they send to Jager. We've got to get rolling." He touched my foot. "Don't worry, Kitten. I won't let Jager screw this up. He doesn't realize it yet, but he's out of his league. I never worked with the chief, but Dick tells me Hargrove is tough, and rips through the bureaucratic BS when things get bogged down. The first thing we must do is to find out about Jose."

Dad hadn't called me Kitten since my early teens. I forced words between my lips, but it took all my strength to keep from bawling. "I hope they're keeping her warm. Who knows if they'll feed her or even know what to feed her."

Dad cleared his throat, then said. "We can hope these are criminals with a conscience, but if it is the cartel..." He didn't finish the awful thought. "I'm emailing the Gray Gumshoes in a few. They have massive contacts on the dark web."

"Don't you?"

Dad admitted, "I'm still learning all the ins and outs of Tor. That's the browser you must sign in to locate anything on the dark web. Trust me, it's way more complicated than Google. I'm reaching out to some of the more proficient guys who can rip through the difficult processes."

"My brain is frozen. I don't know where to start to look for my child." That helplessness, that hopelessness registered as a sharp pain in my gut. This time the tears came in torrents.

Dad stood, walked to the head of the bed, and knelt. Brushing the tears from my cheeks, he said, "Maddie, before you jump feet-first into the investigation, I'd check in with Kurelek and see if you can talk with him. He helped so much last time when you first came home. Call him first. Okay?"

I couldn't get the words out, but I nodded.
Dad kissed my forehead, then my weeping nose.
"Yuk, Dad. Better go wash your mouth off."
"Don't you worry. Get up and call Mike."

# ABOUT THE UNDERGROUND AUTHORS

One afternoon back in June of 2020 I got an email from Caleb Pirtle III inviting me to join an author co-op he was organizing. The purpose of the group would be to promote each other's books. Writing, after all, is easy. Marketing, on the other hand, is difficult. But many hands make light work, and that's what we were hoping for.

In addition to promoting each other's books, and keeping each other up to date on what's happening on the business side of writing, we collaborated on a short story anthology, and are now working on a crime fiction series set in the lovely little Texas Hill Country town of Magnolia Bluff.

The current members are Linda Pirtle, Cindy Davis, James Callan, Breakfield & Burkey, Kelly Marshall, Richard Schwindt, Jinx Schwartz, Joe Congel, Kay McNiven, Rob and Joan Carter, April Coker, and CW Hawes.

They are all fine writers and I'm proud to be associated with them.

*About the Underground Authors*

CW Hawes

# ALSO BY CW HAWES

CW Hawes is a multi-genre author of mystery, paranormal, horror, post-apocalyptic, and alternative history genres.

**Justinia Wright Private Investigator Mysteries**

Sister and brother duo, Tina and Harry Wright, are private investigators in Minneapolis, Minnesota. They live larger than life lifestyles while fighting crime. Especially murder.

The series is contemporary, yet the style harkens back to those mysteries written in a gentler era. The books are not thrillers. They follow the tried and true whodunit formula. The pacing is slower to start and gradually builds to an exciting climax. There are quirky and fun characters, plenty of humor, and loads of sibling rivalry.

If you like puzzles, if you like a romp through good food and wine, if you like to vicariously chase down bad guys — these books are for you.

**Pierce Mostyn Paranormal Investigations**

If high action and adventure in the world of the Cthulhu Mythos is your thing, meet Special Agent Pierce Mostyn and the world of the Office of Unidentified Phenomena. There be monsters here!

Here is what one reviewer wrote of *The Medusa Ritual*:

**A Thrilling Read!**

*Bam! Brarwsh! Boom! Those are the images I feel when Mostyn and his team are fighting the bad guys.*

*Mostyn and his crew are looking for a book that is ancient and evil. It has brought Medusa back to life and has inspired Medusa to get back to turning people into stone.*

*They are stymied by a man wearing a mask. And he and his henchmen are not giving up their freedom.*

*A lot of rambunctious action is going into the war. Will Pierce Mostyn win this battle?*

If you like monsters and plenty of action, Pierce Mostyn is for you!

**The Rocheport Saga**

The world as we know it is gone. An unknown plague wiped out most of humanity overnight. The survivors are now faced with the challenge of what to do next.

Bill Arthur knows what needs to be done. The world must be built again. Only this time better. Eliminate the mistakes made the first time around. And that is what he sets out to do.

Bill, with a small group of friends, settles in Rocheport, Missouri and begins to rebuild. The only problem is not everyone agrees with how he wants to recreate a new world.

The small community is beleaguered with problems. Bill wants to quit, but knows he can't. But will he be able to build his dream? Or will he have to settle for second best?

The Rocheport Saga has been called the thinking person's post-apocalyptic series.

Dig in and see if Bill can pull off his dream.

**Other Works**

Being a multi-genre author, CW has other books and stories to satisfy your reading itch.

You can find all of his work on the My Books page of his website. Just click, tap, or scan the QR code!

# ABOUT CW HAWES

CW Hawes is a multi-genre author because he is a multi-genre reader. He's penned The Justinia Wright Private Investigator Mysteries, The Rocheport Saga: A Post-Apocalyptic Steam Powered Future, the Pierce Mostyn Paranormal Investigations series, and assorted alternative history and horror offerings.

Born and raised in the Buckeye State, CW spent 49 years in the Land of 10,000 Lakes, and now proudly hails from the Lone Star State.

He hasn't met a pizza he doesn't like (okay, he detests pineapple), is something of a tea snob, and rocks out to Handel and Vaughan Williams.

Tap, click, or scan the QR codes to catch up with him on Twitter/X:

Facebook:

And on his website:

www.ingramcontent.com/pod-product-compliance
Lightning Source LLC
Chambersburg PA
CBHW071214250626
47159CB00001B/311